God's Rat

Michael Bookman

AmErica House
Baltimore

Copyright 2000 by Michael Bookman.
Photo by Matthew McCarthy

All rights reserved. No part of this book may be reproduced in any form without written permission from the publishers, except by a reviewer who may quote brief passages in a review to be printed in a newspaper or magazine.

First printing

ISBN: 1-893162-76-1

PUBLISHED BY AMERICA HOUSE BOOK PUBLISHERS
www.publishamerica.com
Baltimore

Printed in the United States of America

To my wife Mona
In memory of my father, Frank Bookman.

Acknowledgments

To those who accepted, unbidden, the burden of being my editors during the year and a half I wrote my first novel and whose remarkable dedication allowed *God's Rat* to be born: Mona Bookman, Bernie Cohen, Bob Bookman, John Chiarkas, Bob Schlesinger, John London, Aaron Margulies, George Pittell, Leo & Meri McCarthy, and Miriam Chipman. And to those whose affirmation of my novel after its completion allowed me to remain steadfast in my quest to insure God's Rat's exposure to the light of day: David Saperstein, author of Cocoon, Susan Schulman, Literary Agent, Leslie Epstein, Director of Creative writing at Boston University, and author of *King of the Jews* and *Ice Fire Water. A Leib Goldkorn Cocktail*, Kathryn Hellerstein, Poet and Professor of English and Yiddish at the University of Pennsylvania, Elizabeth Abel, Associate Professor and Co-Chair of English at the University of Berkeley, and author of *Virginia Woolf. The Fictions of Psychoanalysis*, Yuri Yanover, online editor and publisher, Professor Bernard D. Cooperman, Louis L. Kaplan Chair in Jewish History, at the University of Maryland, Robert Eshman, Managing Editor *LA Jewish Journal* and Stuart Lishan, poet, and Professor of English at Pennsylvania State University. And to Elana Chipman whose efforts at The Central Archives for the History of the Jewish People at The University of Jerusalem put into my hands Abe Shoenfeld's vivid and indispensable sketches of the East Side demimonde.

In memory of Donald Davis, *God's Rat's* first fan.

"The dagos don't work our whores; don't bust up our crap games; don't pick our pockets."

Big Jack Zelig, a.k.a., "The People's Protector", 1915

"There is no fouler blot on the fair fame of Justice in the United States than that of the conviction and execution of Lieutenant Charles Becker."

From the Forward of "Sacrificed," a compilation of the transcripts of the trial of Lieutenant Charles Becker, edited by Henry H. Klein, 1927.

The word is an abyss through which the whole world strides.

The Legend of the Baal-Shem, Martin Buber

part 1

"Death thou shalt die."
John Donne

July 18, 1914

    Fifteen year old Abie Isaacs froze when he saw the slate colored Packard turn East into a now deserted Forty Third Street. He watched intensely as the car slowly glided down the street like a hearse and came to a stop in front of the dazzling electric lights of the Metropole Cafe. Four men piled out and moved up the sidewalk close to the café. The driver remained at the wheel. Abie recognized the three life takers, and Hymie Vallinsky. The life takers loitered near the car. Vallinsky climbed the steps to the vestibule of the Metrapole, and entered. Suddenly a fifth man emerged from the Packard. It was Morris The Pimp Schiff. Abie saw him walk past the life takers and slowly climb the steps to the café. At the vestibule, half hidden by a potted palm, Morris stopped and waited.
    A few minutes later Vallinsky walked out of the café, brushed past Morris, and galloped down the steps. Herman Rosenthal followed carrying his seven copies of *The World.* Morris greeted him warmly. They walked down the steps chatting. At the sidewalk Morris turned and faced Herman. Abie saw the gun pointed at Herman's face. It burst into flames. He heard the shot. "Gotcha," screamed Morris. The life takers drew their guns. Three more bursts of flame; three more shots. Abie thought he heard laughter. Herman crumbled. Released, his seven copies of *The World* separated, the

pages fluttering in the gentle summer's breeze. Some of them scampered playfully down the street. Most landed on top of him. An inky stream ran to the curb and formed a pool in the gutter.

One: Fear

January 24, 1915

Tuesday, 7 AM, Sing Sing Prison. Lieutenant Charles Becker, New York City Police Department, awoke on what he knew was the last day of his life. In less than 24 hours he would be dead, executed for masterminding the murder of Herman Rosenthal; a crime he didn't commit. Becker realized only the condemned on their final day on Death Row can calculate with sickening exactitude their every *last*. Last word. Last shit. Last pang of desire. All hope is removed. A bedridden ninety year old can deceive himself through the day, one day at a time, but for Becker, on his last day on earth, hope as a palpable living barrier - a mental ectoderm against the fear of death - had been violently torn away. His punishment was to be utterly possessed by fear. To see, hear, touch, and breathe nothing but fear. To be driven insane by fear.

Becker had always been able to manage his emotions; today would be no different. He could not protect his life - that was theirs. His reputation, however, was up to him. He might indeed be driven insane. But only one man would know it. Charley Becker.

Immediately he had to deal with the preliminary rituals of manufactured death and was led to a small brightly lit windowless room painted white - a white stool in the center, the only furniture. Two guards in white smocks were waiting. One held a scissors, the other a razor. They averted their eyes, looking so guilty Becker was tempted to comfort them. He was a brother in the copper fraternity. That he might have killed a two bit Yid gangster was irrelevant.

His hair was shaved off; his shoes were exchanged for a pair of black felt slippers; he was helped into a black cotton suit with no metal buttons or snaps. It reminded him of pajamas. The whole effect made him think of Mama preparing him for sleep. In the evening she always smelled of talcum and soap. "Mama," he heard himself saying, "They're going to kill me. I'm going to die." He felt himself succumbing to the cleansing cataclysm of self pity. He closed his eyes effectively damming the flood of tears. "Ma, thank God you're gone. You died proud of your son."

He wrote his last letter to his wife.

My heart's blood,
Your dear letters came and with them a whiff of cheer. As I hope to see you today I shall say nothing, except to tell you my heart cries out for you, for our love and your caresses. There is no way I can tell you all you are and have been to me. You are simply the flower of my life, the guiding star of my hopes and my comfort in my anguish of soul. This I know, my spirit shall ever hover near you until we meet in the green pastures beside the still waters in the great beyond.

Your lover,
Charley

His brother Robert arrived to bid him farewell. Becker noticed his kid brother was turning gray. His face had always been soft and pudgy - like Mama. But now the fat was yielding to gravity, coalescing into an ungainly portrait of jowled middle age. *I'm aging better than him,* Becker thought. Wallowing in the irony.

Small talk was impossible. The silence was excruciating.

I always treated him like garbage, Becker thought. *He loved me anyway. Why?*

Becker remembered a game he played with Robert. "What time is it?" he'd ask. The kid would start to squirm, whimper, "C'mon, Charley I don't want to play that stupid game."
"That's right. It's Beat the Shit Out of Bobby Time." Then Becker would pound his little brother with fists until the kid cried, and screamed for Mama

Becker looked at his middle-aged kid brother and smiled. "Guess it's Beat the Shit Out of Charley Time. You win."

"Fuck you Charley," said Robert.

Becker saw the pain in his brother's eyes. It was more guilt than sorrow. "I am so ashamed," the eyes were saying, "at the joy I feel knowing it is you who are going to die and not me."

Real communication is impossible between the living and the dying. The living choke on their sense of relief; the dying choke on their rage.

He turned down his last meal.

One of the guards gave him the first of the morning newspapers. In 30 point type the headline boomed:

"On the Eve of His Death Whitman Flays Becker."

It referred to a singularly cruel editorial written by DA Charles Whitman whose prosecution of "The Killer Cop" raised his status from party hack to The Peoples' Choice for the State's next Governor. The editorial - full of libels against Becker's character - was intended to counter the considerable sympathy being generated for him on the eve of his execution.

Becker was enraged and demanded paper and pencil.

His Priest, Father Cashen, protested. "Charley, don't bother with the newspapers today. You're facing eternity."

But Becker - on the last day of his life - was determined to defend whatever remained of his reputation. He wrote feverishly. It was the truth and the truth would reach beyond the grave. Writing the letter was an act of faith. A prayer. Life after death. His rosaries. He completed it in an hour. It was published - in the *New York Times* - on the morning of his execution, one hour after his death.

Soon after he finished the letter, Martin Mantin, his lawyer arrived. Mantin was a thirty four year old Irishman. His face was round and baby ass smooth. Becker realized he would never see the day his lawyer stopped looking like a goddamn overgrown altar boy. Right now, like an altar boy about to cry.

"Why am I holding up better than everyone around me?" He began to hate all those who were not condemned; who took for granted the only thing that mattered. Tomorrow.

Suddenly he felt a chill. He was back home on the family farm in Sullivan County. It was late autumn, a chilly evening. Eleven year old Charley and five year old Bobby stood near the barn feeling diminished by the great expanse of pasture, mountain and starry sky. The world was suddenly devoid of humanity. Empty except for the two of them.

Earlier in the day, a cow miscarried. The fetus was only a few weeks away from term, and appeared to the boys a normal calf. When his father and uncle treated it like garbage the brothers were deeply disturbed. "What's the matter, boys?" asked his father. "It's dead. Ain't worth a sack of shit."

Now, a couple of hours later, Bobby crying softly, asked his big brother, "Are we all going to die Charley?"

Guess so," he said.

"You?"

"Sure."

"Mama?"

"Yup."

"Pa?"

"Yup."

Bobby, sobbing: "Grandma, Grandpa?"

Becker felt helpless. He was tempted to deliver platitudes about God, heaven. How we're all going to be together for eternity. But he couldn't do it. He loved this little tortured kid; he wanted to make the pain go away. He did the best he could.

"How old are you?" He asked.

"Five."

"Seems like a lot of time, don't it?" The little head nodded.

"Well, you and me, we're going to live at least another sixty years." Charley counted to sixty on his fingers. "Ain't that a long time?"

Again, the little head nodded. The sobbing stopped.
"Let's eat supper."

Becker looked at his lawyer. "I'm going to die in twelve hours Mantin. I was supposed to live another twenty five years."
Mantin looked at his feet.
His three sisters poured in, gushing. How frumpy and middle-aged they'd become. It was a terrible distraction. He was relieved when they left, taking Robert with them. Becker did not cry.
Nor did his brother.
His Priest, Father Cashen, was chanting in Latin. The prayers fell like drops of ice on Charley Becker's heart. Becker's mind kept picking at the half-healed scars of his recent past, deriving some pleasure from the pain.

2:45 AM on the morning Herman Rosenthal was murdered. The phone rang. It was a reporter Becker worked with downtown: "They shot Herman. Everybody's hysterical. You better get down here."
When he arrived at 3:30 AM the body was already at the station house. He was ushered into a small ante room to see it. Becker remembered feeling numb. The body was lying on a plain table covered by a sheet blotted with blood. The copper on guard pulled the sheet back. Becker forced himself to look. Rosenthal's face was gone. The chubby cheeks, the Hebe nose, the smug self satisfied smile blasted to blood, gore, gristle and bone.
He had seen worse. But this was different. Becker killed Herman Rosenthal. Sure, he didn't pull the trigger; didn't mastermind the murder as charged. Still, he was guilty as hell.
His knees went.
The station house was filling with cops in and out of uniform. And reporters. His superiors barely acknowledged him - keeping their distance. The reporters asked if he knew Herman had spent an entire day speaking about him to the DA? Wasn't he relieved Herman Rosenthal wouldn't be going to the *World* with anymore stories about him? Wasn't he glad the squealer Herman Rosenthal

was dead? And, finally, from the only woman reporter, Did he usually collapse at the sight of dead bodies?

They smelled copper blood.

Becker clutched the bars of his cell. He saw Herman Rosenthal's fat face in front of him. It was minutes after he raided Herman's gambling joint. Herman was crying, actually crying - like a kid whose toys were just broken by the neighborhood bully. Which, when Becker thought about it, was pretty close to the truth. All around him his special strong arm squad of coppers were using fire axes and baseball bats to bust up everything in sight. The wheels, crap tables even the furniture. And of course they were "wetting down" - pissing on the brand new silk Persian carpet - on everything that wasn't already busted. It was the *coup de grace* to every raid. The stench of urine drenched silk was stifling. Herman, tears running down his face, whimpered, "What you do to my place Charley? Our place? My **home** for chrissake. We was partners. Why you do it? And without no warning? I could'a hides the tables and wheels. Could'a pulls up the fucking rug. It Persian, real silk - legit."

Flora Rosenthal lurched through the door. Insane with grief. "My home. My home youse bastards," she screamed. It was a terrifying keening wail. She flung herself on the floor rolling, frothing, in the piss and debris. Herman suddenly looked middle aged, much older than his thirty five years. "Look what you done to my wife, Charley. You's gonna to pay for this, you fucking Dutch prick. You's gonna to pay for this." Herman's eyes were full of conviction. "I will obtain justice. I will even the score."

Becker knew then, Herman Rosenthal was going to rat. And pay the price.

Ten PM., Becker was to die at six AM.

He was told his wife Helen had arrived. She was waiting for him in the keeper's office a few cells down. As he left his cell he noticed the white curtains that had been stretched across all the cubicles of the narrow corridor so the other inmates of death row would not see him as he started his long walk toward the execution chamber. He entered the keeper's room. It was the rumpled lived-in office of a man who considered his place of work as secure as his home. Helen Becker was sitting stiffly at the worn red velvet couch. She smiled bravely.

That's exactly how she'll look at my funeral, he thought.

The guards left the room and were standing outside the door. Husband and wife embraced and he was immediately swept by a flood of passion. It was the first time they had been alone in almost a year. Once the guards went through the door it was understood they were going to fuck. Another gift from the copper brotherhood.

Helen Kelly was lace curtain Irish Catholic. They met on a blind date about ten years ago while Becker was still hobbled by the sudden death of his first wife, Mary. Helen was a school teacher who introduced him to new worlds of literature and theater. Her love was healing and devoted. What he remembered most was a glow - a radiance that gave her fair Celtic skin a lambent translucence; her eyes a soft inviting glimmer as if lit by candles. In the beginning he treated her like fine ivory, or China. Good Catholic girls were so pure and fragile. The sexual desire he felt for Helen Kelly had been his dirty secret. After their marriage he was frightened, almost repelled when he discovered her capacity for lust. But what at first seemed threatening gradually fused with passion and transformed into an exhilarating act of carnal blasphemy. Now as he watched her take off her clothes his passion froze. *It's as if I'm not here; as if she's alone in our bedroom; as if I'm already dead.* Her body was as beautiful as ever, but now abstract - merely art; a memory. She touched his cock; his hardon was also a memory. He thought of Lena Isaacs; passion returned.

My last act of love is an act of betrayal.

It was as if fifteen years had never happened. There was no loyal, adoring wife; there was no electric chair. Only the dashing young copper, Charley Becker, and the beautiful young whore, Lena Isaacs, fucking like they did the first time. He remembered the weird munificence of Lena's orgasm, a warm furious deluge, like the licking of a thousand tongues. He understood why she was called Lena The Lake - he and Lena the Lake fucking forever.

His thoughts of Lena were compulsive. He knew he should be concentrating on Helen - repaying her for all she had done. Her meetings with lawyers, politicians, and the press. The mindless cruelty of the people on the street.

But while his body mechanically fucked his wife, his mind reached out for Lena.

The first time he saw Lena Isaacs was on Allen Street, the biggest open air brothel in the world. As usual the whores were lounging in front of the tenements or sitting nonchalantly on stoops, knees spread, their brightly colored kimonos in studied disarray. How out of place she seemed. With her blond hair in a demure bun, her severe businesslike jacket, her purposeful walk, he was sure she was a school teacher, or one of those pain in the ass social workers from the Henry Street Settlement House. He could still feel his outrage when an Irish trucker hauling a load of coal through Allen Street reigned in his horses, leaned over so far he risked falling out of the carriage, and yelled at Lena, "Three beans moll, to soften me up."

Becker began walking over to the mick to give him a taste of his club when the proper young lady turned, hand on hip, her open jacket revealing full, freshly ripened breasts. She shouted, "I'm taking lunch, paddy, but for four beans I'll fast."

The Irishman was about forty. His wide blue eyes seemed perpetually amused. "You's an angel with horns, Lena. From me kiddies mouth you's sucking food. Three beans."

"But I speaks French, Paddy. Three and two bits." Her tongue grazed her upper lip. Becker recalled his fury transferring from the trucker to the whore. He could still see the three young girls standing on the sidewalk, feigning indifference, watching. Learning. The whore threw them a knowing glance.

Suddenly Becker was all over the driver swinging his club. "Move along mick, you're backing traffic to Delancy." The trucker scurried off without a word.

Beneath him his wife was compliant. Without passion. *She's being fucked by a dead man who's thinking about someone else,* he thought. *What do I expect?*

Now facing the whore, still feeling furious, he realized she was very young. And beautiful. Her lips were prominent, sensuous; her Semitic nose peeked somewhat incongruously between high Slavic cheekbones. Her skin milky white, luminescent, radiating youth. Under the sweep of a broad forehead made more prominent by the soaring swirl of thick blond hair her green eyes - the pupils contracted, damp and lidded from opium - looked frightened.

"I's gonna to tell Morris, copper. He ain't gonna be happy."

It was at that moment he began to drown in a pair of green eyes liquid from too much hop. Too much sorrow.

He befriended her and put the word out to the other coppers that she was to be treated right. He bought her gifts; took her out to the nicest places. Her pimp, Morris Schiff, was enraged at all the attention he was paying to his whore and beat her up.

Even now Becker had to smile at the beating he gave the pimp in return, almost killing him with his billy club - *If I killed the little Hebe prick I wouldn't be here today,* he mused sadly. He was still embarrassed by the thought of what happened next.

He proposed to Lena. Asked her to convert to Catholicism and move back home with him to New Paltz, the family farm in the Catskills. Her mocking reply ripped at his stomach, "I's honored Mr. Charley Becker, but that the dumbest thing I ever heard." Then she stood there and laughed at him. Flat out laughed. The next day the entire East Side knew about his proposal.

He never forgave Lena. And he never stopped loving her.

Under him Helen was moving furiously. *She wants to end this farce,* he thought. He complied, simulating his own orgasm. A wave of nausea swept over him. It was the last time he would ever fuck anyone.

As they dressed Helen trembled and cried. For the last six months she had dedicated her life to save his. And now it was over. Her husband was going to die. Life had no meaning. Love had no meaning. Even their child was born dead. Becker drew her to him. But his embrace repelled her.

He was already dead.

Two: Cooked

January 25, 1915

It was 5:15 and the sun hadn't yet broken the night. The thirty five official witnesses, mostly newsmen, stood waiting in the yard. Collars were up against the near zero cold; frozen hands tried to thaw frozen ears. At 5:30 the company got word to move along. Night turned to day as the huge lights set up by the motion picture cameraman were switched on. The cameras rolled and the witnesses filed through the exercise yard into the hulking gothic building that was Sing Sing State Prison. The newsmen were led through the prison execution chamber to the witness box - a tiny glassed-off enclosure barely able to accommodate them. There was no place to sit; which seemed appropriate - the least they owed Becker was their discomfort. All eyes turned toward the electric chair. It was brown and newly varnished. Straps dangled loosely from its arms and legs; above it a twisted length of wire hung from a gooseneck iron fixture.

It reminded one of the reporters of " *--a voracious Frankensteinian monster sleeping off its last meal; sated and soporific, waiting to be awakened for the next deadly repast. By the genius of Science, Justice has been rendered incarnate in this almost living creature of Electric Death.*"

In back of the chair and a little to the left stood the executioner, a small sharp featured man dressed in a gray sack suit with a pink striped shirt, a winged collar, and pointed patent leather shoes. In spite of the intense heat generated by the electric chair he sported a purple scarf. At five forty two the back door of the death room swung open and Becker entered.

"The Lord have mercy upon me," he was saying in a loud clear voice. It was a response in the litany of the holy name read by Father Cashen who followed a few strides behind him. The cut black cloth of his right trouser leg flapped wide as he walked. His short black coat was unbuttoned, and his black linen shirt was buttoned at the neck. Becker carried a silver crucifix.

GOD'S RAT

To some of the witnesses he looked like the second priest.

Charley Becker hid trembling behind his brave front. He had finally succumbed to pure terror. His strained bowels were losing their resolve. His heart's frenzy was deafening. *I will not give them my shit. I will not give them my tears.* He looked at the newspapermen through the glass partition. They had been his real jury; but now he was their judge. He held their collective gaze until they turned away.

The electric chair was in front of him. Suddenly he was crushed by fatigue. He had lost the fight for his life and was simply tired, welcoming the chance to sit down.

Once in the chair, five prison guards began feverishly tossing heavy straps about and buckling them around his knees, ankles, wrists and chest. Because they were fond of him and wanted to get it over quickly they neglected to buckle one of the straps across his chest.

The blindfold was tied on. It brought him some measure of peace.

The last thing he heard as they put the broad strap across his mouth was a voice he recognized as his own: "Into thy hands oh Lord I commend my spirit."

At that moment one of the prison officials standing by gave a signal, the dapper little executioner took his hands out of his pockets. He threw the wooden lever - 1,850 volts of current pierced Becker's brain. His huge body heaved upward. The unbuckled strap made it seem, for a terrifying second, he would fly out of the chair. But the other straps held, pulling him violently back, causing his head to flail about as if anchored to his shoulders by mere rope. Spit flew from his mouth; his eyes remained open, but the eyeballs were gone, vacuumed into his skull. Suddenly from Becker's left temple an incandescent blue flame blazed. To one of the witnesses it looked like *"--electric blood spurting from an invisible wound."* The executioner looked away. He finally pulled the lever back.

When the two prison doctors examined Becker they found his heart not only beating, but pounding strongly. Now the loose strap was buckled, the priest and doctors stepped back on their protective rubber mats, and over the droning of father Cashen's prayers, the lever crunched again as another jolt was applied. When the doctors moved forward they found the heart was still pounding.

(*The electrocution dragged on for* ***nine minutes****. It was the longest and messiest execution in the thirty-year history of the electric chair.)*

I'm dead, thought Becker. *Why is the pain still tearing me up?* He felt cheated even in death. He believed death was Nothing. Only peace. And sleep. Relieved, he realized he was merely dying, not yet dead. *They can't even kill me. I must give birth to my own death.* Electrons were implanting searing seeds of obliteration. It was not enough. He must abet his own Sweet Obliteration. So he welcomed the waves of hideous pain. *But what if I abort Death?* The thought took hold. It amused him. "I won't die," he roared. " I won't die," he screamed. "I won't die," he bellowed. He convulsed with the hysterical laughter of the truly insane. "I WON'T DIE. I WON'T DIE." *(Some of the witnesses thought they heard Becker emit a sound. Almost articulate. Almost a word.)* He saw Mama. She smelled of burning flesh. *It's not quite time, son. I can wait. I can wait a little longer,* she said.

* * * * *

January 25 1915, Sing Sing. 6:am & 20 seconds.

The blindfold on his eyes became as transparent as glass. I can see, thought Becker. *Death has no power over me. He scanned the two rows of witnesses. Suddenly his eyes disengaged from their sinewy moorings to flit in front of the witnesses like curious birds. He could feel their breath; smell their sweat. He experienced a rush of compassion for his captive audience.* No one should have to watch a man die. *Suddenly Becker felt a new jolt of electricity. Breathing deeply he swallowed pure fire. The pain was sickening.* Morris Schiff appeared. His face was a mess. Blood and snot were everywhere. His nose and jaw were broken. I beat him to within an inch of his miserable heathen life, Becker remembered. Morris put his battered face within inches of Becker's. "Thinks I forgets this copper? Morris don't forget nothing. Now we's square copper." Suddenly Becker was ravaged by loneliness. "Lena, Lena I need you," he shouted. Lena Isaacs came to him in the fullness of youth. Naked. Every pore open. Sweetly, she beckoned. They fucked. Becker felt her orgasm; it was convulsive, a liquid projectile forcing him out - making him afraid of his own response. His coming met force with force. A flood of pleasure; but it did not drown the scalding pain of the fire consuming him. He smelled burning flesh. Will I burst into flames? We are dying together. I am taking Lena with me. Thank God I'm not alone. I won't let you go, Lena - not this time. *Now he was floating with Lena above Allen Street. The whores shouting at the truckers. Grabbing. Cajoling. Smiling. The flash of gold teeth splitting crimson lips.* "You make me so wet Mr. handsome I feel like I'm pishing in my pants." My God, thought Becker, they forgot how to smile. Lena my angel whore - Mary Mother of God save us. Becker looked down at Lena, her legs were spread apart. Her face bathed in sweat. She was giving birth to her first and only child, Abie. Abie's father cast an enormous shadow. It threw the execution chamber into total darkness. He was the only man Lieutenant Charles Becker feared. How could she? *thought Becker.* How could she have fucked **him**? *Becker plunged his hands deep inside Lena and yanked the infant from her womb. It made a popping sound coming out.* "It's a boy," said the nurse. "His name Abraham Isaacs," said Lena. Becker looked at the infant. He smelled of mother's milk, had green eyes, and smiled sweetly. "Papa," he whispered. Becker leaned forward and kissed his eyes. Then he tore his head off.

part 2

And Abraham stretched forth his hand, and took the knife to slay his son.

GENESIS 22

GOD'S RAT

One: Stanton Street Boys

July 11, 1914

Abie Isaacs was proud of his new sling shot. It wasn't the kind kids made. Hand tooled from solid mahogany, he had traded it from the fence, Bella Weinshenker, for a gold watch. "Be careful Abeleh," she told him. "This is a life-taker. You use it, aim good. You misses and the bastard know you tries to kill him. So don't miss." In this case "the bastard" was a huge rat the size of a cat. It was emerging from a deep filthy puddle formed by a recent, violent, July thunder storm. Oblivious to Abie, the rat hoisted its inundated, rancid self onto a huge boulder, gratefully greeting the sun. The boulder's rounded surface afforded scant space for the rat's bulk. It teetered, almost falling back into the murky puddle. Finally it reclined with an almost audible sigh, a living, breathing gob of East Side filth at peace with itself and the world.

Abie and the rat were in a long thin strip of a garbage-strewn, weed infested vacant lot, an alley really, that ran the length of a city block. A few feet to their left was a forlorn and battered solitary four story, illegal, rear wooden tenement, one of the few that still remained on the East Side.

Twenty five feet to their right towered the backs of the six and seven story brick tenements of Stanton Street. The rat was only five feet from where Abie stood, so close he could smell it. Rat smell: shit, rot, and death. Now the creature caught Abie's scent and turned. They faced each other, eye to eye; predator to predator. Brothers. He heard the rush of his blood; he felt his mouth turn to dust. He lifted the sling shot into position. His left hand was steady as he pulled back the leather pouch containing the rock. The elastic was taut. He worried it might tear under the pressure. Suddenly the rat bared its yellow teeth, then lunged. Abie would never forget the rat's eyes; intelligent, eerily human. He released the rock. The rodent's head exploded, splattering Abie with brains, blood, and bone. The body thumped at his feet.

Abie was sure he didn't taste any of the rat. But some gore did land on his lips which was close enough to make him throw up violently.

"Hey Abie," shouted Sugar Davey Saperstein as he galloped down the shaky wrought iron steps of the solitary tenement, "Why you's puking?"

Then he saw the dead rat and the gore on Abie's face. "You's fucking bugs Isaacs, rat that big could kill you." He ran back into the house, quickly returning with a newspaper. "Wipe off that *schmutz*. Wants I should puke?"

Sugar Davey Saperstein was beautiful - darkly perfect. Under lashes that seemed long enough to be feminine, large very dark eyes, verging on black, gazed insolently. His full lips bore a perpetual smirk. Buba Bluastein assured everyone her grandchild's face was kissed by God. Her husband, however, was sure it was the horned god. "Davey, he uses his face the way some men uses a knife or gun."

At eleven he lost his virginity. Now, at fifteen, he was the youngest pimp on the East Side. His father, a highly regarded East Side Rabbi and Talmudic scholar had disowned him.

Abie nudged the dead rat with his foot. "I's gonna bury it." Sugar Davey spit in disgust. Abie reconsidered. *It still only a rat,* he thought. Vehemently he kicked the carcass. "Let's go."

The boys turned the corner and entered Stanton Street. The sidewalk was an almost impenetrable clutter of merchandise disgorged from the darkened maws of cellar shops with no names or visible differences. There were cartons and crates stuffed with used everything - scuffed shoes, battered hats, hopelessly worn suspenders attached to trousers scrubbed to a shine but still sporting visible ghosts of a thousand meals, underwear, buttons of all shapes and sizes, pins, thread and sewing needles to mend and darn garments irredeemable to all but the most desperately poor. Mamas and *bubas* picked gingerly, ever hopefully, at this sorrowful collection of rags like goats at garbage.

Abie and Davey made for the gutter which presented a harrowing tumult of pedestrians and vehicles. Everybody was in everybody's way. Movement was defined by inches. Nerves were raw.

Davey brushed past an ancient, bearded, creamy eyed beggar who thrust an open can, a *pishkeh*, in his face demanding a penny for, *"--the holy men who grovel in Jerusalem for our pathetic souls."*

A truck nearly sideswiped Abie -- "youse goddamn Hebes is slow as niggers," yelled the driver. Abie responded by scooting under his dray horse, and throwing a vicious right fist into the creature's balls.

Slowly, front legs pawing furiously as if to help the ascent, the horse rose to an unsteady, but full vertical stance - like a young circus horse training to pirouette. Eyeballs fled their sockets; lips curled in a profound grimace exposing two rows of perfect white teeth; saliva drooled in copious streams from the sides of his mouth. The horse emitted no sound - its pain too deep to utter. No one breathed. Stanton Street was transfixed. Finally the spell was broken by a horrible scream that seemed human.

"C'mon," said Davey, grabbing Abie by the arm. "He fall he bring the whole damn truck down." But Abie was awed by the magnitude of the reaction he caused. Almost like starting an earthquake by jumping too hard, or burning down the whole damn East Side by flipping a cigarette into a bunch of old newspapers. The horse landed on all fours. The boys moved on.

Davey laughed, "With your strength Abie, you might've knocked his balls off and has them roll down the street like they was marbles."

But Abie was solemn now, stunned by what happened. The look he gave Davey silenced him. Having lived with it all their lives, the boys were oblivious to the raucous din of Stanton Street - the clatter of hooves and wooden wheels on cobble stones, the junkman's bell, a hundred mamas screaming at a thousand ragged children who were screaming at each other; peddlers performing vocal heroics to be heard at all, and the newest insult - the rasping cough of the combustion engine.

An unfamiliar sound caught their attention. In the gutter, near the curb, stood a fat Italian with a long drooping black mustache, methodically grinding a hand organ. At his feet, was a monkey in tattered, faded blue military regalia, including peeked hat and badly scuffed boots. He was holding a battered tin cup full of coins. Forming a semicircle around the monkey and the organ grinder, a group of six Little Mamas was dancing to the grating chords of the organ. The girls, between eleven and fourteen, seemed rapturous, lost in the music, released, if only for seconds, from their eternal burden of "watching" younger siblings. Abie focused on a petite beauty who bore a striking resemblance to his friend Sugar Davey Saperstein.

"Why you don't cop a feel Abie? She let you." said Davey in disgust.

Abie flushed with embarrassment. He'd known Rosie Saperstein since they were practically babies. They liked each other and flirted around. Tiny as she was, Rosie always chided Abie about his size. "You better starts growing Abeleh, I ain't gonna marry no man what smaller than me." Abie actually believed one day he was going to marry the beautiful Rosie Saperstein.

But a short while ago Rosie began to change. She stopped going to school, and began hanging with a rough crowd outside of the neighborhood. It was even rumored she was seen with Nigger Bialick, a young business rival of her brother. Some of the boys swore she was sporting a rose tattoo on her left breast. The last time Abie saw her she wanted to know why he never stopped by her flat when Mama wasn't home. "I's growing up Abie, pretty soon I won't give it away." She thrust her body against his.

Brushing past her he spat, "Just what the East Side need, another whore." She mocked him with her laughter. *Still sound like a little girl,* he thought. And cursed his hardon.

Suddenly the music stopped.

The monkey, a fallen soldier, was lying in a fetal ball still clutching the tin cup, now empty. The fat Italian, brandishing a machete, was running around in circles, beside himself, screaming. "Sonnamabitch, Jubastid, cocksukah I keel you. *Morti Christo.*"

The boys looked at each other. "Freak Show," said Abie.

Mendy "Freak Show" Barovick, fifteen, arrived from Odessa at the age of thirteen. His entire family fashioned buttonholes for men's vests on a piece work regimen. At six he was horribly maimed when he fell under the wheels of a truck. As a result his body came to an abrupt stop at the knees. He stood 3' 8" including the rags he used to cover his stumps. His size allowed him to snatch wallets and instantly disappear in a crowd. Considered the best pick pocket in the gang.

A block away, they found Freak Show sitting on a curb brazenly counting his loot.

Abie pretended disgust, "A monkey you's rolling, holy shit, Barovick."

"A dago monkey," insisted Freak Show.

"What the take?" Davey wanted to know.

"Three bucks."

"Richest monkey in the world," laughed Abie.

"Was," said Davey.

"Gotta pay the rent," shrugged Freak Show.

Abie, Sugar Davey, and Freak Show were walking west on Stanton Street on their way to Seward Park. Here they were going to meet the rest of the gang, Klopper Benny Zlotnick, and Sheeny Mike Levine.

The gang was known as the Stanton Street Boys. The East Side had hundreds of youth gangs. If you belonged to a gang you smoked, spit, "shot crap", copped from pushcarts, cut school, played street sports, and walked with a strut. Passionately territorial, you were willing to fight to the death "protectin'" the little patch of East Side you called home.

GOD'S RAT

The Stanton Street Boys were known to the police as a "rough" gang. Their agenda, included boosting wallets and pocket books, prostitution, protection rackets against local merchants, and a tendency toward extreme violence. Invariably they were armed. Knucks, shivs, blackjacks, sling shots, and slung shots. Klopper Benny, the boss, carried a gun.

The boys arrived at Seward Park. It was an attempt by the City to rescue and isolate a bit of nature from the brutal, relentlessly urban landscape of the East Side. Abie loved it. The winding dirt paths, the sight and smell of perennials, foliage, and mowed grass made his head feel like it was about to explode. He experienced deep and painful longings. Of rescuing Rosie Saperstein from drunken Irishers; of a death so beautiful it made him want to cry.

"It like a fairy tale," he said to no one in particular.

Sugar Davey heard him. "You's a strange kid," he said.

"What the fock a ferry's tail? " asked Freak Show.

Then almost on cue, around a wooded bend came a witch.

I gotta snap out of this fairy tale shit, thought Abie.

The three boys froze at the sight. In winter rags, taking small steps, as if larger ones would cause her to lose all her bodily fluids, her left hand clasping what must have been a wound to the left side of her face, lumbered an authentic piece of East Side flotsam. As the creature approached, the smell of urine and booze became suffocating.

Suddenly a light of recognition flashed in Sugar Davey's eyes. "That the whore Morris The Pimp cut." He felt a rush of professional pride when he said it. "Her name Mushy Bum. She use to like fucking for nothing on Morris' time. Some of the whore's feels sorry for her, lets her work as a towel washer."

Abie realized he was the object of Mushy Bum's attention. She moved her face close to his. Her mouth was a gaping hole spewing spit, and gibberish. "Abela -- Lena -- Morris." In between he could make out, "cocksucker", "bastard", and more than one, "fuck." Finally she came so close her nose was practically touching his.

Speaking coherently for the first time she said, "He home, Abeleh. Papa home."

And then she was gone.

Around a wooded bend.

"Jesus," said Freak Show.

Abie resisted the temptation to run after her. *She crazy this Mushy Bum,* he thought. *And maybe I don't wants to know.*

Exiting the final curve, the boys were confronted by a rather large circular plaza. Forming the periphery were wooden benches, fronting a six-foot high wrought iron fence. In the center was something that looked like the ruins Abie remembered from textbooks - a concrete pool irrigated in the center by a chubby, naked concrete boy, water spuming through puckered lips - cheeks painfully ballooned by the mighty effort. Sometimes Abie wished he was the concrete kid. With nothing to do but spit on the world.

The pool was swarming with real naked kids. Someone standing near the pool was waving at them. "It my sister," said Sugar Davey.

"Where the hell Sheeny and Klopper?" Freak Show wanted to know.

As usual Abie was shaken by the sight of Rosie. "I thinks we's gonna find out," he said. Rosie was smiling maliciously, enjoying their confusion. Her hand was on her hip. She was wearing a faded blue cotton dress; it was amateurishly altered to reveal her budding cleavage. Abie could clearly see the beginning of a blood red petal peeking above her lowered bodice.

Sweat showed through her dress, making him feel he was touching her body with his eyes. Moving closer to Abie she said, "I got a message from Klopper Benny." The smell of her sweat sweetened by cheap perfume made him dizzy.

Abie felt a flash of jealousy. *Everybody got a piece of Rosie Saperstein.* But somehow this was the worst. She knew Klopper was Abie's best friend. Now she's acting like she his girl - his goddamn gun moll. *Why I gives a shit. Why I wants to kill her?*

"He says the racket's on for tomorrow," she said. "Ten O' Clock at Baxter Street. Like youse planned. Bye, Bye Abie, boys."

Davey and Freak Show turned away. Abie hesitated; he looked at Rosie. She closed her eyes and parted her lips. He grabbed her, pressing his lips hard on her mouth. After a few seconds he felt her pulling away and released her.

"Your friends is leaving," she said.

Abie caught up with boys. They hadn't seen the kiss.

"Your sister, Davey," said Freak Show, "a real criminal she turning into."

* * * * *

January 25, 1915, 6:01 am and 02 seconds, Sing Sing.

Another jolt of electricity. Becker felt the inside of his head begin to boil like soup in a cauldron. Words from a half-forgotten poem taunted him. When the words came to him he embraced them with every ounce of passion he had left: "Death be not proud, though some have called thee mighty and dreadful, for thou are not so." Herman Rosenthal appeared and walked toward the electric chair. "It hurt Charlie?" he asked. Even now, thoroughly dead, Rosenfeld dazzled in his hundred-dollar blue plaid wool suit; his yellow silk shirt, and soft felt hat; his gold rings, watch, bracelets, and diamond tie tack. His eight gold teeth, however, were gone as was his nose, his left eye, and most of the top of his head. It was the same face Becker saw at the precinct. A face gouged beyond recognition by five well-placed bullets. "Let me tells you about pain Charley. You gotta be shot in the face. And you gotta look into the cokey eyes of your executioners. "And you gotta understand the only man you ever respected, love like a father, Big Tim Sullivan, was behind the bullets. You knows bullets is hot Charley? Bet you never thought of that. Like they's burning my face off, Charley. First Morris shoot. Morris the Pimp. Never thought he got the stomach for it. Then the punks was laughing and shooting. The pimp had a hardon. I sees it. Like they was fucking me to death. I dies like gash Charley. Like a gang-banged skank. And them kids, Charley. The Gyp, Lefty, Whitey, they work for me sometimes. I treats them good. You knows what I think Charley while they's shooting me? Got to talk to these damn verdiners about this tomorrow. You kills my dream Charley. You was my partner. I was uptown with my own joint. Had it made, but you runs a graft with Bridgey and Morris. How much they pay you to raid me? I would have met the price. How your wife Charley? What a nice kid. She know you screwed me? See you in Hell copper." He was gone. I didn't sell him out for chicken shit, *thought Becker.* I want him to know that. *Becker screamed after Herman into the void,* "Ten thousand dollars, Herman - pure sugar."

GOD'S RAT

Two: Abie 'Cracks'

It was as hot as a goddamn *shvits*. Abie couldn't believe it, ten o'clock in the morning and it smelled like eight at night. The thousands of pounds of produce piled on the hundreds of pushcarts cramming every inch of Baxter Street were rotting in the fierce July heat: the melons, the pears, the potatoes. Even the cabbage, which smelled like garbage to start with. And the fish? An East Side mama wouldn't feed it to her starving baby. Not to mention the meat alive with worms.

Abie was worried. Soon it would be too late - hundreds of venders were already pleading with thousands of mamas to take the putrid stuff off their hands. In a half hour the pushcarts would be gone. Then the streets would be as empty as Shabbis. Abie and the gang had run this racket at least fifty times; the bigger the crowd, the better it worked. It was so simple and safe, it wasn't even much fun. All you did is stage a commotion, like a phony fight, or accident - the more realistic the better. Once the crowd is engrossed one of the gang plucks money and jewelry - as easy as picking berries. But you need the crowd. *So where the hell were the boys?*

Then he heard Sheeny Mike screaming, "There the little fuck, let's kill him." Sugar Davey, Sheeny, and Klopper Benny hit him hard. As in all good performances, preparation is everything. Abie was ready. He knew exactly what he was going to say. Something that would get the attention of the greenies - make their skin crawl.

In Yiddish he shouted, "Pricks. Your mamas eat pig, and your papas eat your mamas." It got everybody's attention. Klopper Benny was pretending to bash Abie's head on the sidewalk while Sheeny Mike was giving him some dangerously realistic kicks to the ribs. There must have been a crowd of fifty adults.

Freak Show got some damn good loot by now, Abie figured.

The crowd was yelling for them to stop. "Just like the *shkutzim*," a horrified Mama kept insisting. Suddenly the crowd was looking someplace else. The boys got up and followed their gaze. There was Freak Show and Sugar Davey getting the shit kicked out of them by about ten micks wearing black derbies. Gophers, an Irish gang from Hells Kitchen. They already had Freak Show's bag full of wallets and jewelry - now they were just having fun.

The crowd murmured disapproval, but was intimidated by this American style pogrom. One immense kid, about eighteen, with knucks, kept slamming on Sugar Davey's beautiful face. Abie felt a rush of anger so intense, he could taste it.

He was strong. Mama would say, "Big deal a Jew what strong? Brains you should have." He lunged for the Gopher who was hitting Davey; grabbing his arm by the wrist and elbow, he smashed it against his knee. The bone broke but never pierced the skin. The kid's arm looked like a broken twig in Abie's hands.

Strangely there wasn't a cracking sound. The crowd was deadly silent. Stunned. Sheeny, Klopper and Abie grabbed their wounded comrades and began walking away. Klopper stopped and went back to where the dazed Gophers were staring stupidly at their friend's busted arm. He retrieved the bag with the loot. An old Jew with a beard and *tsitsis* whispered something to him. Later Klopper told Abie what it was: "Irisheh dreck, better his *farshtinkener* neck you should've broken."

The gang was flying. Freak Show, a grotesquely skipping, stumbling bundle of unmitigated glee sang, "Abie cracked the fockin' mick."

Sugar Davey announced to no one in particular, "You's looking at the strongest little Jew in the world what name is Abie the Mick Cracker."

"Not the Mick Cracker," interrupted, Sheeny Mike, "Abie McCracker." Now the gang was on the pavement laughing hysterically. Except Klopper Benny who was on the second count of the money.

"Names," he said importantly, quieting them, "is serious business. Your mama name you Yankle after your dead uncle; your big brother say it ain't American and he change it to Jake - it don't mean nothin'. But when the gang give you a name that who you is.

And what Abie did today deserve a name. Not no joke - I say we calls him Abie 'Cracks'."

Abie knew the whole East Side was going to hear of Abie Cracks. He wanted to feel exhilarated. Instead he felt sick. The mick wouldn't feel sick if he did it to Abie. He wondered how Klopper would feel? Or Freak Show? His friend Benny Hartman the best amateur lightweight in the neighborhood, told him, "It was easy fighting the guys in Sammy's Gym, ---but when I fights a dago, Zulu Joe, it got real tough - first punch like throwing my fist through glass. Then it got easy again." Sometimes Abie wished he could be bad without second thoughts. But Jews were cursed with second thoughts. Even tough Jews.

There was no sign announcing Bella's Candy Store, just a couple of huge barrels by the door filled with chunks of chocolate. Boisterously the gang tumbled in. The store was tiny and very dark - a clutter of barrels and giant jars brimming over with chunks of chocolate, hard candy, and halvah took up most of the floor space. A small counter with a display of freshly rolled cigars and packs of cigarettes fronted a drawn velvet curtain through which the store's only source of light escaped in frail wisps.

GOD'S RAT

Three: Bella

"Bella," screamed Klopper.

From behind the curtain emerged a woman so huge she made the store look like the set of a Punch and Judy show. She stood at 6 1" and weighed over 240 pounds. Her robe was askew, revealing much of her enormous breasts. Bella Weinschenker, hop head, part time prostitute, and the biggest fence on the East Side.

"Fuck you *gonifs* want? I's trying to conduct business."

"Forget business a minute," said Klopper.

Klopper began telling her about Abie and the Irisher.

From behind the curtain came an angry male voice. "Bella, for this I's paying good money?"

Bella shrugged, and disappeared behind the curtain.

The boys left the store and began to "shoot crap."

Impromptu, pick up "crap games" were as common as stick ball on the East Side. One of Abie's earliest memories was being paid by some older boys to protect a crap game by yelling "Chickie" if he saw a cop. He didn't see the cop, a big Irishman who swooped down like a hawk and lifted him by the scruff of the neck. "Damn Yids, they pays babies to be criminals." Still holding him by the collar he began carrying Abie to the police station. "You's spending the night in jail you little Jew bastard. Maybe that gives you some fear of the law before it too late." Abie dissolved into tears, sure he'd never get out of jail. His little life was over. Then without explanation the cop put him down. "Now, get on with you," he said almost gently. Abie still lived by the lessons he learned that day. Always hate coppers. Never get caught.

Finally a middle-aged man emerged from Bella's. The gang went back in.

"Nu," asked Bella, "Tell me about Abie." Now her robe was completely open.

Klopper told Bella about the incident with the Gophers on Baxter Street. How Abie earned his new name.

She softened. "*Boychicks*, such news is sweeter than bringing me a watch without no monogram. Chocolate for everybody - but just one piece youse greedy bastards. For you Abeleh, Mr. Abie 'Cracks', two pieces. And a special treat." She hugged Abie, almost smothering him in boundless folds of damp cold flesh, reeking of sex and sweat.

"But first *gonifs*, let's see the swag."

Carefully she examined the goods; three pocket watches with monograms, and a gold pince-nez.

After some hard negotiations she placed five singles into Klopper's hand. "A finif for this *chazirai* - pig shit. Maybe I's getting soft. Now gets the fuck outta here."

Abie stood frozen in his tracks. At the time Bella made her offer he felt a rush of anxiety. His sexual experiences had, to that point, been fitful and incomplete. He had never fucked anybody. He wanted to run. She grabbed his hand and walked him through the curtain to the adjoining room. He watched her body bump against her open robe. Suddenly she was no longer Bella, just an enormous apparatus designed, gloriously by God, for his pleasure. Abie never thought much about God. Religion was just part of the strange, musty baggage the old people brought with them from Europe. Why did his hardon make him think about God? Dogs get hardons. Cats. Rats. Probably roaches. Still the prick that had been pathetic and shriveled, was now staunch and proud. *It work*, thought Abie joyfully. *And I gonna fuck Bella Weinschenker.*

They entered the room. It was an enormous warehouse full of swag - like a giant pawn shop. The shelves were stocked with everything imaginable, from musical instruments, to all manner of clothing, to enormous piles of jewelry. None of the items were tagged. Holding him firmly by the hand, Bella led Abie toward an unmade cot which, at first, seemed just part of the clutter.

"How Lena doing?"

"Fine," he lied.

He felt a rush of love for this woman who was about to grant him his manhood at fifteen. The flat features of her dark fat face were always repugnant to him. Now she looked exotic. African. Raw and sexual.

"Good. I never understands why she leave the business."

The mention of Mama and her former profession almost cost Abie his hardon. They sat on the unmade cot.

God she big, he thought.

"*Tataleh* take your clothes off," Bella whispered. Abie felt like a little kid getting ready to be bathed. His raging hardon now seemed incongruous. Silly. Something that belonged to an adult male and had somehow wound up between his legs. There was a moment of panic. *What's I doing here?*

Bella sensed a problem. She slipped off her robe and began running her hands over his body, breathing into his ear, "Fuck me Abie 'Cracks'." Lust returned.

Abie couldn't believe he had permission to touch anything he wanted. Anything. He didn't know where to start. Mounds of soft damp flesh were everywhere. At first it was hard to distinguish her breasts from the rest of the fat. When he found them their weight was even more startling than their size. *How she walk straight?* He was surprised how easy it all was. *This Bella,* he thought. *Big bad Bella the fence. Under me. All around me.* He attacked her with his mouth. He wanted to devour her. All of her. He was a mouse consuming a house-sized chunk of cheese. He had forever. His appetite was boundless. Then pleasure crystallized like a blazing diamond. A blinding coruscation that radiated from somewhere deep within his pelvis. His quest was to pursue the light. Expand it. Make it blind him. He penetrated her cunt with his fingers. Now the light pulsated like an incandescent heart beat. Bella grabbed his cock, and pushed it inside her.

Abie saw himself gripping the Irisher's arm. He watched as it broke in his hands. Then explode. When his eyes opened he was on the floor; he had fallen off this huge, middle-aged naked woman as if from the side of a mountain. He felt empty and weak. Sinew and bone seemed to have melted. Gravity oppressed him, defying his will to stand. When he finally pulled himself up, he noticed the cot was empty. He smelled opium. Along with the smoke Bella's strangely disembodied voice wafted toward him from some hidden corner of the storeroom.

"Go home, Abeleh. Say hello to Moma, Morris."

* * * * *

January 25, 1915, 6:01 am & 56 seconds, Sing Sing.

I'm between life and death, *Becker thought,* Between pain and Nothing. *He clung to the pain. Desperately. Already parts of his body were numb - his head, and his extremities. I'm dying in pieces. He could hear Father Cashen:* "Hagios o Theos. Sanctas Deus. Crucem tuam adoramus, Domine: et sanctum." *Now it was Mama's voice,* "-- resurrecionem tuam laudamus et glorificamus." *Mama came to him.* "Let go, son. For God's sake, let go." "They won't let me, Mama. God nor the Devil." *He reached out for Mama and touched eleven year old Katherine Schillenhouser.* "Kathy," he said, "I forgot how beautiful you are." "Walk me home, Charley," she said. *Becker desperately wanted to hold her hand. He could smell the soap in her hair. Their hands touched as they walked. She was gabbing about Miss Frost their sixth grade teacher.* "I think she hates me Charley." *How can anyone hate Kathy Schillenhouser? he wondered. He took her hand in his - if she pulled it away he would die. Warily he looked in her direction and saw a young Lena. They were on Division Street, walking toward her flat. Suddenly she was transformed - Abie's Mama - her youth and beauty gone.* "Time has not been good to me, Charley," she said. "You're still beautiful to me, Lena," he said. "I was never beautiful Charley - just young. I was dead Charley. A toilet for men to flush twenty seconds of pleasure into. Then I got pregnant. Out of filth come life. For the first time in years I feels alive. Abie still my miracle - all I got. Now they want to kill him, Charley." *Becker reached out to embrace her - she was gone.* "Die with me Lena. Come back. We don't have to be alone."

Four: Little Christ Killer.

When Abie hit the street, he breathed deeply. It was as if the filthy East Side air was a cool spring, and he was dying of thirst. As he walked home he thought of Bella asking him about Morris Schiff. Why did everyone assume Morris was his father just because he was once Mama's pimp? Mama was vague on the subject. She'd say things like "You's just like Morris." But when he was acting up - getting into trouble with his teachers, the coppers - she'd say, "I wish you father was here. He makes sure you act straight."

Abie figured half the men on the East Side could be his father. *Did a whore,* he wondered, *really know who fathered her child?* Sometimes he fantasized who his father might be. A big time gambler, gangster, or politician. Maybe even a goy. Mama didn't ask her tricks their religion. The idea he might be half Christian excited him. Could be he didn't belong on the East Side - that he was a real American and could live anywhere.

His one memory of his father was more like a dream. A nightmare actually - being held out a window six stories up; a powerful hand clutching a fist full of his hair. He remembered wishing the hand would release him so the pain would stop. He knew he wouldn't fall, but fly away like a pigeon. Nearby, Mama was sobbing. Over him a male voice rolled like thunder. It could have been Morris; it could have been anybody. It wasn't a dream.

Suddenly Abie realized he was on Pell Street, in the middle of Chinatown. The Gophers often hung out in Chinatown.

I's dead, he thought.

He cut into Dyer Street, a direct route to the Bowery, and safety. Dyer Street was more a long winding alley than a street. It was extremely narrow, no more than twenty-feet wide, walled on either side by the backs of seven story tenements. Its surface was cobble stones; there was no sidewalk. And very little sun

He was half way between Dyer Street and the Bowery, when he became aware of the silence. The only sound, his heels on cobble stones. Finally, rounding the last curve, he could see the Bowery. His relief was short lived. Six kids, between eleven and thirteen, turned into Dyer and began to walk toward him. They all wore black derbies.

Shit, Baby Gophers. Abie was about to turn, when he heard a voice behind him.

"Where you rushing, Abie Cracks?"

It was Kenny Jackson, leader of the Baby Gophers. Jackson, thirteen, was very blond with a broad forehead and wide set blue eyes. He was smiling. His deep blue eyes were friendly. Inviting trust.

Abie was tempted to relax. But he remembered Nick Scordato - how Jackson knocked out every tooth in Scordato's mouth. Abie's right hand was in his pocket holding his knife; he opened it with his thumb and forefinger.

Jackson and the three Baby Gophers formed a loose semicircle around him. Their black derbies, were pushed forward, almost covering their eyes. Abie knew them by sight, not by name. One was pounding his right fist into his left hand; he was wearing knucks. The other two had link chains wound around their right hands, running across their chests, disappearing over their left shoulders. Abie knew the last link was attached to a small lead ball - slung shots - ugly weapons. Used correctly the slung shot could bust open a man's head as easily as a bullet. The second group of Baby Gophers joined the rest of the gang completing the circle.

The stink of whiskey was overwhelming. Jackson was still smiling.

"We visit Toohey at Saint Joe's," he said. "He in a lot of pain; arm all taped, but he don't hold no grudge. Funny thing, his Mama ain't so nice. 'Kill the little Christ killer,' she says, 'What he done to me Jimmy ain't human.' "

The smile was gone. Abie realized he was looking at the same face Nick Scordato saw before his mouth imploded: flared nose; narrowed eyes; lips receding above whitened gums.

Look like the rat I kill, Abie thought.

One of the Gophers handed Jackson a knife. Abie felt the pain; it tore through his body like a grisly hand clutching and ripping at whatever got in its way. First his heart, then his lungs. He couldn't breathe. *I's dying,* he thought. He fell to his knees. Slowly he moved his hand to the source of the pain, his heart. There was no entry wound. No blood. He opened his eyes. No deadly kids with black derbies. Gradually his breath came back. He looked toward the Bowery. Traffic moved as if nothing happened. Had he been lying there dead, the trucks, cars, carriages, and busses would have continued unabated, indifferent. This frightened him almost as much as death.

Abie understood why he was still alive. He was too important, his crime too heinous, for mere Baby Gophers to kill. Retribution could not be left to a bunch of kids. Right now Jackson and his boys were looking for their big brothers. Abie ran home.

GOD'S RAT

Five: Lovers

Abie arrived breathless. Mama was passed out in a chair, an empty bucket of beer at her side. Entering his room and throwing himself on the raggedy, filthy mattress that passed for a bed, Abie pressed his lips to the pillow. He thought of Rosie. Then slept. A loud banging on the door woke him

In the parlor Lena Isaacs dreamt a hand clutching a hammer was pounding against her skull. The pain woke her. Someone was banging on the door. She staggered to her feet.

"I don't wants to see nobody," she yelled. "Go away."

A deep baritone male voice announced he was Lieutenant Charles Becker. She opened the door.

Lena couldn't believe her eyes. She hadn't seen Charley Becker in fifteen years. His angular face was softened by time, thicker, less fierce. But there was still something of the wolf about him. It was his piercing blue eyes that never seemed to blink, probing, always making her feel vulnerable; and the way his nostrils flared even when he wasn't angry. She had forgotten how tall and muscular he was. Now she remembered Becker's physical presence always made her feel uneasy. Naked he was complete. When dressed, his clothes seemed unnecessary. An aberration, like pants on a panther. She imagined she could see the muscles rippling beneath his blue, freshly pressed uniform.

"I hope I'm not troubling you, Miss Isaacs," he said, "but a James Toohey was brutally attacked and possibly crippled by a young Hebrew."

"Fuck that gotta do with my Abie?" She asked.

Charley Becker was no less shocked at the sight of Lena Isaacs. She was transformed. He was actually going to apologize for knocking on the wrong door. But the familiar, pleading, soft green eyes began to clear, like a warming sun after a storm, the clouds of time. He recognized the proud broad forehead; her lips were still thick and full. But now unpainted, cracked, and framing ruined tobacco stained teeth.

"The fuck it has to do with your Abie, Miss Isaacs," he said, "was a positive identification of a little Jew named Abraham Isaacs."

Lena was confused. *A fight between Jews and Irish,* Lena thought. *A broken arm, nobody killed. No big deal for the East Side. Why this bring a copper to my door? And why **this** copper?* She knew Becker's reputation. He was considered the most corrupt cop on the East Side. Her friends in the underworld had a complicated relationship with him. He cost them a fortune, had his hand in every till. Yet there wasn't a pimp, or gambler who didn't owe his livelihood to Becker's protection. *But why he here?* She wondered *Still hate me after all these years? Still love me?*

When Becker first heard about the little Jew boy who broke Big James Toohey's arm he was amused. Once he realized it was Lena's son he knew what he was going to do. Although he wasn't sure why. *Why don't I just walk away? What could I do to her that she hasn't already done to herself?*

Suddenly her face was wet with tears. "After all these years you's coming after me? You wants maybe I should apologize for laughing at your stupid proposal?"

It began to come back to Lena. The open air bordello of Allen Street. Fancy Lena Isaacs from Albany - an aristocratic butterfly amidst the East Side vermin. An Allen Street whore without an Allen Street history - without any history, fending off suicide with slivovitz and laudanum. And then came Charley Becker, the tall young copper; beautiful, and sculpted like a god. He actually fell in love with her - wanted to protect her. He proposed to her. She laughed at him. Now laughing and crying the way only women do, she said, "What a nar you was Charley. I was a whore for chrissake. You was protection; you was fancy restaurants; expensive gifts. And sometime, if I's drunk enough, you felt good inside of me. But love?"

She was a whore. And she had loved him; the more she loved him, the more she felt like a whore. She needed to hurt him; to make him go away. She punished him for loving her. And now, after all these years, the pain had brought him back.

Looking at her flooded, green eyes Becker saw the twenty four year old Lena the Lake. It made the anger worse. Lena felt the force of his rage. It was physical; terrifying.

Why he want to kill me? For God's sake, Why? Then she remembered - not that she ever really forgot. *How could she?* It was after she laughed at his proposal; it was the canker at the heart of his pain - and hers. Monk Eastman on top of her. Naked. Fucking. The front door crashing down. Footsteps. Becker. *How did he know she was here with Monk?* She remembered seeing herself through Becker's eyes. *He kill us both.* Becker was over them. The blows came crashing down. Inside of her Monk withered. His body collapsed; she felt the full force of his weight. Blood warmed her face. She screamed. "Don't kill him, Charley."

"Maybe Abie should've been yours, Charley; it didn't work out that way," she said. "Let it go."

Becker was watching himself lose control. All he could do was watch.

"I'm going to arrest the little bastard."

Abie, standing behind the half-closed door of his room, heard the shouting; he considered going out the window and down the fire escape.

This copper crazy, he thought.

Instead he walked into the parlor just in time to see Mama, all teeth and nails, jump on the cop. He watched Becker go for his gun and slam it on the side of her head. Slowly Abie approached. Becker saw him and jammed the gun into his mouth, chipping a tooth - blood gushed. Becker looked at Abie long and hard.

Lena, next to him, sopped her bloody wound with a worn and dirty hanky. She was crying. Becker started to talk. Very polite - desperately trying to regain control of himself; to quiet his body's terrible rage.

"You see Mrs. Isaacs, or can I call you - - Abie, did Morris ever tell you what they called Mama?"

She was on him again. He hit her again.

"Lena the Lake. Ask her why."

GOD'S RAT

"Don't hurt Abie 'cause of me Charley."

Watching the copper and his mama fighting made Abie feel strangely secure. Like having two parents. Sure it was all hate, rage and violence. But where there's hate there must have been love. It was good to know someone once loved Mama. Even if it was this lousy copper. And happened a million years ago.

One thing Abie knew - he would never ask Mama why her name was Lena the Lake. Never.

Very friendly now, almost conspiratorial, Becker said, "As I was trying to tell you Miss Isaacs, being we have a mutual acquaintance Morris Schiff - and the last thing the East Side needs is another little Hebrew lad in the Tombs - I ain't going to abide by the strict letter of the law and arrest the kid." His eyes froze - blue ice. His lips barely moved, the words a harsh hiss. His expression had an almost physical impact on Lena. "Miss Isaacs, it was only going to cost you a dollar a month to keep Abie out of jail. But because of your unladylike behavior it will cost you a fin." Becker left.

"Look at us," said Lena, "we looks like the emergency room."

"Somebody should kill that *momser*," said Abie, playing with his chipped tooth.

"He love me once, Abeleh. But then I was young and beautiful."

Abie didn't remember Mama when she was beautiful. He was glad she turned fat and ugly. Nobody would pay two cents to fuck her. He couldn't handle it if she was still working. Being the son of an ex- whore and a drunk was bad enough.

"Maybe if I didn't turn into such a fat broken down zlub it wouldn't of been so bad," Lena said. "Goddamn Cossack - hit me, hit my kid. Find Morris, he's stooling and collecting for Becker now. Maybe he can calm him down. We can't afford no five dollars a month."

*****

January 25, 1915, 6:02 am 30 seconds, Sing Sing.

Becker's lungs were filling with liquid. He saw himself at twelve, alone in the woods behind his parents' house with his rifle. The rabbit was on the crest of a hill, sixty feet from where he stood; he lifted the rifle; put the creature in his sights, and pulled the trigger. The rabbit disappeared. Heart pounding, Becker raced over the hill, down to the little brook at the bottom. The rabbit was in the water, bleeding from the gut, and drowning at the same time. Becker's lungs continued to fill. We're both drowning, *he thought. Then, suddenly, his lungs cleared.* Nothing can kill me. Fire nor water, *he thought. Mama came to him. She kissed his forehead.* "Let them take you son. For God's sake - let go." *The pain again. The pressure behind his eyes was intolerable. He saw a wooden tenement in flames. There was an explosion. All the windows blew out.* "My eyes," *he screamed.* Suddenly Becker was a twenty five year old cop on Allen Street; it was July, about nine PM; the heat was oppressive, a Mama - wearing a sheitle, the horse hair wig of the orthodox wife - began pulling on his sleeve. She spoke no English, but Becker, like most East Side coppers, understood some Yiddish. He was about to sign off for the night. "What do you want, dammnit?" he asked. Jews, *he thought,* always complaining. Probably the toilet isn't working; or her husband is missing; or the border won't pay his rent. *He was about to brush her off until he looked into her eyes; they were wild - staring at some private vision of hell.* "Come please," she said. "My children. My children." *She pulled him toward a tenement. Inside, the smell was overwhelming - burnt chicken fat and onions, and the reek from hall toilets which always overflowed. It was pitch black; he stumbled up the steps, following her to a third floor flat into the kitchen, and through the long hall to the parlor. Four children, all girls, were staring out the window. Mama screamed at them to get away - pulling their hair. They wouldn't budge; like chasing flies from meat. Finally they turned and noticed Becker - staring at him with more anger than fear. He looked out the window. An elevated train came steaming by. It was about five feet from the window; the noise, an ear splitting terror, tore at his brain; the apartment shook so violently it seemed to become the train. He was nauseated by the suffocating crude oil stench of its wake. The little girls came back; edging him out of the way. They were staring through the interstices of track and wooden cross planks at the tenement across the street. He followed their gaze to a second floor window; he saw two people fucking. The girls see this all the time,* he thought. *Bet the damn whore always has the window open. It was Lena. He recognized Monk Eastman. I should have killed him,* he thought. ***That*** *would be worth dying for.*

Six: *Lena in Hell*

Albany. Spring, 1893.

When Fourteen year old Lena Isaacs discovered she was accepted to the all Christian Albany Academy for Girls she was less than enthusiastic.

"Just my luck," Lena confided to her best friend Gertie Halpern, "Papa would become rich in time to buy me into this finishing school for fancy *schiksas*. So fancy they think their shit doesn't stink."

"Yours does to high heaven," Gertie giggled.

"Of course, it's Jew shit."

It wasn't easy being a Jew in Albany. But the chill wind of hatred blew coldest through the arch Victorian corridors of the Albany Academy for Women.

"No matter what I do, they hate me," she complained to Gertie. "The more I try, the worse it gets."

If she dressed expensively, she was trying to buy friends. When she got A's she was too smart to be a real lady. And, of course, any overtures toward friendship confirmed her pushiness. Lena's loneliness was exquisite. She found consolation in fantasy, disfiguring her imagination with the gluttonous consumption of dime romantic novels.

She was bright, and articulate. But her beauty and intelligence hid a deadly flaw - a fissure at the center of her being. It was always there, forcing her to watch her every move, draining her of spontaneity, making her feel like a fraud. After three and a half years at the Academy the small fissure had become a huge crack.

"God Gertie, I hate the Academy. I hate Albany. I hate being a Jew."

Lena did not hate the way she looked, and invariably spent a lot of time in front of the mirror.

How could that be me, she thought. *That girl is beautiful.* Sometimes she would stand before the mirror naked and imagine she was seeing herself through the eyes of one of the heroes in her novels. *I would want me,* she thought and felt a glimmer of sexual excitement. These were her best moments.

Math was her only academic deficiency. Whenever she entered Mr.Schilkraut's Advanced Mathematics class boredom, anger and fatigue converged to create an incredible knot of pain somewhere deep inside her head. She found his logarithm lectures incomprehensible, filling her with a profound sense of inadequacy. The D on her first quarter report was considered highly inappropriate. Young ladies at The Albany Academy for Woman did not get D's. Especially Jewish young ladies.

As Mama reminded her it was, " -- an honor and responsibility to be the first Hebrew admitted to the Academy. An opportunity, my dear, your sisters were denied."

An opportunity, to turn my life into a living hell.

"You're saying, Mama, my sisters wouldn't have shamed the family with a D in Math."

"We want so much to be proud of you dear," said Mama.

One night Papa came home with the news that Mr. Schilkraut had visited his store.

"The man was distressed, Lena. He said if you don't improve in math he would have to fail you." They were having dinner, the five of them. Mama, Papa, and Lena's two older sisters, Flo and Birdie. Blanche, the black servant who was hired on the day of Lena's birth, was serving them.

"I'm trying Papa," she said.

"What will become of you if you don't graduate?" asked Mama.

Lena looked at her two sisters. "They're enjoying this," she thought .

"Woolworth's is hiring," offered Flo, the oldest.

Birdie thought this was the funniest thing she had heard in at least a week. Papa's look silenced her. Lately whenever Papa had dealings with his youngest daughter he tasted bile. Why should someone so beautiful and brilliant be unhappy? It was this goddamn country. *Some Golden Land! Feh, back home such a beauty, seventeen years old with a wealthy father, would be married into a family with* yichus, *maybe scholars, rich merchants. Babies she would have by now.*

But they weren't back home. In America she should be an American. What better place than this gentile Academy? Here she would become a full-fledged American girl. Still Jewish, of course, but a Yenkee - ready to marry one of those Americanized German Jews. She would have little blond, green-eyed babies, and join a huge Temple where the men and women sat together and spoke to God quietly, respectfully. In English. She would be safe and secure. A real Jewish *Americaneh* filling their hearts with pride.

But instead of being grateful for all they'd done for her, Lenaleh was distant, cranky, and defiant. Now she might not even graduate. Papa looked over at his daughter and noticed her tears.

I should cry, he thought. Papa watched her eyes narrow.

She began to scream. " I hate the *schiksa* school that makes me feel like a freak." Her voice shrill. Unhinged. Her beauty creased beyond recognition.

Lena's hysteria brought Papa back forty years.

He was five, at the funeral of Fraidle, his baby brother. Mama's grief grew until it became a living thing that entered and transformed her - a demon bearing her likeness but was not Mama; was something fearsome; ferocious.

"I hate Mr. Schilkrout who makes me feel stupid," Lena said.

Its voice not Mama's voice; its eyes not Mama's eyes.

"I hate you, Papa, for sending me there."

The Mama Thing threw itself on Fraidle's tiny corpse; tore at its shroud. The Rabbi tried to restrain it; but the Mama Thing thrust him away with such force he flew backwards nearly tumbling into the grave.

"I hate you Papa," Lena screamed.

"The Mama Thing turned toward Papa; its Mama face, now dangerous; it screeched, "Why isn't it you wrapped in the shroud you little bastard. Please God, I give you Moitle; bring back my baby, my Fraidle."

"I hate you Papa. I hate you." Lena was standing now. Hysterical.

He had to stop this Daughter Thing that was no longer Lena.

Furiously he rushed toward her.

The next morning Lena woke shuddering at the memory of her nightmare. For reassurance she touched her face.

"Oh my God, it actually happened."

After three days the swelling went down and the blood red of her left eye faded to pink. She returned to school. But nothing would ever be the same. Before the beating Papa's love was as inevitable as breath. Now everything was open to question. Will the sun greet the morning? Will her eyes greet the sun?

Papa. Papa. Papa.

Every Saturday after sundown Lena attended the post Shabbis dance at the Albany YMHA. Here young unmarried Jews came to find the rest of their lives. It was held in the gymnasium, a room not much larger than Lena's dining room. The walls were painted an institutional green. Foot-high bold black letters warned: **NO WOMEN ALLOWED IN GYM AREA.** The wooden floor was sweat stained and buckling. The lamps, improvised for the weekly fete, seemed to initiate more shadow than light.

"Show some enthusiasm for God's sake," said Gertie.

"The only thing exciting about this place Gert, is the smell of men's perspiration."

"I think it's disgusting."

"Are you sure?" They both giggled.

Lena wished she could be more interested in the assortment of males parading before her. Some were handsome; some were amusing; a few were quite rich. A husband would solve a lot of her problems. For one, it would get her out of the Academy. Mama and Papa would trade a rich son-in-law for a diploma any day. Why did it all make her feel so empty? *What's wrong with me?* she wondered for the thousandth time.

"May I have this dance, Lena?" It was Louie Klaff. The Klaffs' were the oldest Jewish family in Albany. More important, his father was Klaff's Department store. She liked him in spite of the fact he would make Mama and Papa so happy. He was a tall good looking young man. And there was an earnest sincerity about him.

Manny's Chamber Orchestra doled out another off-key waltz. They danced.

"So Miss Isaacs, how are the fine young ladies at the Academy treating you?"

"With extraordinary forbearance, Mr. Klaff."

"Very Christian of them, Miss Isaacs. Seriously Lena, you seem unhappy."

She felt him hard against her thigh. Even through the crinoline. That's when she noticed Morris Schiff.

Morris often worked as a recruiter for Rosie Hurtz the most powerful madam on the East Side. He scoured the country recruiting young women - a sexual alchemist seeking to turn flesh into gold.

Not just any flesh. His instructions from Rosie were clear.

"*Schiksas* we's looking for Morris - real Christians, blond hair, blue eyes. It what the greenhorns wants - Yenkees. Believe me, our Jewish girls *schtuping* for nickels and dimes make my heart bleed. But that business," she shrugged - "supply and demand."

Morris was taking the night off - no *schiksas* at a YMHA dance.

Then he saw Lena. "God she beautiful."

Lena had never seen anyone like Morris Schiff.

He wore a white cotton suit, pink silk shirt, and yellow tie. His dark skin compounded the startling mosaic. Instead of the conventional stiff straw boater, his hat was floppy and wide brimmed, constructed of softened straw. The huge diamond stick pin attached to his tie caused Lena to blink. She counted six gold, gem studded rings, three on each hand. His full lips bent slightly upward at the corners into something less than a smile.

There was an intriguing quality about him Lena found difficult to define. Defiant. Dangerous. His presence in the gym created waves of anxiety. "I may only be a stranger," he seemed to announce to the assembled dancers, "but you will justify yourselves to me."

"He looks like a gangster," said Gertie. "And he's looking at you."

No one had ever looked at Lena like that. *God doesn't he ever blink?* she wondered. *And why am I staring back?*

"Who does he think he is?" asked Louie Klaff. Purposefully, he walked toward Morris.

"Isn't he brave?" said Gert.

Gert and Lena were transfixed by the confrontation between Morris and Louie. It was theater. They watched as Louie extended his hand in welcome. Morris hesitated. For the first time unsure. He scowled; his hands remained deep in his pockets. Louie's extended arm was stuck in space. His smile froze.

"Poor Louie," Lena whispered to Gert.

Then Morris smiled, pulled his hand from his pocket and grasped Louie's. Immediately the two men were engaged in intense animated conversation. It wasn't long before Louie motioned Lena and Gert to join them.

"Lena Isaacs, Gertie Halpern, this is Mr. Aaron Margulies, President of one of those exciting little upstart manufacturing companies on the East Side of Manhatten. In fact Mr. Margulies is going to be presenting his spring line to me a week from this Monday."

"You honor me with the opportunity, Mr. Klaff. Will your father attend?" Asked Morris.

"He will be delighted."

Manny's Chamber Orchestra began another approximation of a Straus waltz.

"May I Miss Isaacs," said Morris The Pimp, "be so presumptuous as to ask for this dance?"

Lena's beauty, wealth and social grace presented Morris with a unique challenge. But he was undaunted - like a shark sensing blood, he tasted her loneliness, anger, and despair. As they danced his words poured like wine, making Lena drunk on possibilities. He tore at her fragile defenses, inventing a New York City of earthly delights - of glittering theaters, and fine restaurants. Of golden gambling palaces teeming with beautiful women and wealthy men. He promised endless nights of laughter without tears. Morris anticipated every nuance of Lena's resistance with brilliant improvisations. A girl like Lena would never visit a single man's apartment alone. So he invented a chaperone - his sister Sarah, a teacher, who shared his spacious Fifth Avenue apartment.

"It's amazing, Miss Isaacs, how much you and Sarah have in common. You two would make swell friends. Perhaps you'll meet her one day."

"I'd love that, Mr. Margulies."

Morris looked at his watch. It was important not to appear eager. He had all the time in the world. "I must catch the first train back to the City in the morning - the early bird gets the worm. It's been a pleasure, Miss Isaacs."

Lena felt a door slam in her face.

Will I see you again, Mr. Margulies?" She heard the desperation in her voice, and didn't care.

Morris at first looked doubtful; then brightened. "I do have that presentation to the Klaffs' next Monday."

"We can meet here then," said Lena.

"Perhaps, Miss Isaacs. It's been a pleasure."

He was gone.

Lena was certain she would see Mr. Margulies again. Nobody had ever looked at her like that. For an entire week the memory of his brown eyes warmed her nights. *Am I in love?* she wondered. When Saturday finally came she was in a state of near hysteria. Perhaps he wouldn't come. Why would a gentleman of such wealth and stature care about meeting a silly school girl in a stinking old gymnasium? She arrived early with Gert.

Manny's Chamber Orchestra was warming up.

"For your sake Lena, I hope he doesn't show up," said Gert. "I don't trust anyone who dresses like a gangster and speaks like a gentleman."

GOD'S RAT

On cue Morris appeared. He seemed worried - preoccupied. He brushed past Lena with a curt, "I must see Mr. Klaff."

Lena watched while Morris spoke intently to Louie Klaff. She saw Louie put his hand on Morris' shoulder sympathetically; they shook hands. Morris turned toward Lena. "I'm sorry Miss Isaacs, I must return home immediately."

Lena wanted to die. "How could this be happening?"

He explained, "I just received a wire at the hotel from Sarah. Momma's quite ill. I simply must go now."

His face was drained of color. The tough guy smirk was gone. *He looks like a frightened little boy,* thought Lena.

Morris kissed her hand. "I'm sorry Miss Isaacs," he said, and turned toward the exit.

As if standing outside her body, Lena heard herself call after Morris: "Please Mr. Margulies, I'd like to join you."

Morris turned. "That, Miss Isaacs, would be impossible." He wore the expression of an adult speaking to a difficult child.

"I could be of help. I worked as a volunteer at Mt. Sinai Hospital. Beside sir, I insist."

"In that case, we have a train to catch," said Morris.

Once on the train, Lena became frightened. She had no money; no clothes. She hadn't even stopped to tell Gert - afraid it would give Mr. Margulies the opportunity to change his mind.

Mama and Papa are going to be crazy, she thought. Probably go to the police. She was aware her behavior was strange. Far beyond anything she had done before. The train was permeated with the smell of coal drenched steam; it was nauseating. Lena turned her head to the window. Dusk seemed to linger forever in early June. The bucolic landscape of upstate New York was a soft golden silhouette fading to black; the rush of dimming trees, farm houses and cows as monotonous as the metronomic click of the metal wheels on the metal track. The huge overhead fan created a gentle draft. Drifting off to sleep, she dreamed of Mama's hand soothing her hair. The train jerked. Her head fell against Morris' shoulder. He was unresponsive.

Sleep silenced her questions.

The next thing she heard was Morris: "OK girlie we here. Let's go."

Out the window all she could see was steam. The aisle was full of passengers struggling with luggage. Morris grabbed his bag and disappeared in the crowd. Lena's body was drenched in sweat. Her eyes filled with tears. *Dear God, what have I done?*

For a harrowing three minutes she couldn't find Morris. The crowd pushed her off the train. She found herself in a dark, cavernous tunnel. The rush of passengers was a river flowing furiously up a concrete walkway. At times her feet weren't touching the ground. She looked hopefully toward the only source of light, gas lit chandeliers; but they were feeble stars casting dull shadows in a man made night.

Lena was dizzy with fear. *If only I was eight years old I could cry,* she thought. *Tell someone I'm lost; 'Please help me find Mama and Papa.'* But she wasn't eight years old, and Mama and Papa were a million miles away.

Would the dark tunnel ever end? Finally she saw light. Entering the massive vestibule of Grand Central Station she was blinded by the brilliance of the electric lights. From man-made night to man-made day. The vastness of this huge secular cathedral overwhelmed her. The entire city of Albany would fit in here, she thought. Yet the enormity of Grand Central Station was strangely comforting. It reminded her why she was in New York City.

"Think you was lost, girlie?" Morris was smiling. He grabbed her arm and began pulling her toward an exit. His touch was comforting. She leaned against him.

Her fear transformed into excitement. *Maybe this will work out. I'm in New York City and my whole life is in front of me.*

Outside Grand Central Station, Lena was astonished by all the activity - trucks, buses, carriages, thousands of pedestrians. It was late, nine in the evening. At this time in Albany the streets are deserted. Even the police are home asleep. Morris hailed a taxi. Inside, Lena peered out the window. She found the soaring height of the buildings suffocating. Her breathing became labored. "I must find the sky," she thought. But no matter how she squirmed in her seat and twisted her head she couldn't see above the upper floors.

Morris was amused. "They's called skyscrapers girlie"

"My name is Lena, Mr. Margulies," she said sternly.

"Sure it is."

Albany, if you travel a mile in any direction, comes to an end. Manhattan's vastness seemed endless - the ride interminable. Morris said nothing; his silence, tangible - a festering malignance. Again Lena was seized by panic.

Nothing in her life would ever be the same. "I've stepped off the edge of the world."

Lena noticed the streets becoming more crowded. People were overflowing the sidewalks, flooding the gutter - the swarm of humanity so intense it slowed the taxi to a virtual standstill. Faces pressed against the window. *Who are these people? Why aren't they asleep?* she wondered. Kids with hard eyes; men with broken noses and golden teeth; women whose furiously painted faces were grotesque, rouged masks.

Lena no longer felt protected in the carriage. Her role as spectator crumbled. It was as if she were at a theater and the actors suddenly left the stage to watch her. She heard as much Yiddish as English. Morris finally told the driver to stop. Lena had never seen so many people in one place in her life. Hundreds of unescorted women. Thousands of kids, half of them barefoot. The men wore the expression Morris had when she first saw him; an upward thrust of the lips never quite resolving into a smile. Like Morris their stares were unrelenting.

On both sides of the street, separated by a mere fifty feet, seven story tenements loomed like walls. Looking up Lena could see a slim slice of sky, the stars wan, overpowered by the street lamps. The second floor of many of the buildings had been converted into dance halls. She could hear the raucous, syncopated music; see the dancers swirling. She thought of the gym at the YMHA. It seemed far away

Why was I so desperate to leave? I'll never see it again, she thought.

By now she realized it was all a sham. Mr. Aaron Margulies was someone called Morris. He was well known to the low lifes, cut throats, and whores on the street. There was no sick Mama. No sister Sarah. No apartment on Fifth Avenue. Lena was inundated by feelings of unreality. Mama, Papa, her sisters, Gertie, Louie Klaff, Mr. Schilkrout, even her tormentors at the Albany Academy for Women, were gone - the breathing mirrors confirming who she was. Without them she felt invisible.

"I'm Lena Isaacs, I'm Lena Isaacs, I'm Lena Isaacs," she chanted. But the chant became a taunt - a mocking reminder that Lena Isaacs cast no shadow. Her knees weakened. She clutched Morris' arm.

They reached their destination - a brilliantly lit saloon - its name spelled out in hundreds of little bulbs: **SILVER DOLLAR SMITH'S**. Lena was confronted by two large swinging doors. As she was about to enter, Morris grabbed her by the shoulder and shoved her toward a battered brown door with the inscription, in hand written black ink, "Women Only."

Inside, the noise was deafening. But most striking was the glare. Beams of piercing light flared from the thousands of silver dollars that tiled the floor. It stung her eyes like the sun. In the distance a tenor trilled, *Wild Irish Rose* to an off key piano.

A huge bearded gentleman in regal attire greeted them. He grandly introduced himself as Mr. Silver Dollar Smith. His gold teeth glittered when he smiled.

"Morris, you runty procurer, what green fruit have you plucked from the vine?" He asked.

"Her name is Lena, Mr. Smith, ain't she a beauty?"

Smith directed his gaze toward Lena. "From whence was you harvested, my dear?"

Morris turned to speak to some huge whore he called Bella.

Lena saw an opportunity. She whispered in Smith's ear, "Stolen, Mr. Smith. From Albany."

Smith's eyes hardened. "Moisheleh ain't no thief my dear - just a pimp."

He led them to a crowded table. Lena wasn't introduced. Beer was brought by the bucket. For the first time in her life, Lena drank beer. It tasted like ashes. The conversation regarded some card game called stuss, crooked cops, race horses, Jenny the Bug turning forty tricks, a dog named Rabbi who stole pocket books for a kid named Crazy Butchie. Morris kept filling Lena's glass.

The din was ear splitting. Looking up through the blue haze of smoke Lena was amazed to notice a second tier. Never had she seen so many people in one place before. At the table next to them two men stood up, and began screaming at each other. A skinny whore in a huge feathered hat was crying bitterly. The men looked like the kind of gentlemen who frequented Papa's haberdashery; spending an entire day in deep consultation with Manny the tailor and dropping a couple of hundred dollars without blinking an eye. One was short and squat; the other quite tall, at least six feet; his thinning grey hair and sharp angular features reminded Lena of Mr. Schilkrout. Suddenly he pitched forward onto the table with such force all the drinks went over. The back of his head was thick with blood. The white table cloth turned red. Two hands grabbed him by the shoulder and flung him off the table, onto the floor.

His assailant was one of the most bizarre men Lena had ever seen. Standing about five-five he had a bullet shaped head that sat on a short bull neck. His heavily veined sagging jowls were horribly scarred as were his cheeks. His nose was broken. He was wearing a checkered suit so tight fitting it made him look like a sausage about to burst. Awkwardly perched on his overly large head was a derby many sizes too small. In one hand he held a large wooden club. His face was twisted by rage. "Where the other guy?" he screamed, "Where the other guy?"

Lena was relieved the short squat gentleman was nowhere to be seen. Morris stood and called to the man with the club. He came over and shook Morris' hand. His presence silenced their table. He and Morris conferred quietly; Morris seemed cowed by this strange man. Lena noticed he wore a belt with a gun in a holster. As he spoke to Morris he looked at Lena. Finally he walked over to her.

"Monk Eastman," he said. "I's the sheriff of this place."

His face was softer now. Lena was surprised she didn't feel afraid. "Sorry if I causes you any fright, Ma'am - but them fancy assed goys from uptown comes down here, thinks they owns the joint. Moishe tell me you's from Albany. Hope you enjoys you stay on the East Side."

"Lena Isaacs, Mr. Eastman - pleased to meet you."

Eastman smiled, turned, and disappeared into the crowd. Lena sat back down and took a long swig of beer. Mr. Smith sat next to her. He moved so close she could feel his whiskers, smell his sweat.

"Easy with the beer," he whispered. He pressed a coin into the palm of her right hand.

"Go home," he said.

She looked at the coin. It was a ten-dollar gold piece.

Morris stood up. "Time to go girlie."

Outside the crowds had thinned. A cooling breeze lifted from the East River caressing her face. With great pleasure she imagined the river, its boats and passengers. They had destinations, and families, and lives far removed from these foul man made canyons.

On Essex Street they walked north to East Houston. Here the crowds evaporated. There were no saloons or dance halls. Just darkened tenements and store fronts with signs in Yiddish.

Suddenly the silence was interrupted by the sound of something crashing to the ground at high velocity. Lena jumped.

Morris laughed. "Just a bag of garbage, girlie."

"They throw it out the window?"

Morris was indignant. "Maybe in Albany they walks down seven flights of stairs to throw away garbage. On the East Side we got more sense."

This is the closest they came to having a conversation since leaving the gymnasium. For Lena it created an illusion of normalcy.

"Why did you lie to me? Why did you bring me here?" she asked.

Morris' answer was a violent slap across the face. She tasted blood running from her nose.

He gave her a hanky. Walking in silence, they turned north on East First Street. Finally, they reached their destination: a nondescript three story tenement, its frayed canopy inscribed, The Hertz Hotel.

Inside it was dark, empty, and sparsely furnished; a small bar, a few battered tables and chairs. Each table had a small dimly lit lamp. There was a strong smell of stale beer, cigar smoke, sweat, and cheap perfume. Dulled by alcohol and drenched in fear Lena convinced herself she was dreaming. Soon Mama will wake her up. "It's time for school, dear. What in the world were you dreaming about? You must stop reading those damn novels."

Lena's hand was in her pocket clenching Smith's ten dollar gold piece. The bartender brought over a bucket of beer and three glasses.

"Rosie will be right out, Morris," he said.

Rosie Hertz entered from an interior entrance. She was stout, and dressed plainly. Lena, in her confusion, was sure it was Mama's sister, her *tanta* Essie.

"Nu, Moisheleh?" Rosie asked Morris, kissing him hard on the cheek. "Like a son I misses you. You eat *tateleh*? Food, we got plenty - Izzy, go to the kitchen..."

Morris assured her he couldn't eat a thing.

Looking at Lena she asked Morris, "So what you got for Momma Rosie?"

She placed her hands on each side of Lena's head and gently pushed it back.

Carefully she appraised her face like a jeweler would a diamond.

"Such a beautiful *punim*. Blond hair. Green eyes. Without the Yid nose she be a perfect little *shiksa*. Morris, you outdid yourself this time."

Morris was pleased. He had the look of a little boy who brought his mama a report card with all A's.

"Stand up girlie," he demanded.

Lena complied.

Rosie shook her head. "A little on the skinny side. But we fix that, *tsatskeh*," she said to Lena - playfully poking her in the ribs.

She poured her a beer.

Morris took a small silver box from his pocket, removed a tiny white pill and placed it in Lena's drink.

Lena remembered what happened next as if it were a dream.

She was weightless; floating, rising above a strange room. Papa's voice reassured her: "You are returning to God, my daughter." She heard the chanting prayers of a thousand Jews; saw their upper torsos genuflecting violently. She drifted above them, their white prayer shawls, the sea. They are praying for my soul, she thought. My body is dead. The Jews yanked at their beards. Tears ran from their eyes. They threw themselves on the floor, a thousand prayer shawls becoming one billowing sheet of satin.

"Look away, my daughter," said Papa. Lena could not. She saw herself naked on satin sheets; her eyes closed in drugged sleep. A door opened. Some foul beast approached. He was naked. Lena screamed. Morris tore into her. The pain was exquisite. Morris came. Lena's pleasure, like the blood, covered her in shame. She heard Papa weeping.

After Morris, there were more men. Now she felt only pain. *Tanta* Essie came to her with food and maternal caresses. Later she realized the food was drugged.

Wakefulness seeped through layers of pain, and waves of nausea. Lena opened her eyes to see a young black woman entering the room. She carried a silver tray laden with food: sweet rolls, bagels, bialys, a whole white fish, lox, pickled herring. In the center of the tray was an ornate silver tureen of steaming tea.

The sight and smell of food made her want to puke. Rosie bustled in.

"*Ess, gueleebte*, we gotta fatten you up." She leaned over and kissed Lena on the forehead. Lena realized last night never happened. It was not to be mentioned. She picked at the food. Rosie filled the room with idle chatter. She explained how lucky Lena was to be in the greatest city in the world. Albany was a joke - no place for a beautiful, bright Jewish girl.

"All my girls marry well, *leibling*," Rosie assured her. "More than a madam, I's a matchmaker. One day even your mama and papa will thank me." Rosie took Lena shopping. They went to finest stores. Money was no object.

Once Lena called Rosie, "Mama". When they returned Lena was shown to her room; a tiny cubicle consisting of a bed, a closet, a chair, and a dressing table with a mirror. Under the bed was a chamber pot. The door was locked from the outside. Alone, her head completely clear for the first time in over twenty four hours, Lena was determined to escape. She searched for Silver Dollar Smith's ten dollar gold piece. It was gone.

Where would I go? she thought. *I don't even know who I am anymore. How can I ever look at Papa, Mama? I'm a whore, I slept with God knows how many men. The first time I even liked it.* She could still smell the men, the sex.

She looked in the mirror. Rosie had done her hair. It was swept up, tied in a bun. She looked older.

"*Kurva*," she heard herself saying. "Whore."

She watched the tears roll down her face. Suddenly she relaxed. A feeling of peace swept over her. *I can go home,* she thought. For the first time in forty-eight hours she smiled. She went to the bed, reached under it, and retrieved the chamber pot. Returning to the mirror she put the chamber pot on the table and gazed at her reflection. She undid her hair and undressed. Her body seemed strange, stained. "No one would want this filth."

Then she imagined she was home in her own room. Her body was beautiful again. She smiled. Lifting the chamber pot over her head she hurled it into the mirror and picked up a shard of glass from the dressing table.

There was no pain. She lay down on the bed. "Good night Mama, Papa."

Her next recollection was an excruciating pain coming from the wound on her right wrist. She opened her eyes and saw a short, painfully thin man of about fifty, formally attired, sporting a gray goatee, and a gold framed pince nez bandaging her wounds. He introduced himself as Dr.Greenbaum and told Lena how fortunate she was to be alive.

"If Mrs. Hertz didn't hear you smash the mirror, dearie, you'd be dead. She saved your life."

"Protected her investment," mumbled Lena.

"Don't be so hard on Rosie dearie," said Dr. Greenbaum. "She loves her girls."

His breath stank of schnapps. He reached into his battered black leather bag and took out a bottle of laudanum. Lena noticed his hands were shaking.

"This will assuage your pain dearie, and your dolorous spirit."

The doctor left. Greedily Lena gulped the laudanum and drifted off to sleep. Later she was awakened by someone running a hand through her hair. It was Rosie.

"Mama Rosie loves you, *liebling*." She put a bottle of slivovitz in Lena's hand. Then, not bothering to even close the door, she left.

GOD'S RAT

Seven: Hoodlum Bar Mitzvah

East Side, NYC. July, 1914

Abie's search for Morris took him to Segal's Cafe a low life hangout on Second Avenue that was home away from home for every manner of Jewish criminal on the East Side. Guerrillas, gangsters, pimps, lifetakers, strike breakers, pipe fiends, gamblers, *gonifs*, gun molls, and prostitutes. At three in the afternoon it wasn't very crowded. The heat was oppressive, and the place stank of burnt onions, stale fish, chicken fat, and sweat. In the rear there were card tables for stuss. A couple of games were going on.

Morris wasn't there but a few of the Cafe's denizens, Sam and Meyer Boston, Little Keever, and Chaim the Mummy, asked Abie to join them. The Boston brothers were notorious guerrillas, part of Big Jack Zelig's gang. A couple of years ago their murderous exploits in Boston got so out of hand all the gangs wanted them dead and put a hefty price on their heads. They were both enormously fat with blond hair and goyishe faces. To Abie with their pug noses, and squinty eyes they looked like pigs.

Chaim the Mummy was a pipe fiend whose perpetual state of quasi consciousness led to his street name. Little Keever stood under five feet tall and was considered one of the best pickpockets in the business. He had a thick black beard and tiny puckered red lips making the lower part of his face look like a monkey's ass. Whenever Little Keever opened his mouth Abie smelled shit.

As the men talked, they gobbled pieces of honey cake, semi-stale rolls and bagels, herring, jellied calve's feet cooked in onion and garlic, and chunks of halvah. Along with the food were bottles of slivovitz, cognac, and beer. The Boston brothers totally dispensed with utensils. It seemed to Abie their concession to propriety was using their hands as opposed to the direct application of their bloated pig faces to the food.

Still, Abie felt proud sitting with these luminaries of the underworld. He wished Rosie Saperstein could see him .

GOD'S RAT

"Abeleh," said Meyer Boston, "we hears what you done to that Gopher, Big James Toohey. For this you deserve a drink. Gusseleh," he shouted to the wreck behind the bar, "bring a glass." When the glass arrived, he filled it with slivovitz. "Drink, eat, boychick."

Break some poor bastard's arm, you get laid and a free meal, thought Abie.

"So Abeleh, they gives you a name. 'Abie Cracks'," murmured Chaim the Mummy in a barely audible monotone.

"You know that a very good name," pronounced Meyer Boston barely interrupting licking his greasy fingers as if they were a half devoured calve's foot.

Sammy Boston staggered to his feet and declaimed drunkenly to all the tables, "Shutup youse dumb *gonifs*. And ladies," he glared murderously at a table of gaggling whores. The silence was quick and total. Even the stuss players put down their cards. Abie imagined the roaches stopped dead in their tracks. Sammy motioned for Abie to stand up.

"As many of youse low life's knows, this young man is Abraham Isaacs, a true son of the East Side. His mama Lena is one of us, and if God knows who his papa is, probably a low life too."

Polite laughter. "Abie a fine thief. He and his boys run as good rackets as any young *gunsils* on the East Side. I ain't saying nothing, but Shlomo what owns the fruit stand on Essex and Grand, ain't gonna turn down no honest grafters no more. Not after that terrible fire what almost got him killed, that fucking cheapskate."

Abie's chest swelled at the words, ' -- his boys'. Good thing Klopper ain't here to hear this bullshit, he thought. He was less happy about the mention of the fire.

"But today, he graduates; it's his hoodlum Bar Mitzvah." Sammy stopped, his pig eyes demanding a response for such sharp wit.

"Some of youse know the overgrown piece of mick dreck, the Gopher, Big James Toohey, a Yid hating cocksucker if there ever was one. Well, starting today he gonna to think twice before fucking with Yeshiva *buchas* and *alte cockers*. And here's why."

He grabbed the chair Abie had been sitting on, lifted it high over his head and smashed it violently on the filthy floor. The grubby crowd at Segal's Cafe was thoroughly rapt. Sammy was left holding one of the chair legs. He handed it to Abie and continued.

"Today this Toohey bastard was smashing that poor cripple Freak Show Barovick in the face with knucks--"

Abie forgave Sammy the lie, it was for dramatic effect. Although the ladies would have been more sympathetic had he told the truth. No punishment would be good enough for the prick who tried to disfigure Sugar Davey Saperstein, the most beautiful face on the East Side.

"--our little Abie grab his arm like this." Sammy grabbed the arm of Little Keever by the wrist and the elbow." Keever was terrified. His eyes rolled like one of those white fools in black face.

"Abeleh, shows them what happened."

Holding the three-inch thick mahogany leg, Abie began to sweat profusely. He was terrified the damn thing wouldn't break. It wasn't his personal humiliation that worried him. *Sammy'll kill me I don't bust it,* he thought. He hesitated out of fear. The hesitation appeared to be for dramatic effect. He brought the chair leg down hard against his knee. It cracked. There was a loud cheer.

Shouts of "Mazel Tov" rang out. Just like at a wedding after the groom smashes the glass.

Sammy quieted the crowd. "The drinks is on Sammy and Meyer Boston." He raised his glass, "To Abie 'Cracks' the East Side's newest *schtarker.*"

Abie had his moment. A gangster among gangsters. But the table leg was easy; an act of pure strength. He couldn't help but remember Toohey's arm, the initial thrill - the feeling he was a Jewish avenger, possessed by a demon, a *dybuk*, hell bent on wreaking pain, havoc, and death on all the Jew bashers. And then seeing the kid writhing in pain, his own nausea - the regret. Suddenly the nausea returned. He felt he was going to vomit.

"What the matter, you sick," whined Chaim the Mummy, "Too much schnapps?"

Sammy looked at Abie hard. "For a *schtarker* there never enough schnapps." And he refilled his glass with slivovitz. Abie realized he couldn't throw up. Unless he wanted Abie 'Cracks' to become Abie 'Puke'.

"You know the junk man Wexler?" Meyer asked the table.

Abie was relieved; he was no longer the center of attention.

"Sure, the schmuck what think he can takes on Yushke Nigger and his horse poisoners," said Little Keever.

"A real *macher* this junk man. 'I knows people at Tammany. I ain't giving youse bastards nothin.' Fuck you.'"

"It worse than that. I hears he beat the shit out of one of Yushke's boys," whispered Chaim the Mummy, his eyes half closed.

"Bastard," shouted Sammy slamming his fist on the table so hard it knocked over Abie's glass of slivovitz.

"Nigger can't put up with that," said Little Keever.

"He didn't," smiles Meyer. "Yesterday Wexler on Mott Street when his precious horsy start farting like a gas engine blowing smoke. It getting the junk man sick. Then he notice the horse growing bigger, like a balloon. Next thing it start dancing, and making noises like it drowning."

Everybody's laughing, Tears were coming out of Sammy's eyes.

"The junk man jump out of his wagon. Then the horse stop, just stand there like a statue. Real quiet. Wexler figure, "Everything OK now - maybe it got indigestion." Meyer's laughing so hard he can't speak.

"So finish the damn story," demanded Sammy.

Meyer tried but all that came out was spit and flecks of halvah. Finally he caught his breath. "It ain't got no indigestion, it fucking dead."

"On its feet, it dead?" asked Chaim the Mummy, suddenly wide awake.

"Good for Yushke," announced Sammy.

Abie wanted to ask what happened next. Did the horse finally fall? Did the wagon topple over? But he realized these are the wrong questions. It was essentially a moral tale; the point had been made.

"Nu Abeleh," Sammy asked, "Why you wants to see Morris?" Abie told them. Even showed his trophy, the chipped tooth.

"Becker was sweet on your mama," mumbled Chaim the Mummy.

"Lena changed," added Little Keever. His monkey's ass mouth puckered into a caustic smile. Abie smelled shit.

"Becker's famous," said Chaim the Mummy, sinking fast. "You reads what Herman Rosenthal says about him in *The World*?"

"Herman a rat. He gotta die," shouted Sammy. "Got a beef with Becker, keep it downtown. Not in no papers. You's Big Tim Sullivan's mutt. Get the Irishman to talk to the copper for you. A gangster don't yap to no reporters. Now everybody riled up. Rosenthal ain't just squealing on a copper what's fucking him. He squealing on all of us. Why the whole world gotta knows our business?"

Meyer sensed they were doing too much talking in front of the kid. "So Abeleh, Morris gonna help get Becker off your ass?" He said. Gratefully, Abie took the hint and got up. "Yeah, I better find him." He forgot the two glasses of slivovitz. On his first step, the floor came up and slammed him in the head. The men laughed the same way they laughed at Wexler's horse. Without mercy.

* * * * *

January 25, 1915, 6:03 am, and 2 seconds, Sing Sing.

Behind the glass the witnesses were growing impatient. "They want me dead. Only my death will make their shame go away," he thought. "Die Becker. Die Becker. Die. Die. Die." Fists were raised; mouths twisted into predatory snarls; spit like rain splashed against the glass barrier. His face became wet; it was a cold driving November rain - the small canopy he was under provided scant protection. A drunk stumbled past. Suddenly out of the shadows two figures emerged. It's Sammy and Meyer Boston, *Becker thought,*

GOD'S RAT

They're kids, like when they were run out of Boston. *Sammy was laughing; he pointed to Becker strapped in the chair.* "Meyer," he said, "Ain't this a sight - them cooking their own." "But he ain't dead yet Sammy," said Meyer, "--maybe we should help?" *Meyer put his gun to Becker's head. Angrily Sammy knocked the gun away.* "Schmuck - You crazy? Dying horses you shoot. Not no copper." *Sammy spit in Becker's face. Then he turned toward the drunk and smashed him across the knees with a foot long lead pipe.* "Remember this, copper?" *Sammy asked. The drunk went down, losing his hat; Meyer whacked him on the head with his black jack. The brothers deftly stripped him of his wallet and jewelry. The drunk rolled onto his back. With his hat off they clearly saw his face.* "Shit it Mendy the iceman," said Meyer. *The iceman moaned and opened his eyes.* "He seen us," said Sammy. *Each brother drew his gun - pointed it at the iceman's head; they blew his brains out.* "We was doing our job, copper," said Sammy. "But what you do? Just stand there like you don't see nothing." What could I do? *thought Becker, watching the brothers disappear in the rain - listening to their laughter.* The Boston's are with Eastman. We all work for Tammany. *Becker began to cry.* What could I do? *He tried to pray; but no words came. Another jolt of electricity tore through his body. The pain was terrifying. But it was all he had left of life. It was life.*

Eight: The Boss

Abie knew Morris could often be found with Senator Big Tim Sullivan, at the center of political power on the East Side, Tammany Hall's downtown headquarters, The Occidental Hotel on the corner of Broome Street and the Bowery. The battered three-story wooden structure was once a famous dance hall, but now the garish orange paint was a peeled and fading memory; the baroque wrought iron gates, guarding the second floor terraces where expensive young hookers once embraced wealthy old men, forever locked.

To Abie it looked like the body of a old dead whore nobody had the decency to bury. In fact the place would have been knocked down years ago except for the sentimental whim of Boss Sullivan; it was the original hangout for his old gang, the Whyos.

Abie couldn't remember a time he hadn't heard of Big Tim Sullivan. He was King of the Irish, and the Irishers were the aristocracy that ran the East Side. The name Boss Sullivan radiated with legend. Like the time he was eighteen, a bouncer at McGory's Armoury Hall on Hester and beat a man to death for insulting a prostitute named Barbary Jane. "With his bare hands he done it - not even no knucks," Morris once told Abie.

After Sullivan took over the Whyos, a notorious gang from from the old Five Points, their violence and mayhem escalated to a point where the police were advised to disperse rather than confront them.

One day The Honorable Frances X. O'Boyle Tamaney's Big Boss summoned young Sullivan to Headquaters for a chat. "Tim," he's reputed to have said, "There more to life than running whores, breaking heads and raising hell."

"Mr. O'Boyle," replied the gang leader, "I appreciates you talking to me like my father and my priest, but I got ten times the money me pa' ever dreamed of, and I could buy any Church on the East Side. I means no disrespect sir, but why in the name of all that holy should I stop doing what I's doing?"

O'Boyle laughed uproariously. "I ain't your pa' -- your priest, you dumb mick. I's the bloody devil. Your soul going straight to hell. I just got a better deal." Sullivan stared at him.

"Join us," said the Honorable Frances X. O'Boyle.

A year later, in 1886, at the age of twenty three, Big Tim Sullivan was elected state Assemblyman. From that time on you didn't rob a bank, run whores, set up a crap game, roll a lush, or get a City job or contract in the Fourth Ward without paying your most humble respects to Boss Big Tim Sullivan.

It was hard for Abie to imagine Sullivan as a nineteen year old gangster. These days he weighed just under three hundred pounds. But beneath the sixty five years of caloric anarchy there still lurked the wiry leader of the Whyos. Maybe it was only his reputation, but still, he projected an awesome physical presence for a fat old man.

Abie turned into Broome Street and stopped. The place looked closed. The Occidental never closed, and here it was only five in the afternoon. He tried the door, it wasn't locked. Opening it as narrowly as possible, he slithered in. The inside was as huge as his old school's auditorium. The curtains were drawn, the darkness broken only by a small gas lamp at the far side of a very long bar. Its dull glow barely illuminated Morris and Big Tim. Although the men perceived themselves to be alone, they were whispering. Abie wondered whether the last two people on earth would whisper if they were ashamed of what they were saying?

He knew he should leave; he had no business overhearing what they were plotting. But he was too scared to move; and, he had to admit, too excited. His heart pounded so hard he worried the racket would give him away. He was crouching where the four-foot wall separating the bar area from the enormous ball room ended. Peeking from behind the wall he faced the men straight on, at a distance of only ten feet. Big Tim was talking.

"I loves Herman Rosenthal like a son, and here we's talking about having him killed."

"It ain't that complicated Mr. Sullivan. Herman Rosenthal is getting hisself killed," said Morris.

He sounded like a teacher explaining something quite basic to an honor student who had somehow lost half his brain.

At this point terror overtook Abie. Each breath became an effort. "I shouldn't be here," he thought. "I shouldn't be hearing this shit." He looked away from the men, trying to subdue a new wave of panic. His eyes drifted upwards. In the dim light he could just make out the fresco of frolicking fat nudes on the ceiling. He pictured Bella and immediately got a hardon. Her taste and smell were still with him. He thought of the hot, pungent aroma that rises from the weeds, wild flowers, and garbage in vacant lots on Delancy Street in late Spring; an exotic, dizzying, scent of infinite promise and filth.

"Look, Mr. Sullivan," continued the pimp, "none of us is angels. We steals each other's whores; we snitches to the coppers on each other's gambling houses; and there ain't one of us what don't pay *schtarkers* to break heads - and God help us - do the Big Job. We does what we got to do to survive. Self preservation is the first law of nature. But Herman go too far Mr. Sullivan. They says there's no honor among thieves -- but that ain't the same as no rules. We don't fuck each other's wives, or girlies; we don't associates with no copper we can't buy; and we don't go to no newspapers and puts our private business under every citizen's nose."

Abie noticed Big Tim was looking past Morris. He figured the old man was thinking about dying. What else do old people think about?

Finally, he looked at Morris and said, hopefully, "OK, we beats him to within an inch of his life."

"Damn it, Mr. Sullivan, he still drags his bloody broken ass to the New York World and tell the whole story, names and everything to that putz reporter Herbert Swope. Sure Herman had a run of lousy luck lately but that no excuse--"

"Thought his luck changed," interrupted Sullivan.

The door opened. Abie shut his eyes against the brilliant light, hugging the wall as footsteps whispered across the carpet, then clicked crisply - leather heels hitting the parquet wood of the barroom floor.

GOD'S RAT

Abie peeked around the wall. It was the copper Becker. The big Irishman turned away from Morris to face the cop.

"You wanted to see me, Mr. Sullivan?"

Sullivan put his left hand on the Lieutenant's shoulder. Abie could feel the copper shrink.

"Charley," he said, "You was Herman's partner, Why you raid him? Herman finally moving in on the fancy uptown goys. It wasn't just his place of business, Charley. It was his home. Your boys pissing on his fucking rug - it nearly drives him crazy."

Now the Irishman placed his right hand on Becker's left shoulder. Both hands forming a loose stranglehold around his neck. "I had money in the place too, Charley. It was my rug your boys was pissing on. You fucking knew that." He sighed deeply.

"I got pressure from my own people," said Becker, "Especially Inspector Hughes. They figured I was too tight with Herman - I had to treat him like everybody else."

Abie held his breath. Becker was lying. A crooked copper wouldn't raid a joint he had money in. Somebody paid him - paid him a lot. Morris took out his knife and began to clean his fingernails.

The big man's hands tightened around Becker's neck. "Your fucking raid was Rosenthal's death warrant, Charley. He has to rat you out after that." With great effort the copper held Sullivan's stare, squinting as if looking directly into the sun.

Big Tim brought his face so close, Becker could feel him breathe. Abie remembered the big Irishman's Whyo past, how he had killed someone with his bare hands. Becker, so formidable just a few hours ago, terrorizing him and Mama, now seemed broken. Full of guilt, regret. Fear. Everybody knew Big Tim was close to Herman Rosenthal; always picking him up after he fell. Loaning him soft money. Making excuses.

He gonna kill him, thought Abie.

But the Irishman moved his hands up from Becker's neck to his cheeks. He pinched them hard. "Don't worry Charley, I's too old to break your neck. Too tired. All I can think about is going to sleep.

They says age bring wisdom, Charley. Don't believe it. Just fatigue." He placed his hands on the bar, and looked at his image in the mirror.

To Abie he seemed drawn. Very tired. His heavy jowls sagged; hanging from his jaw like a beard. He turned to Morris. "Herman a rat. Cook him."

Becker slammed his fist hard on the bar. "Herman gets killed Mr. Sullivan I take the rap. Who has more reason to kill him then me? I'm out of this." He left. In his wake, silence.

Finally Morris spoke. "He in it whether he like it or not."

"We setting him up," Sullivan said. "We knows it; now he knows it."

Still staring at the mirror Sullivan yawned loudly; to Abie it sounded like a sob. "Do it right Moisheleh," he said. "Fast. Talk to Zelig, we need his best life takers. And get word to Herman we got fifteen thousand, gold. All he got to do is collect it, and leave town. It got my guarantee."

"Herman getting nervous, Mr. Sullivan. Sure he'll show?"

"For that kind of money he'll show up wherever we wants him. Prompt too. You got a time and place?"

Morris, preoccupied removing an offending bit of gunk with his knife from the inside of his thumb nail, replied without looking up, "Why you wants to know sir? Wants to be there? Kiss him good-bye?"

Sullivan smacked him hard against the side of his face. Morris didn't flinch. "Tomorrow at the Metropole, two AM." Complaining of a headache, and how he's getting old, Big Tim rose to go to his room on the second floor.

Watching him, Abie had the feeling the huge aging body already died and only by pure will was the old Irishman lugging three hundred pounds of dead flesh up the stairs. One step at a time.

* * * * *

GOD'S RAT

January 25, 1915, 6:03 am & 39 seconds, Sing Sing.

Becker felt the pain of betrayal; a pain as profound as eighteen hundred volts of electricity. Mr. Sullivan knows I'm innocent, he thought. Suddenly Sullivan was standing in front of him, opening an envelope the twenty two year old Becker had just given him; he removed the six hundred dollars - Becker's "fee" to become a cop. Becker felt Sullivan's arm on his shoulder. "It the best investment you ever made, son," he said. And laughed. "Me and you, copper. We gonna to make each other rich." He turned toward the dapper executioner. "This man is innocent. He didn't want no part of the murder of Herman Rosenfeld. We sets him up - me and Morris The Pimp Schiff. Stop this execution." "Fuck you," screamed the executioner. "You have no authority here." Suddenly Sullivan became the notorious nineteen year old leader of the Whyos; he pressed his black derby hard against his ears and put on a pair of knucks. Becker felt safe. "No one ever beat Sullivan in a street fight." But Sullivan disappeared and became Abie Isaacs, his newsboy cap tilted low over his right eye. Abie was holding a stack of papers under his right arm. He gave Becker a paper. The headline screamed: **Boss "Big" Tim Sullivan Found Beaten to Death in Railroad Yards.** Sullivan reappeared - an old man now - filthy, covered with grease and mud. His face battered; his neck busted. Without the support of a neck his head listed heavily to the right, resting on his shoulder. "Sorry what happened, Mr. Sullivan," Becker said. "I heard how they found you dead in the train yards. Said you were getting old and feeble. Wandered off. Must've lost your mind. Yard bums found you. Beat you to death." And Sullivan - or what was left of him just smiled. Becker was impaled by a new jolt of electricity.

Nine: The Death of Kings

January, 1915. NYC.

Feeble waves of consciousness interrupted the old man's death coma. He knew where he was; the cold steel of a railroad track burned the back of his outstretched right hand. It was the playground of his childhood, these railroad yards between 11th Avenue and the river, beginning at 60th Street and running north for a half a mile.

The stench of grease and burnt coal and livestock and chickens. Him and his boys running through the box cars, dodging the yard bums and the yard cops - fighting the other West Side gangs, first with fists and sticks and then with knucks, and knives and slung shots - all for the rights to the one boxcar that mattered to them, even though it was ancient and rusted and surrounded by deep weeds; but it was magical - full of rotting tufts of straw still redolent of cows and their shit and their piss and their milk; and it made the boys think of a world they had only heard of where there were no tenements or concrete, or drunken papas beating up on sick, tired, drunken mamas; a world with places called Omaha, and Kansas and the land's only interruption, the horizon.

Big Tim knew why he was drugged and dumped here to freeze to death, or to be attacked and torn to pieces by the feral bums who roamed the yards in packs and killed for sport; he knew they knew he intended to do the unpardonable; do something that would destroy the System - a near perfect mesh of greed and power; of politicians and cops and gangsters that ran and plundered the richest city in the world. He himself had murdered to protect the System. Why else was Herman Rosenthal dead? And why, in a couple of days, the copper Becker? Maybe he was just getting old and feeble - not because he was going to the press to tell the truth about Rosenthal's murder - even if that would implicate him and blow the whole System to high heaven - or hell; but because he talked about it to the Tammany hacks - half of them relatives - who for forty-five years he had protected and made rich and who he knew would stop him and do what he had taught them to do for the same forty years - defend the System at all costs. Maybe he just wanted to fucking die. And then he heard footsteps, and he knew it wasn't the yard cops because tonight they were told to go home early.

Ten: "Herman Rosenthal Dies Bravely."

July, 1914. NYC.

Morris arrived at the Tombs early next morning to see Big Jack Zelig. It was not the first time he had been in the Tombs; it was the first time he was there voluntarily. The jail got its name because the prison it replaced in 1878 had been modeled on an Egyptian tomb. It was a gray brooding, chateau-like structure built on piles on the site of the old Collect Pond of New York's colonial days. The pond had never been properly drained and the cells constantly dripped with moisture; the lower tiers were often ankle deep in water forced back by faulty pipes. Morris could swear the building rose and fell with the tide. He always felt he was entering a cave. A dank, stinking bear cave hewn by millions of years of erosion into a fit, perhaps even wondrous, domicile for beasts. For humans it was death. But, to Morris, it was no injustice. "Serve us right, scumbags that we is. But first they gotta catch us."

Zelig's cell was located in a lower tier. Morris was impressed. The lower tiers were reserved for the worst and most feared offenders. To reach the cell he had to walk along a narrow corridor. On his right, a brick wall; on his left, separated by a five foot wooden walkway, the cells; in front of him, the guard, an enormous key hanging loosely from his belt, walked slowly. The only source of light was tiny windows twenty feet above the surface.

Finally the guard stopped in front a cell, placed the key into the key hole and swung open the gate. The light was so sparse Morris could barely distinguish anything, but he knew the layout by heart. The cell was about seven feet by three-and-a-half. A man had barely enough room to stand between his iron cot and the opposite wall. There was no running water, no sanitation except for tin pails, and no ventilation save for small chutes like chimney flues which pierced the massive walls to the roof above. It didn't help that the weather was in the nineties and humid.

GOD'S RAT

At twenty six Jack Zelig had become a legend on the East Side. He began to make his mark as a baby faced pick pocket whose ability to cry on cue kept his juvenile rap sheet short. As he reached the age where his own tears failed to break hearts he'd hire a young, scrawny pipe-fiend whore to show up in court as his "wife" to do his crying for him. "Your honor," he would plead, "my baby died of consumption and as you can see my wife starving. I is a desperate man." Few judicial hearts could withstand this pathetic onslaught.

Zelig was a brutal thug and fierce street fighter, but to the desperately poor Jews struggling to survive on the East Side, he was more than just another *gengstah*. He stood up to the gentile tormentor. In this case the Italians. Whenever Italian mobsters encroached on anything Jewish, Zelig and his boys would extract quick vengeance. His credo was simple: "The dagos don't work our whores; don't bust up our crap games; don't pick our pockets." This gained him an unlikely moniker, "The People's Protector."

People's Protector my ass, thought Morris. *Jack protecting his money - Jewish money for Jewish gonifs. Which OK by me.*

In the darkened cell Big Jack Zelig was just a shadow. Morris was tense. There were rumors on the street, he set Zelig up.

"Nu Moishele," said Zelig, "Tell me about the sky. Tell me about the sun. Tell me about the garbage on Christie Street. Tell me about a couple shots of schnapps. Remind me, boychick, what a naked woman body feel like. Look. Smell. Tell me you see my sister Shandele's kiddy, Sadie? You tells her you's gonna see her Uncle Jack? You tells her, you little mockey, pimp, that it because of you he buried alive?"

Zelig's voice didn't waver; his body remained motionless.

Morris heard the dripping of water. He remembered how at three in the morning each drop was like a crash of thunder. He felt the sweat poring off his body. Zelig could snap his neck like a twig. Morris was beginning to feel dizzy. Along with the lack of oxygen, the stench of raw sewage made him reluctant to breathe at all.

"Jack, why I tell your sister's little *schein'heit* such a thing? Better I tell her that I's bringing her uncle home. That in my pocket

I got a fifteen hundred dollar check for the bail. That her uncle, a hero on the East Side the way he stand up against the enemies of our people, and for this reason alone is plagued by the Irisheh coppers who then starts rumors what set Jew against Jew so that we should all kills each other and make their job easy, is gonna be hugging and kissing her and buying her nice things again."

"I should thank you Schiff because you's buying your own life with money you's getting back?"

"Not all of it. And Big Tim's fixing those bullshit charges. Can I sit down now? I got business we should discuss."

Morris hated this; it was almost an apology - he never felt the need to apologize. As he sat down on the cot his body made a thumping sound as it hit the hard metal surface.

Zelig laughed. "You was expecting a mattress, schmuck?"

"Yankleh, this is important."

"Sound like someone going to die."

"Herman."

Zelig liked Herman Rosenthal. Did a lot of work for him. But business was business. Sure he would have liked it better if Herman was sitting here now, telling him Morris the Pimp had to die. But life was war on the East Side. "We soldiers. We do what we's paid to do."

"What the *shtanges*?"

"A thousand dollars, next day."

"Who behind it?" asked Zelig.

"Everybody."

"Sullivan?"

"Yankleh, maybe you got a problem?" asked Morris. "We could go to the damn Italians. They ain't happy with Herman yapping neither. We don't wants no *Talainas* cooking one of our own. But the job gotta to be done."

"Morris, I can't do nothing in this stinking dungeon. Get me outta here."

"Who the shooters?" Asked the pimp making sure he's getting his money's worth.

GOD'S RAT

"Gyp, Lefty, maybe Whitey. Now get me the fuck out of here."
"Sure Jack," said Morris.

Gyp The Blood Horowitz. Lefty Louie Rosenberg. Whitey Louis Seidenheimer. *Not a bad day after all,* he thought. *I just buys the best life-takers on the East Side.*

Herman Rosenthal checked his gold pocket watch, a gift from Bella Weinschenker presented at the last birthday bash he threw for himself at the Hesper Club. It was 1:15. His meeting with Morris wasn't until 2 AM. He was standing at the second floor vestibule of his brownstone on West 45th Street.

"Be careful Herman," said his wife, Flora. She was a chunky 35 year old former prostitute who defected from Morris to work for Herman.

"Why careful? Ain't Big Tim behind this?"

"He ain't what he used to be; couldn't even get his cousin elected sheriff - remember? And everyone want you dead."

"Everyone want me quiet. Dead, *I's* headlines in every paper in the city."

"I's scared Herman." She began to cry. Her tears were rivers creating canyons of rouge.

Herman put his arms around her. He really loved this big, stupid, loyal woman. She used to be his best whore. But after their marriage he insisted she retire. "A Jewish wife shouldn't be no trotter," he explained magnanimously. Even now, when times were rough, he wouldn't let her 'help out'.

Herman left. He was on his way to collect the money for keeping his mouth shut - fifteen thousand dollars.

Nellie "Chink" Bartfield brought the news. "Herman," said Bartfield, "you meet Morris at the Metropole Cafe, tomorrow, 2: AM. He be there with the money. Next day you's out of town."

"This kosher Chink?" Herman asked.

"Why you worry?" asked Chink. "Sullivan say the *bruchas*. Ain't he your Rabbi?"

As Herman began his short walk to the Metropole Cafe, a bar in the lobby of the Metropole Hotel, on 43rd Street between Sixth and Seventh Avenues, he felt things were finally looking up. It had been a rough couple of years. First Albany passed an anti-racing ordinance that put all his telephone horse parlors out of business. Then he got Big Tim to back him in a high class gaming establishment right smack in the middle of the Tenderloin, the City's night time gold mine - the fanciest gambling joints, whore houses, restaurants, and saloons. The Tenderloin ran north and south from 42nd Street to 53rd; and from Sixth Avenue on the east to Eighth on the west. No Jew had been allowed to venture that far north before. But within three months his arch rival Bridgey Webber got Tammaney's big boss Tom Murphy to back him in a joint right across the street. Staying in business was going to become very expensive.

It wasn't long before Chief Inspector Hayes invited him out for dinner and asked for a thousand dollars. But Herman got stubborn. He explained to Flora, "You goes that high and there no end to it. Soon you working for the coppers." Of course he was raided. His expensive equipment was busted up. Herman was out of business.

But Inspector Hayes wasn't finished. He went to the press with a bullshit story that made Herman the laughing stock of the City. The headline read: **"INSPECTOR HAYES TRICKS ROSENTHAL INTO CONFESSING."** Herman grimaced as he remembered Hayes' quote in *Times*: "I suggested to Mr. Rosenthal that his wheels and card games might be less than honest. Mr Rosenthal with a show of pride boasted, 'Inspector, I run the most honest wheels, crap tables and stuss games in the City.' It was tantamount to a confession. Judge Goff agreed, and gave us the go ahead for the raid." Then he added, "That's not one smart Jew boy." Hayes was forced to apologize to, " --all the honest and intelligent Hebrews that help make this City great."

He never apologizes to me, the lying bastard, thought Herman. Soon Herman got his mentor, Sullivan, to back him in yet another venture in the same location. This time he thought he had foolproof protection. He took on a partner: Lieutenant Charles Becker.

After Becker screwed him, his situation could not have been much worse. He was out of business, and quickly running out of money. Maybe he should listen to Flora and let her go back to work. That's when he remembered Herbert Bayard Swope. Swope was a brilliant young reporter for *The New York World* with a taste for the fast life. He frequented gaming houses of the highest and lowest order. Always looking for stories, he could be trusted not to reveal his sources.

Herman sought Swope out. "Herbert," he said, "Maybe we can help each other."

To Herman, the reporter Swope looked like a college boy. One of those rich pampered kids who inhabit the world of real power. Power that builds railroads, bridges, and skyscrapers; buys Senators and Presidents, not coppers and ward politicians. The kind of easy, frictionless goy power that puts a kid like Swope into an office on Park Avenue to write articles that make crooked Lieutenants and Inspectors shit in their paints.

"I got no teeth left, Herbert. No money, no joint, and my rabbi, Sullivan, he getting old. They's closing in on me."

"How can I possibly be of help, Herman?" Swope asked pleasantly. He knew exactly what was coming.

"Maybe if the public learn how the coppers and politicians is abusing their public trust - how they making a big splash in the press squeezing one little Jew gambler who down on his luck while the big boys is raking it in. Maybe if my enemies know I going to hang their dirty laundry from the front page of the World every time they fuck with me, they think twice. Like I was taught in school, Herbert, for the five or six years I goes, the pen more powerful than the sword. Which I figures also includes the gun, the shiv, the slung shot, and knucks." Swope put a comforting hand on Herman's shoulder, as if he was the one who was ten years older. He looked, squinted really, through thick round glasses, deeply into Herman's eyes.

"Herman," said Swope, his eyes soft, comforting, " this city is a quagmire of filth and corruption. Only when public spirited citizens--"

"Excuse me, kid," interrupted Herman, "I don't mean no disrespect or nothing, but one reason I quits school, aside from wanting to make money, is I always fall asleep during civics class. Look, let's keep it simple. I's just a criminal looking for revenge and leverage - maybe you can help me?"

"Have you ever met our esteemed District Attorney Charles Whitman?" asked Swope.

"No, I never had the pleasure," said Herman warily. The only time men like Herman met a District Attorney was to cop a plea after an arrest. *Where he going, this rich man's kid?* he wondered.

"Whitman's a man deeply committed to rooting out the crime and corruption that beset this city, Herman."

"I hears he committed to moving his family to the Big House in Albany."

"Extreme ambition, Herman, is not a detriment to achievement. Often just the opposite. The point is he will find your allegations very interesting. You see I am acquainted with the man. After he reads our piece in the paper, I have a feeling he'll want to see you."

"This is a good thing, Herbert?"

Swope laughed, and again placed his arm on the gambler's shoulder. "He's the top cop in the City of New York. His job is to arrest bad guys. He will be very grateful to whoever helps him do his job."

The article ran. It was to be the first in a series. It detailed Herman's relationship with his former partner, Lieutenant Charles Becker. Herman Rosenthal became the most famous gangster in the city. And, among the fraternity of low life's, the most hated.

As predicted Herman was invited, along with Herbert Bayard Swope, to meet with DA Charles Whitman. For the first time, while on official police business, Herman Rosenthal was accompanied by someone other than his lawyer. The meeting did not go unnoticed.

GOD'S RAT

Now, as he walked north on Broadway on his way to the Metropole, Herman was buoyant, full of himself. He turned the tables on all his enemies. Becker had gotten himself a lawyer; and the local politicians, and gangsters - prodded by Sullivan - had agreed to put together enough cold cash to allow him to start fresh in Chicago. Fifteen thousand dollars!

He turned east on 43rd Street. The street was thronged with the usual crowd of actors, actresses, gamblers, wise guys, politicians, boxers, and prostitutes. These were Herman's people. Night stalkers looking for angles that could only be seen in the dark. The heat was a tangible oppressive presence forcing off hats, jackets, and ties. The Metrapole was ablaze. All windows were opened wide, shades up, and curtains yanked aside. The entire building, it seemed to Herman, was gasping for air.

Suddenly he stopped, realizing that agreeing to come here was the biggest gamble of his life. He was indeed the most hated gangster in New York. "Flora's right, damnit, everybody want me dead. Shit, if I was everybody, I'd want me dead." He was blackmailing some of the most dangerous men in the city. "What happen if I's wiped out? Next year I's back demanding more money. Threatening to go to Swope again. Or, worse, the DA." Sweat poured off his body. But what was the alternative? Continue to snitch to Swope? Testify in court? That was no gamble. A sure thing. He'd be dead.

Fuck it, he thought. *The odds is better than even. And the pot fat.*

A rag time piano player's cheerful version of "The Bunny Hug" drifted out the open window of the Metrapole Cafe, the all night club adjacent to the hotel. It was in the cafe that the meeting with Morris was to take place. Herman bustled up the steps to the brightly lit entrance leading to the cafe. The revolving doors were folded flat against the jambs because of the heat. As he passed the potted palms lining the steps he noticed they fluttered in the draft of the two giant electrical fans right inside the door.

Entering the cafe he was aware of the stark silence that fell at a table in the corner near the door where several East Side gamblers were clustered. And that the piano player stopped playing in mid-bar. He basked in the notoriety, and took his accustomed seat in the rear.

    Morris, and the life-takers were in the back room of Bridgey's poker joint, nearby, on the second floor of a tenement over a cigar store on Broadway and 43rd Street. It was 1:35 am. They were waiting for Bridgey to come back from the Metropole Cafe telling them Herman arrived; things were OK. Proceed.

    Morris couldn't believe how well things were going. Sullivan was in with them. The loose alliance of gangsters and gamblers who wanted Herman dead had finally come up with the thousand beans to pay the shooters.

    He even had an alibi should things go wrong. I just tells the DA the copper make me do it - threatened to trump up charges, send me to jail, if I don't get rid of Herman. Morris smiled at the thought of sending Becker to the chair for a crime he didn't commit. *Should've killed me with that club,* he thought.

    Bridgey Webber was in too; he and Herman were bitter rivals, snarling at each other since they were kids. Louis Bridgey Webber carried a lot of weight these days since the success of his uptown gambling joint, and him being so snug with Tammany's Number One Boss, Murphy. Unfortunately, having Bridgey also meant Vallinsky. Hyman Vallinsky was a pencil thin sharp featured thug, his swarthy face scarred by childhood acne and too many collisions with high velocity knuckles, blackjacks, slung shots, and knucks. His nose had collapsed under the onslaught. To Morris it looked more like a limp dick than a nose. Vallinsky liked to think of himself as Bridgey's junior partner. To everyone else he was Webber's personal muscle, a lobbygow. Dangerously stupid, and too quick to blow his top

    Even the life-takers - Gyp the Blood, Whitey, and Lefty Louie - arrived on time, although drinking too much, and sniffing coke. Morris wished Zelig was here to control them instead of on the street waiting for the action to happen like some goddamn spectator at a prize fight. Morris poured himself another shot of slivovitz. He was feeling good. The schnapps made him feel better. For ten years he was waiting for this. Sure everybody wanted Herman dead, but not as bad as he did - from the time Rosenthal stole Flora from him. She was his best whore. But it was more than that. He loved her- actually worried about her. Made sure she got her check-ups. Sometimes he even thought about marrying her; taking her off the street; having kids for chrissake. And best as he could remember he never hurt her; not once. Then she disappeared. Two months she's gone. Nobody knew where she was. Could have been dead. Next thing he heard she's working for Herman; he had Spanish Louis beat Herman half to death. But he couldn't have him killed; everybody knew his motive.

So he waited. Got Herman thinking it was OK, let bygones be bygones. But he knew his day would come. Herman was a real boob - a loose canon. Always making enemies.

Abie Isaacs, with a stack of newspapers under his arm, was standing in front of the Cadillac Hotel opposite the Metropole, about three hundred feet to the east. He was selling *The World*. The headline reverberated with the growing Becker/Rosenthal scandal: **"Rosenthal's Allegations Reveal Bottomless Corruption."** It was under the byline of Herbert Bayard Swope. After Rosenthal was murdered Swope focused all his attention on the scandal, working closely with his friend Whitman - becoming his primary conduit for leaking incriminating Grand Jury testimony to the public. By the time Becker was dead Swope was famous - poised to become the most prominent journalist of his generation.

Abie did not fashion himself as an East Side newsboy. He was a gangster; and gangsters didn't hold civilian jobs. None of the other Stanton Street Boys would be seen dead working as a newsy. But like Klopper always said, "You's a strange kid, Abie."

Normally he worked downtown - the Yiddish theaters on Second Avenue, or The Bowery, near the Manhatten Bridge. But tonight was different, the newspapers were just a prop. He was here to stop a murder. *Why I gives a shit they kill Herman Rosenthal?* He wondered. *It how things' done on the East Side. Gamblers gets in each other's way. And sometime somebody get killed - big fucking deal.* He understood warning Rosenthal would change his life forever. What he didn't understand - would never understand - is why he gave a shit.

Abie reached his position in front of the Cadillac Hotel at about 1:15 AM. He was surprised how familiar everything was. After all, this was only the fourth time he had ever been north of Fourteenth Street. It the same crowd as Second Avenue, he thought. One difference. He had never before seen so many tourists and traveling businessmen. They were the "live ones" that made the Tenderloin such a soft touch.

Then he noticed the familiar faces from the East Side - the pimps, guerrillas, and *gonifs*. Benny Yot, Crazy Yudkie, Moishe the Schtarker, Little Doggie, Joe the Greaser. And quite a few others whose faces he recognized but names he didn't know. In spite of the heat he felt a chill. "It really gonna happen. These *paskudnyaks* ain't here for the sights." When they saw Abie they nodded in recognition. "They's wondering what I's doing so far from home."

The East Siders were glaring and jostling the pedestrians and taxis off the street. One smartly dressed young tourist resisted Moishe the Schtarker's invitation to, "Move along."

"Haven't you heard, it's a free country?" he asked. Moishe's look reminded the fop that valor had its better part. He moved. It wasn't long before the crowds and the traffic began to thin.

That's when Abie saw Herman. He was standing in front of the Metropole Cafe and seemed confused. Maybe afraid. Abie could see himself running over to the doomed gambler, "Mr. Rosenthal, Morris is doing a job on you. He ain't giving you no money. You goes in there you's dead." In his reverie he could see Herman Rosenthal look at him. Smile. Cuff him playfully on the side of the head. Maybe put his arm on his shoulder "Thanks, kid. You's like a son to me now." The headline in tomorrow's paper would read: **"ABIE 'CRACKS' ISAACS SAVES ROSENTHAL"**

Still basking in the glow of his little fantasy, he watched Herman turn and bound up the steps to the Metropole Cafe. A couple of minutes later Bridgey Webber followed him in. Abie knew Bridgey and Herman were long time rivals. He also knew what everybody on the East Side knew about Bridgey Webber - he was a snake. In fact, twenty years ago the whole city got to know a kid named Louis Webber. That's when the coppers busted his dog theft ring. What he and his boys did was steal dogs and hold them for ransom. The papers had a field day. "Dognapping" they called it. Abie never quite believed the old timers' story that in his statement to the judge before sentencing Webber said, "Your Honor, I ain't never steals no Jewish dogs - only rich dogs."

After only a couple of minutes Bridgey left the Cafe; he scanned the nearly empty street, crossed to the north side, and walked directly to the canopied entrance of the Elk's Club. There he conferred with a man Abie didn't recognize. The conference was short, furtive. Intense.

Bridgey left and began walking west toward Broadway. Abie figured he was heading back to his joint to tell the killers Herman arrived. Suddenly he realized the man under the canopy was Zelig.

On the East Side no gangster stirred more fear, envy, and yes, even love. Abie picked up his remaining papers. It was time to leave. To defy Zelig was not just being a snitch; it was an act of desecration. Like a yeshiva *bucha* spitting on the Torah.

Fuck it, he thought, *I's goin' home.*

Bridgey arrived back at his joint. "Herman at the Metropole," he announced.

"About fucking time," said Gyp.

"Check you guns," said Lefty.

"Don't need no gun," joked Whitey Louis. "Judge Donovan say my left hook a lethal weapon."

"He never sees you fight," said Vallinsky.

Laughter. They all rose.

"Hold on boys," said Bridgey. "I sees Zelig by the Elk's Club. 'No shooting 'til the Bronx,' he say."

"We knows that," said Whitey.

"Sober, you knows that. Told him youse mugs was so coked and *schikered* up, couldn't find your *schvantz* in a whore house."

"Maybe we can't tell one gambler from another, neither," said Lefty reaching for his gun.

Vallinsky went for his.

"So Lefty," said Morris, the voice of reason, "Maybe you don't want the thousand. Or maybe you figures Zelig don't. Let's go."

Downstairs they piled into a rented, seven passenger, slate colored, 1909 Packard, touring car.

Sitting at his accustomed seat at the Metropole Cafe Herman Rosenthal began to relax. *Just another night doing business*, he thought, lighting up his fat Havana cigar and taking a sip of his drink, a horse's neck - ginger ale with a twist of lime. Scattered on the table in front of him were seven copies of the World he had the waiter bring him from the newsstand in the hotel lobby. Seeing his name in 30 point type brought tears to his eyes. He saw Bridgey Webber talking to the East Side gamblers at the front table. "Think I plays with the prick," he thought.

"Hey Bridgey," Herman yelled, "Been reading The World." Bridgey smiled, and nodded. Not the response Herman expected. He was nervous again. *Nah, it don't mean nothing*, he convinced himself. Webber left. Herman looked at his watch, 1:45. He began feeling nostalgic. One way or another the life he had known on the East Side was history.

Suddenly his life appeared to him like one of those big heroic six reel movies that cost a quarter to see.

He is with Mama and Papa on the steamer that carried them to America from Odessa. It sails through the turbulent waters of New York harbor. The deck is packed with immigrants. Papa points to the Statue of Liberty. Herman sees himself at six, his hair blowing in the wind; his eyes streaming tears; his face set in fierce determination.

(The screen reads:)

"This is the land of opportunity. I better make the most of it."

Now he's in class. All the boys are mouthing English - it's an incomprehensible flow of guttural gibberish. Herman looks confused.

(The screen reads:)

His first day in school.

The teacher, a fat middle-aged Irisher wearing her tight gray bun like a battered old hat, is screaming at him. She keeps shouting the same words. He keeps not understanding them. The boys are laughing at him. Howling. Convulsing. Herman's face is wreathed in pain and confusion. He rolls his eyes.

(The screen reads:)

I must not cry.

Finally one of the boys takes pity and whispers something to him. Herman nods, faces the teacher, and moves his lips:

(He mouths his name:)

"Ich haist Chaim Rossental."

This causes even more hilarity. Cut to the boys shouting in unison:

(Their lips say:)

"Greenhorn. Greenhorn. Greenhorn. Go back to Russia."

We see Herman cry.

(Words move scroll-like across the screen framed by flowers:)

Time passes. Little Chaim Rossental grows up to become Herman Rosenthal, a famous and feared East Side gambler and gangster.

Herman, now an adult, appears, arms akimbo, nattily dressed, his large gold HR cufflinks and tie clasp insolently gleaming. He's standing in the center of a large room full of men sitting at tables playing cards. Next to him beaming like a proud father is Big Tim Sullivan

(The screen reads:)

His first stuss parlor.

He sees his aging Mama on the screen; she's tearful with pride.

(She mouths the words:)

"Now I can die happy."

Herman felt tears welling up. Everything seemed very sad. Tenuous. He had to talk to somebody. He motioned to a couple of thugs sitting at a nearby table to join him. Boob Walker and Bernie Cohen were freelance *schtarkers* who did most of their work for Bridgey Webber. This made them de facto enemies of Herman Rosenthal. God knows they must have blown up at least one of his stuss parlors. He personally watched Boob beat one of his boys, Crazy Izzy Broder, half to death. But this was his last night on the East Side. And he needed company.

Abie froze when he saw the slate colored Packard turn East into a now deserted 43rd Street. He watched intensely as the car slowly glided down the street and came to a stop in front of the Metropole Cafe. Five men piled out and moved up the sidewalk close to the hotel. The driver remained at the wheel. Abie recognized the three life-takers and Hyman Vallinsky. Suddenly Abie's feet had a mind of their own; they were taking him to the Cafe Metrapole. When he entered nobody paid attention. Newsy's were as common as mosquitoes. The dim lights and heavy cigar smoke made it impossible for him to see beyond the first few tables.

Out of the fog he heard a gruff voice call his name. It was the gambler Dudie Tarnoff, a friend of Mama's. Abie walked over to his table. He didn't recognize the other men with Dudie.

"Vi geyt's, Abeleh, What you's doing so far from home?"

"They tells me this where the money is. Maybe you wants *The World*, Mr. Tarnoff?"

"Maybe kid, you should be selling another paper. That paper full of shit."

"I guess shit sell, Mr.Tarnoff."

"Shit stink, kid. You can smell it from here." Tarnoff glanced to the rear of the room.

"Gotta gets to work," said Abie.

He walked toward the back, and saw Herman Rosenthal sitting with two of Bridgey's boys. Arriving at the table he no longer heard the hollow chords of the honky tonk piano; the comforting hum of voices that rose and fell like breath; the clunk of glass against hard wood tables. He heard nothing but his own voice articulating a question that would change his life forever: "Mr. Rosenthal, can I talks to you?"

"Sure kid, go ahead," said the gambler smiling.

"Privately," said Abie, "It important."

He saw Boob Walker's fist clench.

"Important," growled Herman. "A *pisherkeh* like you know important?"

"Herman," asked Boob, "know who this kid is?" The gambler didn't know.

"The little *momser's* the son of Morris the Pimp, and Lena The Lake." Herman's eyes began to bulge. His face, turning red. He coughed, choking on cigar smoke; he made a high pitched barking sound. Then another. And another. He was laughing and gagging simultaneously.

Abie wanted to put his fist through Boob's already ruined nose. Instead he stared directly at Herman.

"They's going to kill you Mr. Rosenthal."

Herman waved Abie away.

As Abie approached the exit he shouted, "They's gonna kill you, you fat putz. And now I knows why."

He felt Dudie Tarnoff's eyes on the back of his head. They were like knives piercing his brain. Or bullets. On his way out Abie passed Vallinsky coming in. He crossed the Street and hid in a narrow alley formed by the Cadillac Hotel and its adjacent building.

Catching his breath, Herman thought about what Abie said. "Fuck'm I laughing?" Boob and Sammy were still laughing.

A voice called to him. "Herman, can you come outside for a minute, Morris wanna see you?"

It was Vallinsky.

Strange, he thought, *Bridgey's man call me to see Morris.*

At that moment Herman knew he was going to die.

(The screen reads:)

Herman Rosenthal dies bravely.

Brightly lit but deserted, 43rd Street seemed like a stage set. Abie tried to convince himself what he was seeing wasn't real. It was a play - a dream. Nobody was going to be murdered in cold blood right in front of his eyes.

GOD'S RAT

Suddenly a fifth man emerged from the Packard. It was Morris. Abie saw him walk past the life-takers and slowly climb the steps to the vestibule of the Metrapole Cafe. He stopped, and half hidden by a potted palm, waited. Vallinsky walked out of the cafe, brushed past Morris and galloped down the steps. Herman followed carrying his seven copies of *The World*. Morris, stepping out from behind the potted palm, greeted him warmly. They walked down the steps chatting. At the sidewalk Morris turned and faced Herman. Abie saw the gun pointed at Herman's face. It burst into flames. He heard the shot.

Then the life takers opened fire. As Herman crumbled they jumped into the Packard. It pulled away from the curb and moved toward Sixth Avenue. Abie saw Morris sitting in the seat next to the window. Their eyes locked.

Abie arrived home breathless. Mama was passed out in the living room chair. Next to the chair was an empty bucket of beer. He woke her; told her what happened.

"Morris saw you? Then you's dead - I dead. You has to go out of your way to save Rosenthal's squealing ass? *Nar*, you's my curse. I smells your papa in you. Get the fuck out of here. I hope they find you. Die -- die -- die."

Abie was used to outbursts like this. He felt no anger. Only a familiar sense of loss. She was his child; and he was alone. So goddamn alone.

He left.

Eleven: The Hunted

On the street everything seemed different. The East Side was the only home he knew. And now, suddenly he didn't know it at all. Here on his own block, little Abie the tough guy, *paskudnyak*, *gengsteh*, a feared member of the Stanton Street Boys had realized an instant transformation. No longer could he saunter into Izzey's and get a free schpritz and a chunk of halvah. Mendel the tailor wouldn't slip a buck into his pocket and suggest he spend it wisely. And he doubted if Big Gus would fill Mama's bucket with all the beer she could drink for a penny. He had earned their tribute and their fear. He was Abie Cracks, the titled prince of Rivington Street - anointed schtarker by a guerrilla king, Sammy Boston. But now he was Abie the rat. Abie the snitch. And even worse - Abie the witness to murder one. Abie the hunted.

It was time to find his best friend, Klopper Benny Zlotnick. At sixteen Klopper was the oldest member of the Stanton Street Boys. His face was narrow, craggy; hard edged as if hewed from rock. His mama, Frenchy Sadie Horowitz was a hop head whoring for quarters with truckers on Canal Street. No one ever met Mr. Zlotnick.

At thirteen Klopper spent eight months on Blackstone Island for rolling a lush who happened to be a plainclothes shamus. He made the best of it.

"To some of these geelicks my ass was virgin pussy," he explained to the boys soon after his release. "Wasn't 'til I cuts this forty year old pervert between the eyes they understand I ain't worth the fuck."

Klopper had the ability to turn shit into money wherever he was. "Pretty soon I has the coppers working for me," he explained. "Bringing in cocaine and laudanum. Soft money. Like Mr.Barnum says, 'There a sucker born every minute.' Suckers thicker than flies on the Island." He did have one regret. "Misses my Bar Mitzvah. Break Mama's heart." He laughed.

Klopper Benny lived on the street since he was eight. Sometimes Lena would let him stay with them. He slept on the floor.

Having Klopper Benny around was almost like having a full grown man in the house. These days Klopper was sleeping under the stars in one of the vacant lots on Delancy Street. Not that he couldn't afford to pay rent. But it was summer. And the price was right.

When Klopper saw Abie he slapped him.

They were standing in front of Klopper Benny's temporary home - a lean-to structured from a woolen blanket nailed at one end to the side of what was left of a torn down wooden tenement; the other end to a six foot long 2 by 4 placed about five feet from the tenement wall. The floor was a filthy old mattress, its fabric dissolving with age, its stuffing bursting through like feathered tears. There were no pots or pans, or signs of a fire. Klopper Benny took his meals out.

As usual he knew everything.

"You a dumb schmuck - sure you's a Yid? You's dead, know that?"

"Yeah, Mama tell me."

Klopper's blue eyes were hard. Unrelenting. "Ain't funny, Abie. Why you warns Rosenthal, chrissake? He was a fucking snitch."

Talking to Klopper Benny must be what it's like talking to a father. Abie felt like an idiot. Every excuse dissolving like fog before he could use it. He tried the truth. "They's going to step on him like a roach, Benny." Only Abie and Lena were allowed to use Klopper's given name. "He ain't no insect."

Now I whining like a baby, Abie thought with disgust. But he noticed Klopper's cold blue eyes begin to thaw.

"Jesus, you's a strange kid," Klopper said. "Lucky the killers is on the lam. Gyp'd break you back."

Gyp the Blood took great pride in his ability to kill a man by snapping his spine.

"And Morris' going to *kish meir in touchas*? He was the first shooter. I sees him -- he sees me. You gotta help me, Klopper."

"Morris? He ain't no life-taker. He telling the boys Becker makes him do it - says he have him and Bridgey locked up for ten years, they don't kill Rosenthal."

Klopper had it wrong. Morris was establishing an alibi; setting up the cop. "Klop," Abie said, "I seen Morris shoot Rosenthal. I knows Becker ain't in this. Morris shoots Rosenthal because he fucking wants to. Morris know I sees him." Suddenly Abie realized the pimp **had** to kill him.

"Mama is home alone," Abie said.

He began to run. Klopper followed.

It wasn't easy running on the East Side. Like swimming upstream. After three blocks the boys reached Canal Street. The traffic was so snarled they had to crawl under wagons and trucks - dodging hooves, horse shit, wheels, and the truckers whips and curses. The gasoline fumes had them lying on the sidewalk coughing and choking. Up and running again. On Rivington they busted up a dago crap game. A short Italian must have been on a roll. He snarled like a wounded beast and grabbed Abie's leg. Abie flashed a knife. The Italian let go. A few hundred yards more and he was home. The boys devoured the six flights of stairs in one panicked gulp.

Abie knocked - no answer. "Open the door," he screamed. "Damnit, either she ain't home, or too drunk to hear nothing."

"Or maybe Morris get here first," said Klopper.

Beads of sweat formed on Abie's forehead. He was pounding furiously now. The door opened.

"Look who still alive. Everybody favorite hero." Mama was holding an unplucked chicken. She seemed sober.

Abie was standing near the window, looking out. It was stained and rippled by age. He saw a slate gray 1909 Packard pull up in front of the tenement. Two men got out.

"The Boston brothers," he said. "Shit, Morris sent the Bostons!"

Lena's lips moved, "Sammy and Meyer Boston." She put the half-plucked chicken in the sink and wiped her hands on her apron.

Klopper walked over to the window and looked.

Abie never saw Mama so scared.

"Even the Bostons wouldn't kill no kid," she said to no one in particular.

"Abie ain't no ordinary kid," said Klopper. "He a snitch."

GOD'S RAT

"It worse than it looks," said Abie. He told them about his, "Hoodlum Bar Mitzvah" at Siegal's.

"Sammy took you in, Abie. Snitching, you makes him look like a boob. He kill you for nothing," said Klopper.

Now Lena was at the window looking over Abie's head. "They's in the building."

"We going to the roof," said Klopper.

Abie hated taking orders from anyone. But Klopper was different. He always knew what to do. It was more than being smart; it was staying alive on the East Side - alone.

Klopper opened the door to the hallway. "Gots to be real quiet." Darkness loomed like a wall. A few flights down the Boston's were stumbling toward them. One flight above them was the roof. The wrought iron stairway to the roof hung flat against the wall - rigged like a fire escape.

Klopper, Abie, and Lena moved carefully up the iron slats a half step at a time; their silence defying gravity. The brothers' footsteps were getting louder. Abie heard their labored breathing and wheezing. He imagined their sweaty pig faces; felt their anger. For the first time in Abie's memory, the door to the roof was locked. Mickey Feathers must have put on the lock after somebody stole his lead pigeon - a White; it almost drove him crazy.

Abie felt the lock. It was new, but attached to braces as old as the building. He yanked it. The braces held. Abie's hands began to sweat. He pulled again. Nothing. A few flakes of rust. Again. This time the unopened lock came off in his hand. They scampered onto the tin roof. Mickey's pigeons were scant protection. But it was all they had. They hid behind the coop.

Their presence caused some movement, but the pigeons kept their nocturnal silence. The stench was sickening. From the roof, through the open door, Abie could clearly hear the Bostons' reach their flat and knock on the door. He felt incredibly vulnerable. What a pathetic shield skin was.

Soon the knocking turned to violent pounding. Meyer was yelling, "Lena, Abie open the door; we just wanna to talk."

"Abeleh," shouted Sammy, "You one of us, What for you worried? We ain't gonna to hurt our own."

Abie thought of Herman crumbling on 43rd Street.

Next to him, Klopper was holding his gun. The pounding stopped.

A new sound. The brothers were trying to push the door down. The idea of the Bostons' breaking down the door to their flat was terrifying. Lena whimpered. Abie tried to say something comforting. No words came out.

Who was comforting him?

There was a crash. The door must have collapsed with the Bostons' on top of it. Abie had to laugh at the picture of the two huge schtarkers on their bellies. Klopper was up in a second - running.

"No Benny," Lena screamed.

Gun in hand, Klopper ran through the roof's open door. Abie heard him clatter down the wrought iron steps. He followed about twenty seconds behind. Klopper was standing over the fallen brothers, pointing his gun at their heads.

For a moment Abie felt a deep sense of loss. The Bostons' had taken him in; made him feel part of their world. Now they seemed so utterly vanquished. Silly even. Lying on top of the smashed door, writhing in frustration and rage like bloated dying fish washed up on a beach. He had an almost unbearable impulse to go to their aid.

"Abeleh," said Meyer as if reading his mind, "Tell your friend Klopper put away his gun before it too late."

Abie said nothing. He felt a sharp pain deep in his stomach, like a belt of broken glass pulled tight around his intestines.

"We had big plans for you, Abie Cracks," Sammy said.

The belt tightened.

Lena joined them.

"Abie, you's OK?" she asked. "You look sick."

"I's fine Mama."

Klopper never noticed Abie's distress. His hand holding the gun was steady. "If I was to shoot the two of youse," he said softly, reasonably, "What the coppers think? Not that no kid shoot youse."

Abie could barely resist the temptation to grab Klopper's gun.

"Sammy and Meyer," said Klopper, "push your guns to me. Abie takes the guns."

Abie picked up the guns. Klopper gave his gun to Lena and took the two guns from Abie. One in each hand pointed at the brothers' heads.

"Now boys" said Klopper, "Turn over on your backs please."

It was the first time Abie heard his friend say please.

"When the coppers finds youse," said Klopper, "they figures youse got into an argument - bang, bang youse shoot each other. Case closed."

Abie felt as if his bowels were filling with blood. He wanted to run to the toilet in the hall; he couldn't move.

Lena was silent. Cold. Klopper's gun was steady; pointed at the brothers' heads.

Lying there, staring up at their own guns, the Bostons' looked like trapped rats. More angry than scared.

Klopper cocked both guns. He fired one, then the other. The bullets tore into the wall. Through the stench of burnt gun powder Abie picked up the distinct smell of piss. He saw a running stain enveloping the right leg of Sammy Boston's white cotton slacks. From the look on his face Abie figured Sammy would rather be dead.

"I wants the two of you out of here. This ain't no public toilet," Lena said.

They left quickly. Without a word.

"Time to go home, Mama," Abie said. Home was Albany New York, Lena's birthplace. To Abie it was unreal - a place shrouded in mystery, and magic. Sometimes late at night, when very drunk, Lena would talk about the big house on Madison Avenue. "It had chandeliers like a dance hall, and a twenty-foot wide circular staircase which I imagines, when I was very little, was how youse got to heaven." She would talk about her Mama and Papa. "They was angels what only wanted the best for me." According to Lena there was a liveried cook, maid, and chauffeur. And her papa owned *Isaacs' Clothier*. "It the most exclusive men's haberdashery in the city," she told Abie. "Only men from the best and richest families shops there. All gentiles, of course." At first Abie believed her only because he didn't want to think she was crazy. Then one day he saw the picture. It was on her lap where she lay drunk on the sofa. A faded photograph of a family arrayed in fancy summer whites in front of a huge white four gabled house. Three sisters, a mama and a papa. The youngest, about six, was a beautiful child with long golden locks. It was Mama.

Lena looked at Abie as if he just slapped her across the face. "You's crazy, Abeleh, I can't go home. I stuck a knife in their hearts. They has my funeral. I'm a bummerca, a whore. A piece of *schiksa dreck*." She began to cry. First sobs. Then convulsive gasps. It was as if she was vomiting from her eyes; attempting to purge with tears something deep and diseased.

"Jesus," said Klopper, "Do something."

Abie tried to be strong; he wanted to comfort Mama. The strength wasn't there. Finally Lena composed herself. The boys helped her pack.

They had to drag the steamer trunk to Canal Street to find a cab that would take them to Grand Central Station. Klopper never took his hand off his gun. The cab was excruciatingly hot. They all stank from sweat and fear. Abie began to doze. He dreamt he was in a classroom full of everyone who wanted him dead. Zelig. Gyp the Blood. The Boston's. Even the Gopher, Toohey, whose arm he busted, was there. He, Abie, was standing in front of the room near the blackboard trying to explain why they shouldn't kill him. He felt himself becoming younger and younger; his voice softer. He looked for forgiveness in their eyes; he found none. In the back of the room he noticed Mama and Klopper. Herman Rosenthal entered. "Good morning class," he said. "I's your principal." For a second Abie felt hope. Herman spoke. "Kill him boys, he ain't one of us." They all drew their guns. Abie looked for Mama and Klopper; they were gone.

"Grand Central Station, folks," said the driver.

GOD'S RAT

Thirteen: Whore

Albany. July, 1914.

In the cab, riding through the familiar streets, Lena was surprised how comfortable she felt.

"Abie, like nothing has changed. See that house with all the gables? My friend Gertie Halpern lived there."

Abie thought of the busses that toured the East Side full of rich tourists gawking at poor Jews as if they were animals in a zoo. "So this is where they go home."

"Bet they don't even lock their doors," said Klopper. "Bella'd get wet we bring her loot from these places."

Lena glared at him. "This ain't the East Side, Benny. Talk nice."

Suddenly the cab stopped.

Abie recognized the house from the picture he had found on Mama's lap. He felt her shudder.

"*Veyis meir,*" she exhaled.

Standing in front of the massive oak door to her mama and papa's house, after twenty three years Lena knew she was violating their lives again. This mansion and the people who inhabited it had nothing to do with her.

"What if they's gone, Abie? Maybe another family live here now. We should go."

Abie knocked. His fist stung uselessly against the foot thick oak of the door. The impact barely created a sound. Lena giggled. She grabbed the brass knocker and pounded three times.

The door was answered by an ancient black servant.

"Hello, Blanche."

The old woman's expression showed neither surprise, shock, pleasure, or regret. She devoured Lena with her eyes.

"They in the dining room."

"Please tell them we's here."

The woman didn't move. Or take her eyes off Lena.

"Who is at the door, Blanche?" called a voice from inside.

Abie, Lena, and Klopper froze as if caught committing a crime.

"This' bullshit," said Klopper. He brushed past the servant and walked toward the voice. Abie and Lena followed. They entered a huge room. *The chandeliers in the Occidental ain't this big,* Abie thought. Eight people in formal attire were having dinner. He couldn't believe they were somehow connected to him. "Jesus, they looks like royalty."

"Blanche," said a chunky woman in her early forties, "Why did you let these people in here? If they're hungry take them to the kitchen."

It was Lena's oldest sister Flo. Lena looked at the others. She recognized Mama, Papa, her sister Birdie. They returned her look as if she were rat shit in their chicken soup.

My God, they don't know who I am, she thought. *I disgust them.*

Suddenly she was back in the Hertz Hotel facing herself in the mirror, holding the chamber pot over her head. Loneliness, like death, swept over her. Abie noticed Lena swaying from side to side. She collapsed at his feet. One of the diners, an old lady who looked like a duchess, jumped out of her chair and began screaming, "Meine tochter, Meine tochter. Oi Gotten himmel, Lenaleh, Lenaleh."

Pandemonium

Birdie, even heavier than sister Flo, was screaming, "Why, Lena? Filth. You dragged us through the gutters of your stinking East Side. Now you come back like nothing happened." She ran over to Lena, who remained dazed on the floor, and began spitting at her.

Abie grabbed Klopper who was about to swing at Birdie.

Flo pushed her sister away.

Then she began screaming at Lena. "*Kurva,* get out. And take the ragamuffins with you. Which one's your little bastard?"

She turned to Abie with a look of pure hatred. "Maybe you're Morris' *momser*? Get your whore Mama out of here!"

Nobody ever spoke to Abie like that - except Mama when she was drunk. He slapped Flo hard in the face. The shock of the blow caused her to freeze; a statue with tears and snot running down its face. Then someone slapped him in the face. It was a fat, bald little man. "That's my wife, you damn scamp." Before Abie could react Klopper was hammering the guy in the nose until it collapsed into a mushy spout, gushing blood.

"He broke my nose. He broke my nose," the little man screamed on the verge of tears.

Blanche went to Lena and cradled her head in her lap.

I's killing everyone I ever loved, Lena thought.

She lost consciousness, sinking in a pool of blood - drowning in it, gasping for breath. *I must breathe. I don't want to die.* She felt strong arms pulling her from the liquid depths. There was a scream - the sound of a young woman in excruciating pain. An infant squalled. Lena breathed deeply.

Blanche rocked her.

Awake again, Lena heard Papa demanding silence. The tumult stopped; they all looked at the old man. With his eyes on Lena, he began to speak - in Yiddish.

"Lenaleh, life is a mystery. God is a mystery. But there is no mystery greater than you my daughter. Twenty four years ago you shamed us when you ran away with a man who profited in the sale of human flesh, the white slaver Morris Schiff. Now unannounced, you return. We buried you, daughter, said *kaddish*, sat *shiva*. Jews do not welcome back the dead."

He talk just like a Rabbi, Abie thought, impressed.

The old man continued, "From relatives on the East Side we heard how you sold yourself, and associated with low lifes We prayed God should grant us an early death. But our sins were too many. It was His plan; His wisdom to rub our souls in the slime of your degradation."

"Why's we listening to this fancy assed bullshit?" Klopper whispered to Abie.

Abie was rapt; he ignored his friend.

All eyes were fixed on the old man. The men were silent. The women sobbed softly.

GOD'S RAT

Now Zayde looked at Abie and Klopper. "Which one of you is my grandson?" Abie answered with his eyes. Lena winced, knowing what was coming. Papa looked directly at her.

"That our first grandson was the spawn of unwed filth brought me and Mama to our knees. A permanent sadness settled on us. Pleasure was out of the question. But, somehow, we got on with our lives. There was even good fortune - seven consecrated grandchildren."

With some difficulty he got out of his chair and walked to where Lena was still sprawled on the floor. Looking up at her father's implacable eyes, she noticed tears. *Can stone melt?* She wondered.

"Why you come back to us, Lenaleh?" he asked "The stench of your evil fills this house. Please daughter, return to your grave."

Abie felt he should hate anyone who spoke so harshly to his mother. But when he looked into the old man's face he saw the shadow of his own. He didn't know his papa, but this was Zayde his flesh and blood. The ancient pale green eyes were without anger; just a sadness that seemed to have no end.

Abie looked around the room. Klopper was staring intently at the rug. Mama's head was still cradled in Blanche's arms. He had to speak; yet the wrong words would put Mama on the street.

"Zayde, you says I come from filth. Yeah, I's a little *momser*." He looked at Birdie. "And I sure as hell live in filth. I's proud I got family what lives like royalty. And I understands you want no part of us. My mama's a drunk and she used to be a whore, but she still my mama."

Everyone was staring at him.

"And Zayde," he continued - in Yiddish now - "she's still your daughter. You throw her on the street Morris will kill her. She has no place but here with her Mama and Papa." Suddenly everyone was speaking at once.

"Silence," screamed the old man. He looked at Abie.

"Once Morris killed her already. Now he wants to kill her again? Can you explain that to me, Abeleh from the ghetto?"

Abie told how he witnessed Morris and the others shoot Herman Rosenthal; and even worse - he tried to warn the gambler. "Zayde," he explained, "Morris, masterminded the whole thing. I overheard him planning it. Now he's laying it all on Becker. He knows I know everything. Morris wants me dead; he'll go through Mama to get to me."

"But Morris' your papa."

"No he ain't," said Lena; her first words in the house of her birth after twenty four years.

The old man looked intently at his grandson. His eyes narrowed. "Why you warn the hooligan Rosenthal? You put everybody in danger."

Abie glanced at his feet; he shrugged.

The old man spoke to the maid. "Take Lena to her old room. She'll stay here until it's safe."

He looked back at his grandson. "You Bar Mitzvah?"

Abie shook his head.

Zayde lifted his hand --

Abie flinched, expecting a blow.

-- he put it on his grandson's shoulder. Abie felt enveloped by the old man's small boney hand; as if it was something else altogether. Huge, and protective, and forever.

"Stay with us, Abeleh."

Zayde looked at Klopper.

"And your friend, the *schtarker*, he's welcome too. With him here we don't have to worry about no Morris."

"We gotta go, Zayde."

The old man shrugged. "Go in health, Abeleh from the ghetto. Be careful."

Abie and Klopper kissed Lena, and left.

GOD'S RAT

Fourteen: Dead Eyes

Morris couldn't believe only four days ago he was a visitor in the Tombs. Now he was back, an inmate, about to be indicted for murder one. He felt a rumbling in his bowels and thought of the pail under the metal cot. He pictured himself squatting over the pail; living with the stench of his own filth for the rest of the night. "I'll wait 'till I sees Whitman. First thing, he gotta let me take a shit like a man."

Morris was arrested a few hours after the murder. Immediately he asked for a meeting with DA Charles Whitman. The meeting was scheduled in Whitman's office in the State Criminal Court Building, 9 AM. Morris lay down and tried to sleep. Tomorrow was a big day.

The next morning Morris Schiff, in chains, was led across the "The Bridge of Tears", a walkway ten stories up connecting the Tombs to the State Criminal Court Building. The shackles around his arms and legs weighed over fifty pounds. It was impossible to walk normally. The pain caused by the metal clamps chaffing against his ankles was excruciating. He felt blood dripping into his shoes.

Just like that black bear, he thought - remembering a picture he saw in a book when he was a kid, a black bear in chains. The caption read, "Off to The Zoo." The pity he felt for the beast transferred to himself. Then he smiled, realizing the difference. The bear was innocent. He was a killer.

His left shoe filled with blood; it felt as if he stepped into a warm puddle. A cool breeze gusted across his face; he smelled the brine, decay, and seaweed of the East River.

For the millionth time he replayed the moment he pulled the trigger. Everything was going as planned. Looked like he could get Herman into the car without a struggle. "I can't give you no fifteen thousand beans right here in the street," he explained. Herman stopped, looked at him, smiled, and said, "Moisheleh, you knows Flora got religion? Every night before she go to sleep she light a candle. Guess what she pray for?"

Herman waited a second, bringing Morris in.

Morris became impatient; needing the answer. His eyebrows lifted.

Herman smiled. "Your funeral, you little prick," he hissed in Morris' ear.

He know what he doing, Morris thought. *Know I kills him right there on the street. He was taking me with him.*

Two guards ushered Morris into the District Attorney's office. The room was dominated by a gigantic black mahogany desk completely ornamented with intricate carvings Morris took to be Chinese. He was impressed. *It must'a takes a hundred Chinks ten years to do all that work.* In the far right corner was a huge American flag. Directly behind the desk was the portrait of a youngish man with a very serious expression. Morris recognized him from his pictures in the press - the Commissioner of Police, Rhinelander Waldo.

Behind the desk sat Charles Whitman. It was the first time he had seen the famous District Attorney in person. He was uglier in the flesh than his press photos suggested. His face so pale it seemed to emanate, ghostlike, from behind his lips. Or, rather, his absence of lips, as if his mouth was the result of a rough surgical procedure; the lips, crusts of dried blood, a wound that never healed.

Whitman glared at Morris. With great difficulty Morris held the piercing stare. He never saw eyes as cold. *They looks like the eyes of a dead man before someone shut them,* he thought.

The DA spoke to one of the guards. "Unchain this man; then wait outside the door." He spoke in a low, phlegm-clotted growl, like something was busted in his throat; even worse, he was always coughing- spitting in his hanky, examining the foul rag with the intensity of a prospector looking for a glint of gold in a pan full of dirt. He talked in circles, or riddles; starting a sentence in the middle, leaving Morris to figure out how it began.

"Mr. Schiff," said the DA, after the guards left, "You got caught with the proverbial pants around the proverbial ankles."

"It don't look good," Morris agreed.

"'It don't look good,'" Whitman mimicked. He laughed; a merciless wet cackle He kept laughing until his eyes watered. Morris realized he would continue laughing until he, Morris, joined in. Morris, laughed.

Whitman's laugh lapsed into a deep phlegmy cough. Catching his breath he rasped, "You bet, 'It don't look good,' you little hoodlum," his eyes dead cold again. "We have witnesses saw you at the scene when Whitey, Lefty, and Gyp shot Rosenthal. Saw the four of you and Vallinsky jump into the car. Got the plate number. Got a statement from your Limo driver, Shapiro, he dropped you off at the Metrapole and drove you away after the shooting. Bridgey Webber was seen there too. 'It don't look good?'" He was laughing. Again, the racking wet cough.

Morris was suddenly at ease. *He don't know I fires the first shot.*

The DA spit into his hanky, subjecting the deposit to close scrutiny.

"Nasty cough you's got sir," said Morris.

"Mr. Schiff," said Whitman, "You're taking my time. Why?"

Morris leaned over the desk; forced himself to stare into the cold dead eyes. "What you got Mr. Whitman is me, Bridgey, and Vallinsky. Sure you gonna catch the shooters: Gyp, Lefty, Whitey. But it small change. Convicting Jew trash of murdering Jew trash ain't gonna get you to Albany."

Whitman smiled. "And you, pray tell, have something that will?

"The truth, Mr. Whitman."

Whitman yawned, and looked at his watch.

Morris leaned over the desk. Now he spoke in a whisper. "OK, me, Bridgey and Vallinsky; we had Rosenthal killed; we hires Zelig and his life takers. But Lieutenant Becker give the orders - the bent copper, he make us cook Herman Rosenthal."

Morris studied Whitman's face. There was no reaction. Through the open windows he could hear a steamer bellowing its plangent farewell to New York harbor. It took him a second to realize Whitman was speaking, his hoarse whisper barely audible over the din.

"You wanted Rosenthal dead too, Schiff," he said.

Morris was ready. "Yeah, Herman was annoying all of us by blabbing to the press, but he wasn't squealing on all of us; it was Becker he ratting out. The copper say he frame us up we don't cook Rosenthal. He want the boys to cut Herman's tongue out so's he could hang it on a street lamp on Broadway like a warning to all squealers. He was bugs, Mr. Whitman."

Whitman hunched forward. Morris realized he was looking at him differently. "Get your lawyer Mr. Schiff," he said, "we've got a lot to do." Before he left Whitman's office, Morris was allowed to take a shit like a man.

* * * * *

July 25, 1915, 6:04 am & 10 seconds, Sing Sing.

Becker heard noise - a dull roar. Like a distant sea. The sound grew louder; more distinct. It was applause. The reporters began shouting, "Here, Here." The DA, Charles Whitman, in black billowing robes, entered the witness section of the execution chamber and smiled at Becker - his eyes radiating pure love. He's come to claim me, thought Becker. It's only right, I am his. Whitman floated through the glass enclosure toward Becker. He was on top of Becker now. His lips pressed to the cop's ear. "I love you Charles Becker, you're going to make me Governor. I was nothing until I convicted the 'killer copper'. You were sent to me by God. Death Is my gift" The reporters became the twelve men of the jury. How distinguished they seemed; how attentive. Whitman, his lips still pressed against Becker's ears, exhorted: "-- the evidence, gentlemen, proves here beyond a reasonable doubt that the man who inspired, the man who directed, the man who compelled the execution of Herman Rosenthal is the lieutenant of police who had the power to dictate, and the power to accomplish it. I ask you to declare the truth of the evidence before you prove that Charles Becker, Lieutenant of police of this city indicted for the murder of

Herman Rosenthal, is guilty of that murder - - of murder in the first degree." The words poured into Becker's brain like white hot lava. All went dark.

GOD'S RAT

Fifteen: Cop Killers

By the end of the day a warrant was issued for the arrest of Lieutenant Charles Becker for the murder of Herman Rosenthal. Morris got word to Bridgey and Vallinsky to turn themselves in. He had his lawyer Leroy Shaw deliver the message. "Tell them we's copping to immunity. We's trading Becker. It OK."

The next morning, at 8:45, Morris was back on the Bridge of Tears. This time only in handcuffs. Things were looking good. Bridgey and Vallinsky turned themselves in, but Whitman wouldn't see them until they spoke to Morris. *Me and the DA, we's partners,* he thought.

Bridgey and Vallinsky arrived at the Criminal Court Building, accompanied by their lawyers Lawrence Beglin and Robert Schlessinger; they were led into Whitman's ante room. Morris was waiting, along with his lawyer, Shaw, at the far end of a long conference table.

In spite of Bridgey's effort to appear sullen, indifferent, Morris could tell he was scared. Vallinsky, on the other hand, was pissed. Beglin was solemn. Schlessinger, bored. Morris was impressed with Bridgey's attorney. Lawrence Beglin was a top expensive criminal lawyer with political ambitions - and connections at Tammany. In fact he often represented Big Tim Sullivan. Morris smiled: "Wouldn't take the job without Sullivan's permission. Must have cost Bridgey 10,000 beans upfront. Easy."

Robert Schlessinger, Vallinsky's man, was a shyster who fronted half the small time pimps and gamblers on the East Side. His job was to walk in Beglin's shadow.

Beglin cleared his throat. "Greetings Mr. Schlessinger, Mr Shaw. Our expectations were, gentlemen, we would be meeting with the District Attorney as is appropriate."

Morris perused his fingernails. "Mr. Beglin," he said, speaking slowly, carefully; not looking up. "What is appropriate is that you Mr. Schlessinger, and Mr.Shaw leaves the room. I been advised by

Mr. Whitman that what me and your client has to discuss ain't for your ears."

Beglin turned angrily to Morris' lawyer, Shaw. "What your client is asking is impossible."

"Beglin," snapped Bridgey. "Get the fuck out of here. We calls you when you needed."

The three lawyers left the room.

Bridgey was all business. "Moisheleh, we's framing up the copper? What's Whitman's *shmeer*?"

To Morris, Bridgey always looked like a civilian - some kind of salesman, his features too refined, unblemished, unbroken, to belong to a hoodlum. He was bothered, as usual, at how much kinder thirty eight years were to Bridgey than to him. *Still got the twitch, though,* he thought.

Whenever on edge, the left side of Bridgey's mouth moved suddenly upward, as if he were about to break out in a smile, and then changed his mind

"The *shmeer's* simple," said Morris, "we gives Whitman a ticket to the Big House in Albany. Public want a crooked copper's balls - we got the perfect copper. A real piece of shit this cop the way he force us to cook Herman Rosenthal what's only doing his citizen's duty exposing corruption. Maybe we don't love this Rosenthal; but it ain't our asses he biting - it Becker he ratting out. Copper want Herman dead, say if we don't set up the killing we's doing hard time - frame us up. We ain't no killers, but we ain't no heroes neither."

"Giving us immunity?" asked Vallinsky still looking very pissed.

"That the deal. What we got to do is get our stories straight." Morris pushed his chair in closer to the table. He lowered his voice. "I tells Mr. Whitman this low life copper want to cut out Herman's tongue, hang it on a lamp post - a warning to squealers. I think he believe it."

Bridgey laughed, a high pitched girlish giggle. Even Vallinsky cracked a smile. "You tells him," Bridgey asked, excited by the game, "how he threaten to frame us up on a Federal rap so we's in a chain gang in Tupelo getting our raggedy Jew asses fucked by crackers when they runs out of pigs?"

This was too much for Morris; he laughed so hard he fell under the table.

"Enough of this shit!" screamed Vallinsky pounding on the table. "Let's get the hell out of here. In jail, ain't nothing funny."

"Better get used to it, *meeskite*," said Morris.

Bridgey stopped laughing. Vallinsky closed his eyes as if holding back a flood of tears. Not surprising for a man who had spent six years in Sing Sing. Morris reveled in the stunned silence. It was his show; he held all the cards. He explained, "Whitman keeping us in protective custody as material witnesses. No charges. No bail. Afraid the killer copper's friends on the force'd cook us."

Vallinsky bit his lips. "We could be locked up six months - a year." He stood up. Staring down at Morris he shouted, "Fucking pimp why you shoot Herman on 43rd Street? We has a plan."

Morris stayed seated. "Maybe you wants I should tell Whitman you was in it with Becker? Helped him coerce me and Bridgey - the copper's muscle."

"That bullshit," screamed Vallinsky

"If I says it he believe it," Morris answered coolly.

Vallinsky closed four fingers of his right hand. His forefinger was extended to mimic a gun. He pointed it at an imaginary victim.

"Gotcha," he shouted.

Morris stayed calm. He looked Vallinsky in the eye. "Think about it Hymie. We in it together - the three of us. One of us a shooter, nobody get immunity. We was coerced into hiring killers. So why one of us shoot? Give me up, our story in the shitter."

"Schmuck," said Bridgey. "Sit down."

Vallinsky sat.

"We got another problem," said Morris. "The kid Abie Isaacs. He sees me shoot Rosenthal."

"That the fucking newsy what tries to warn him?" said Bridgey.

"It worse than that," said Morris. "Think about it. Why he was on 43rd Street at 2 AM - an East Side newsy? I runs into Little Segal, tells me Abie Isaacs' at his place looking for me same day I's with Sullivan and Becker at the Occidental. Somehow finds me there, hears us talking 'bout killing Herman. Gets scared; sneaks out. Kid know everything. He gotta go."

"Ain't he Lena's kid?" asked Vallinsky.

Morris jumped up; he was in Vallinsky's face "What you saying? My own kid I'd kill? He ain't my kid."

Bridgey stepped between them. He looked at Vallinsky. "What difference who he is. The kid can't be trusted."

He turned to Morris. "We needs a shooter. Talk to Zelig?"

"After the Boston's fucked up, Zelig change his mind - got soft on this. Don't want to kill no kid. Washing his hands of the whole thing," said Morris.

"The Bostons still got a beef," said Vallinsky.

"That the problem," said Morris. "Too personal. And for brains, they's got *kishkas*. We needs a stone cold killer what smart, we can count on," said Morris. Vallinsky and Bridgey waited impatiently. Morris began cleaning his nails. Without his knife he was reduced to using his teeth - right now concentrating on his left thumb nail.

Finally, he released his thumb. "Monk Eastman," he said.

"He in jail," said Bridgey.

"I don't know that, putz?" Morris carefully reexamined the offending thumb nail - not satisfied, it went back into his mouth.

"Moisheleh," said Bridgey, "you swallowing jail dirt - rat shit, roach shit, piss, come, puke, blood--"

Morris ignored him and moved to the next nail. Finally he was ready. "Monk getting an early release. DA want the copper real bad. When I tells him about this Isaacs kid, Abie, how he musta been in the Occidental and seen Becker walk out; hears the copper say, 'I don't want no part of this,' Whitman seen his case busting up."

Vallinsky interrupted. "Tells him the kid see you shoot Rosenthal?"

Morris ignored him, and continued, "Whitman want me to take care of it - our 'little problem,' he call it. What you mean 'take care of it, sir?' I asks. He just stare at me. 'Wrong question Schiff,' he says. 'Question is, Who? Remember what we're asking - a kid, how old? fifteen? Probably doesn't even shave - never had pussy. Who would do a thing like that? What manner of beast Mr. Schiff would stalk and murder a child?"

"He right," said Bridgey

Morris gave Bridgey a disgusted look. He continued, "I asks Whitman, he know a Mr. Edward Osterman? 'No,' he says. 'Mr. Osterman,' I says, 'is a sub human piece of shit. He kill his own mother, the price is right. On the East Side he Monk Eastman.' 'Of course,' Whitman says - smiling now. 'Problem is,' I says, 'Eastman's still incarcerated.' Whitman get up and walk to the window - he look out, real quiet. Then he says, 'My good friend Judge Goff will find many blatant discrepancies occurred during Mr Osterman's trial. He will suggest an early release. I will concur. If, of course, Mr. Monk Eastman agrees to eliminate, 'Our little problem.'"

*****

Albany, NY.

The huge oak door of Zayde's house slammed behind Abie; he felt more alone than ever before in his life. Abie and Klopper were walking toward the Albany station. It was 11:30 PM. Laved by the light of a full moon the huge houses with their porticos, gables, and lawns like miniature parks seemed unreal - as fragile as a dream. Yet this was Mama's world. He remembered Zayde patting him on the shoulder, "Stay with us, Abeleh from the ghetto."

Mama was gone - back where she always belonged.

"Your mama home, Abie," said Klopper, as if reading his mind.

He wondered why he was troubled. He should be relieved. A burden was lifted from his shoulders - Mama was safe. And he didn't have to worry about her moods, her rages, her drinking.

Still, feelings of sadness and loss threatened to overwhelm him.

"You looks like you's about to cry for crissake," said Klopper.

"Hey, Klop," he said, recovering, "think that little putz' nose ever gonna to grow back?"

Klopper looked at his knuckles and realized they were still covered with blood, now dry. Disgusted, he rubbed them on his pants and began walking faster. "C'mon Abie," he said. "We got to hurry; miss the train we never get home."

Abie thought of the flat he shared with Mama on Rivington Street. He could never go home.

Sixteen: The Rat Eaters

By the time Klopper and Abie reached Klopper's lean-to on the vacant lot on Delancy Street it was after three AM. Abie couldn't sleep. The streets were deserted. The tenements, like slumbering beasts, loomed menacingly against the flicker of street lamps and the dull glow of the moon. It was so quiet Abie could hear crickets.

Klopper was asleep on the filthy mattress. Abie heard him cough. *Me and Klopper,* he thought, *is the only people in the world.* A breeze disturbed his hair; he smelled the East River, and imagined a vast and empty sea. Albany was a million miles away.

He heard another cough. It wasn't Klopper. He reached for his knife, and turned toward the noise. His eyes fought against the darkness. Footseps came toward him. He crouched, knife in hand.

"Nu, Abeleh," said Rosie Saperstein, "this how you greets a friend?"

Once Abie got over his surprise, he remembered he was angry. "Thought you was Klopper's friend," he said. In the flicker of the distant gas lamp and the muted light of the moon he saw the thick layer of rouge, and imagined her teeth smeared with lipstick. "Working?" he asked. And was immediately sorry.

"Maybe I should go?" she turned away.

Gently, Abie grabbed her shoulder. "Don't go," he said.

Rosie's expression softened. "Been looking all over for you. Thought you's dead. The whole goddamn East Side want you dead. Abie, What you's gonna to do?"

He ran his hand through her hair. "Stay alive," he said.

She smiled, "Maybe I can help?" and reached into her pocketbook taking out a gun. "It Nigger's, I stole it." She handed him the gun.

Abie placed it carefully in his pocket. "She risking her life to give me this," he realized. Before he could react, Rosie kissed him on the cheek and backed away.

"Gotta go, Abeleh. Say hello to Klopper." She was gone.

Abie awoke at the break of dawn, not convinced he slept at all. His body and hands were splotched with blood; bed bugs. He must

GOD'S RAT

have squashed hundreds of them. *They always win,* he thought. *You kills them, you spills your own blood.* The thought of his body covered with dead insects bound to his skin by his blood, made him vaguely sick.

He staggered out of the lean-to and watched two bums cook breakfast over a sputtering flame of dry horse dung and weeds; he didn't dare imagine what they were cooking. Oily black smoke rose, adding another stain to the early morning sky. He took out his battered pocket watch. Seven o'clock. Each second felt like a minute. Somewhere, on a fire escape, an old dago's rooster crowed. He imagined a place with chickens, and cows, and pigs, and trees. A lump, like he swallowed a rock, formed in his throat.

He sat down amidst the weeds and debris, his head resting on his hands. Then he felt the gun in his pocket. He had forgotten Rosie's gift. Her visit was like a dream. He took the gun out and opened the chamber. Six bullets. He stood up and glared at the two bums still fussing over their smoldering breakfast. In the expanding light he could see it was a rat, skinned, gutted, and dripping fat into the sputtering flames. It smelled like burning leather.

He heard himself screaming at the bums. "Get out of here youse slimy bastards. Bums. Rat eating pieces of shit!"

He was stunned at the extent of his rage. The men turned and began to move menacingly in his direction. They both had knives. Abie waved the gun. The men stopped looked at each other, but continued to move forward. Warily.

Abie pointed the gun. The men turned and ran. He opened fire. The smell of gun powder was intoxicating. He fired again. Then something hit him hard from behind; he went down. Klopper was on top of him screaming.

Abie struggled. He wasn't finished, there were still four bullets in the chamber. Klopper hit him hard in the face. He dropped the gun. Klopper picked it up and put it into his pocket. The boys never discussed the incident; except how Abie got the gun.

MICHAEL BOOKMAN

* * * * *

January 25, 1915, 6:05 am &1 seconds, Sing Sing.

Becker could hear his own pain - a piercing wail; a million sighs; a siren song. "Open yourself to the pain, son," said Mama. "On the other side is silence." "I'm cold Mama," Becker said. "I'm burning to death. Why am I cold?" It was a bitter cold morning in January. Becker, a young beat cop, was on Suffolk Street. A spectacular crimson sun broke the night. In the distance, a woman holding the hand of a young child walked toward him; black apparitions against the golden dawn. Some bastard must have thrown them out of the house, he thought. Then he recognized Sadie Frenchy Horowitz. She was a hop head whore who walked the streets at night with her five year old kid. "Excuse me sir," she would implore, "My husband a drunk what throws us out. A quarter buys a roof and food for my boy." If that didn't work she'd blow the guy for as little as a nickel - sometimes in clear view of the kid. She was darkly beautiful. Like a gypsy witch, Becker thought. Luxurious black hair flowed past her waist, and dancing eyes promised unspeakable pleasure. Her blow jobs were reputed to be the best on the East Side. "Why not?" Becker asked himself. She smiled as she passed: "Hello Charley," she said. "Got to pull you in Sadie," Becker said gruffly. "Orders from the chief." She walked over to him; put her lips to his ear. "Is that what you really want, Charley?" Then she turned to her kid. His rags were scant protection against the cold. He was freezing. His nose ran; his teeth rattled - bare hands covered bare ears. "Benny," she said, "go home and wait for Mama. Don't put no nickel in the gas, we ain't got the money." It was Klopper Benny.

GOD'S RAT

Seventeen: Beast

Monk Eastman couldn't sleep. It was his last night in jail. Every night for five years he imagined he was a bird; not one of the pigeons or parrots he sold from his store, but a hawk. A red eyed predatory presence seething through steel bars, soaring, mightily, over concrete walls to freedom. And now freedom was here, three years early. And freedom meant revenge. *They all turns their backs on me,* he thought. He would swoop down on them; tear them to pieces, the bastards. *All of them. Peruvnicks, yeggs, bums. I makes money for everybody. So what happen? Sullivan take away my protection. Him and his Yids, Sam Paul and Silver Dollar Smith. And my boys, The Eastman's: Crazy Butchie. Zelig. Morris. Kid Twist. Bridgey. Dead fucking silence - four years talking to the walls while they's stealing me blind.*

Even his whores turned on him. *I keeps my trotters safe. Nobody* farshloguen *my* nafkas. *Nobody.*

Yet not one of them visited him. They knew he hated cages; that, when he couldn't get to his pet shop on Mott Street, the thought of his birds locked up all day and night would drive him crazy. Suddenly he smiled; he remembered opening the store in the morning, smelling the bird shit; getting the birds back in their cages. Cleaning the up the mess, a labor of love. Who has his birds now? The thought of his parrots and pigeons, abandoned, brought tears to his eyes.

And where Louie? he wondered. *Best bird I ever has.* He bought him from a broken down seaman for ten beans. A Mexican Double Yellow Head, scrawny, flea ridden, but worth its weight in gold. Him and Tessy the Truck killing the fleas one at a time, fattening him up until his eyes were bright, and his green and orange feathers, shiny and slick. Teaching him to say, "Monk you's the best." Sometimes he'd open the store three or four in the morning and Louie would fly on to his shoulder and say it so clear it would give him a chill, "Monk you's the best. Monk you's the best."

GOD'S RAT

Been a couple of years since he let himself think of Louie. Walking down Boadway with the parrot on his shoulder. Better than a moll on his arm. Who knows? Maybe he'd track Louie down. "Better be just like I last seen him." And what happened to his pet store? Probably some dago fruit stand. "Dagos think they's gonna run the East Side. Over my dead body."

Two days earlier Eastman was summoned from Sing Sing to the Criminal Court Building on Center Street adjacent to the Tombs. He was taken directly to the office of the Attorney of the Eastern District of the State of New York, Charles Whitman.

Whitman greeted him with a big fishy smile, and a stare that made Eastman flinch. He had the guards take the handcuffs off; sent them away, then reached over and shook hands. His hand was dry and cold; soft like a baby's. After elaborately clearing his throat, he began to speak. "Pleased to meet you Mr. Eastman," he growled. "You are a legend on the East Side. It would have been my pleasure to have been responsible for your incarceration. Quite a trophy. I'm sure you have heard of Lieutenant Becker. A menace to society. A real scumbag. It will be my pleasure to be responsible for his legal demise. But I can't do this without your help Mr. Eastman. There is an irony here" - he coughed wetly - studied his hanky and continued. "You are being conscripted to be an agent of the constabulary." Now he was laughing and coughing at the same time. More phlegm. "What is required," he croaked, "is an act of cold brutality. Of course the consequence to the people will be justice. Your consequence sir, should you choose to accept our offer, will be freedom."

Eastman found himself leaning forward trying desperately to make heads or tails what this *meshugeh* DA wanted from him. Whatever he wanted he'd do if it meant getting out of jail. "Just say what the fuck you wants," he thought. His head began to throb. Listening to Whitman was like eating prison slop; fishing through fat, and gristle, and grease trying to find some meat. Finally, after what seemed like hours of fancy-assed phlegm clogged gibberish, certain things became clear.

MICHAEL BOOKMAN

Whitman was trying to cook this Becker. Making it seem like the bent copper coerced poor Morris, Bridgey, Valinsky to have Herman Rosenthal killed. The three of them becoming state witnesses, copping immunity. Should Eastman agree to commit the "brutal act" he will be released. The DA seemed reluctant to tell him exactly what it was he had to do.

Suddenly Whitman stood up, excused himself. As he left the room Morris Schiff entered, glittering in a svelte blue plaid suit, and enough gold to plate the teeth of ten East Side whores. A guard came in behind him.

"Monk," said the pimp as he rushed over to grab his hand. "The East Side ain't been the same without you. Welcome home."

Eastman didn't move; just stared menacingly at his former lieutenant. "*Vantz*, bloodsucker, four years I don't see you, Welcome home," he sneered. "You bastards steals my fucking home."

The guard, a tall, aging Irishman, nervously fingered his holster. After all, this was the notorious Monk Eastman, whose flesh was so torn by bullets a mere mortal would have died a hundred deaths; Monk Eastman, the Jewish Beelzebub, revealing yet another face of Hebrew perfidy: vicious, violent, destructive. More than one inmate confided he'd seen Eastman tear out a Christian heart with his bare hands.

Morris smiled. "Boychick, better you should look to the future; a future, by the way, what's coming three years early. But if you don't relax a little I can't tell you how to get out of this shit hole, because unless you think I's more buggy then Crazy Butchie, I ain't letting this copper out of here 'till's I damn sure you ain't gonna to tear my head off."

Eastman always knew, and now it was confirmed, there wasn't a smoother, slicker hoodlum on the East Side than Morris The Pimp Schiff. Only Schiff could blow the head off a gambler in front of a million witnesses and end up with the DA in his one hundred percent silk, blue plaid hip pocket. And he, Monk Eastman the *k'nocker*, big shot, the pimp's boss for chrissake, in prison stripes with his hand out.

Morris was talking about cutting three years from his sentence. Three years! He could think of nothing sweeter, except maybe opium filling his lungs and demolishing his brain.

Eastman looked at Morris. "OK, putz, tell me what you wants."

With a small gesture of his head toward the door, Morris dismissed the guard. He told Monk what he wanted. Eastman didn't respond; he just stared at Morris who was now examining his fingernails.

Eastman watched Morris capture some jailhouse dirt between his teeth. "Nobody has his own kid killed," he said. "Even you, pimp; even you don't sinks that low."

Morris began to pace. "Look, maybe Abie my kid. Maybe not. Ain't nobody's business. Point is I gotta stay alive. Each man for himself - it nature's way. Starving rat see a fat rat with cheese, he care it might be his kid? Does what he gotta do. Why you gives a shit Monk? Get soft in jail? Want to know why you's here Monk? DA ask me, 'What kind of beast would kill a child?' That why you's here."

Morris knew damn well whose kid it was. He always knew. After Lena left Monk, she came back to work for him, all beat up, nowhere else to turn; she told him she was pregnant, it was Monk's kid. She wanted Doc Greenbaum to kill it. "Monk a *baizeh cheiyeh*, a beast. Moisheleh - feels like I"s carrying a disease, not no baby." But she kept putting it off; got out of the business; had the baby, Abraham Osterman; known to the world as Abie Isaacs. She swore Morris to secrecy. "If anyone know," she said, " it would be a curse on Abie." Morris kept his word, but figured being the son of Monk Eastman was curse enough - even if only God knew.

"How quick you gets me out of here?" asked Monk Eastman. But all the time he's thinking, *They's telling me too much. Don't care what I knows, because after I kills this kid, they kills me.*

* * * * *

January 25, 1915, 6:05 am & 58 seconds, Sing Sing.

Becker saw Monk Eastman walking toward him; twenty four year old Lena Isaacs on his arm. Perched on Monk's shoulder was his trained parrot, Louie. "Hello, Charley," said Lena. Monk leaned toward Lena and whispered in her ear. She giggled girlishly. Becker trembled with rage. *The parrot flew off Eastman's shoulder and landed on his. What a beautiful bird, thought Becker. He could feel the beak at his ear - the parrot spoke. "Copper, Monk and Lena is fucking. They's fucking copper. They's fucking copper. They's fucking copper." It was Morris' voice. Monk stuck his face into Becker's. He was smiling broadly. "Marry me, Lena," he said mockingly. "Become a Christian, Lena. I takes you away from all this." He was laughing . Becker never saw Monk Eastman laugh before. He looked over Eastman's shoulder at Lena. She was crying. Again, the smell of burning flesh.*

GOD'S RAT

Eighteen: *Zelig is Dead*

It was dusk. Abie was waiting for Klopper to return; he had been waiting for hours. Klopper left to look for Big Jack Zelig. Recently he and the Stanton Street boys had done some effective scab busting for Chink Bartfield, a Zelig cohort. Word got back Big Jack was happy with the work they did. Klopper told Abie it gave them credibility. "He know we got the job done; he can use us on other jobs - we can help him with the dagos. He'll call off his dogs."

"You's dreaming, Klop," said Abie. "That was before I tries to tip off Rosenthal. It was Zelig's contract."

"Maybe you got a better idea?" Klopper asked.

Abie looked at his pocket watch - 8 PM. *Six hours,* he thought. He scanned the Delancey Street lot; its demolished wooden tenements, piles of garbage, starving cats, and rats and filthy human wrecks were now blanketed by a hot steamy mist, the result of a recent summer downpour; the lurid reality of the lot was softened, transformed into a weird dreamscape: insubstantial; unreal; intolerably fragile. *It all going to evaporate,* thought Abie, *and take me with it.*

Suddenly, about fifty feet away, and moving quickly toward him were three shadowy figures. Abie thought two of them were the bums he shot at earlier in the day. He reached for his gun, but remembered Klopper took it away.

He recognized Freak Show. Flanking him was Sheeny Mike Levine, and Sugar Davey Saperstein. Abie relaxed. But too soon. Freak Show slapped him hard in the face. Abie's head exploded; his eyes filled with tears. The dwarf's rag encased stumps provided precarious leverage; the force of his blow caused him to fall; he landed on his back, stumps and arms flailing uselessly, reminding Abie of a roach when it flips over.

Then Sheeny Mike hit Abie hard in the midsection, he was wearing knucks; the blow felt like a boulder was dropped on his stomach. Sugar Davey kneed him in the mouth momentarily straightening him, forcing his teeth deep into his lower lip. Abie went down. A shot rang out; everyone froze. The cats, the rats, and the bums.

It was Klopper, his gun at his side, his face hard as stone. He said nothing. Waiting. The silence oppressed like the heat. Freak Show spoke, "He a rat Klop, ain't no better than the rat he tries to warn." Now with tears in his eyes, he looked at Abie, "You turns us into a joke Abie - a bunch geelicks what can't be trusted."

"It costing me, Klop," said Davey, black eyes flashing. "Looses two of my best whores to Nigger."

"Abie Cracks," laughed Sheeny Mike. He put his face into Abie's - so close Abie could count the freckles on Mike's nose. "That what you got Abie," he sneered, "a crack where your balls use to be. We should calls you Abie Gash."

No one laughed.

Abie, not bothering to wipe the blood from his lip, spoke through torrents of pain, "I ain't apologizing for nothing. I done what I did. I do it again."

All eyes turned to Klopper. It wasn't just the gun; the chips were down and they were nothing without him. He spoke, "We knows each other since we's babies. Been through all kinds of shit together. Abie a strange kid; but he our brother. I ain't got no family. None of us got no real family. This our family. Anybody want out; they gets out But youse lay another hand on Abie I kills youse. *Farshtaist?*"

Everybody understood. Nobody wanted out. Klopper told them about his day.

"First I run into Big Lenny Knoll and Louie Bum. I asks where Zelig? Louie slam me in the ear. I's thinking it strange. These guys got no gripe with me - so I don't go for my gun. They just walks away. Don't make no sense. So I walks to Yussie's pool hall. Spooky - no one there. Just Yussie; he drinking a beer - ain't even nine in the morning. Yussie aint no *schikeh*. '*Ve geittus* Yusseleh,' I says; he don't even look up. 'Where everybody,' I asks - 'they on civilian time?' He look at me funny.

"'Where you from?' he says, 'you from Minsk?'"

The boys are sitting now, forming a semicircle around Klopper. His back is toward the lean-to.

"Where the hell has you been?" asked Davey.

Ignoring Davey, Klopper continued. " 'C'mon Yuss,' I says, 'what going on? So he tell me."

"Tell you what, for chrissake?" asked Abie.

Silence.

Abie panicked, maybe they got Mama. But why would Yussie and Louie Bum give a shit?

He looked at Klopper and saw the tears. Abie's head throbbed, blending with the pain in his gut, and punctured lip. He sprang at Klopper, and shook him.

"Fuck going on?" he screamed.

Klopper turned away; he could not utter the words.

"Zelig dead," said Sheeny Mike.

Abie kept his grip on Klopper's neck. He heard the syllables, the words; but he refused to decipher them. Finally he understood and released Klopper.

"Who done it?" he asked

"Not no dago. Red Phil Davidson - a nobody," said Sugar Davey in disgust.

All over the East Side, the newsies were having a field day. "Zelig dead," they shouted. The headline of *The New York World* read: **"East Side Hoodlum Shot to Death."** But it took the Yiddish *Tageblatt* to capture the deeper emotional currents roiling the East Side: **"People's Protector Killed by One of Our Own."**

The front page obituary began:

Today the East Side lost a unique young man, William Alberts, 26 - known to friend and foe as Big Jack Zelig. His tragic and premature death was not a result of his race battles with the Italians. He was shot and killed on a Delancey Street trolley by a small time Jewish thief, and pimp, "Red Phil" Davidson. The reasons are unclear. Some of our readers may be asking, 'Why such a big deal over a gangster?' Yes, he was a gangster. But it was with good reason he bore the sobriquet, "People's Protector." Of course, other gangsters fought the Italians and the Irish. Monk Eastman and his gang waged classic turf wars with the Five Pointers Gang. But it was different with Zelig. For Jack, keeping Italian gunmen and pimps out of our neighborhood was a matter of pride if not principle. Certainly not merely a matter of profit.

One event in particular designated Big Jack Zelig a legend. It happened on a Saturday night sometime in April, three months before his death. And now, on the eve of his burial, it was given a new luster by grief - recalled in saloons, dance halls, brothels, pool halls, and Socialist coffee houses; in synagogues, yeshivas, and Talmudic study rooms.

And in a squalid vacant lot on Delancey Street .

"The word was out," recalled Sheeny Mike. "Zelig taking on the dagos what's bashing the Jews in Seward Park. All the gangs was there to watch - Rivington Street, Forsyth Street, Broome Street. Even the Cherry Street Boys."

"And everybody armed to the teeth," said Freak Show.

"Yeah," remembered Abie. "So we gets there and nothing happening. Just the usual bunch of greenie Jews with their *tsitis* and beards. No Jew bashing wops. No Zelig."

"Then we sees Fat Vinnie and his crew," said Klopper; "Vinnie in his goddamn undershirt - fifty degrees, dumb wop in his *gotkis*."

Freak Show wondered, "Maybe his fat keep him warm?"

"Then come Jonsey," said Sugar Davey, "with his crew - ten guys. Jonsey with that scar on his face what Big Jack give him with his own knife. Now there's twenty wops and no Zelig."

"These dagos," said Davey, "they's men, we's kids. So Klop you takes out your gun, remember? I says, 'Klop, What you gonna to do, shoot them all?' "

"Then Augie Two Cents pull this big greenie's beard," said Abie. " 'I gives you a quick shave kike,' he says. Remember his expression when the beard come off in his hand?"

"I remember his expression when he see it Zelig," said Sheeny Mike, laughing.

They spoke for hours.

How Zelig went to the local Rabbis to get their cooperation in keeping the real *frum* Jews out of the park that night; how he got his friend Thomashensky, the great Yiddish actor, to help with the disguises; the caftans, the *tsises*, side curls and the beards and for the whores, and gun molls - shapeless long dresses, and horse hair wigs. He convinced Big Tim Sullivan to clear the area of coppers for thirty minutes.

They spoke of the shock of seeing orthodox Jews fighting back. Even if it was only an illusion. But mostly they spoke of the violence. Abie remembered Bald Jack Rose who was sitting on a bench pretending to read a paper get up and charge Fat Vinnie, his shiny pate like a speeding bullet. "Vinnie go down and stay down, five minutes," said Abie.

Sugar Davey took a proprietary interest in the ladies - the whores and gun molls who fought side by side with the men, screaming at the top of their lungs, their knives and straight razors a fearsome, slashing juggernaut creating bloody havoc. "Little Solly's whore Faigaleh," he exulted, "she cut Frank Nicolo so bad, side of his face open like a mouth puking blood."

They spoke of Gyp the Blood smiling insanely behind his fake beard and side curls as he slashed and slammed - a knife in one hand and a black jack in the other - at an enemy virtually incapacitated by shock; and of Sammy Boston and Big Alec hoisting Tony The Lump De Gregorio high over their heads, him screaming, "Mama Mia," and crying like a baby as they lowered him, ever so gently, on the wrought iron pickets that topped the Seward Park fence.

And finally, in what was their greatest moment as a gang, they spoke of getting caught up in the bloodlust - no longer satisfied being spectators, joining the battle, their weapons drawn, putting an end to whatever resistance was left on the part of the enemy, becoming a part of what they sensed would be their moment in history.

GOD'S RAT

They spoke throughout the night, their voices mingling with the crickets, the caterwauling toms, and the nauseating noises drunks make when they sleep. The conclusion of the front page obituary in the *Tageblatt* read:

And so, led by Zelig, the crooks, gangsters, gamblers, pimps, punks, and whores, the despised underbelly of the East Side, experienced a transcendent moment when their un-Jewishness became righteous; a mighty sword of retribution and vengeance. On that night they perpetrated a Jewish pogrom against the gentile tormentor. Jewish because it was ultimately defensive; a pogrom, because it was merciless and unrelentingly violent. On that night the East Side's low lifes and scum were able to be themselves while, at the same time, making their mamas proud.

We will miss you, Big Jack Zelig.

In the morning after Zelig was killed Monk Eastman was back on the street. Everything was the same; and nothing was the same. It was still his beloved East Side - the jostling, screaming sea of peddlers, beggars, orthodox Jews, working Jews, tough Jews, and a million raggedy, barefoot kids. Of course there were changes.

He noticed more combustion engine vehicles, the smell of gasoline overwhelming the stench of horse shit; his mind's eye rejecting the notion of hundreds of horseless vehicles defying gravity by sputtering, east up Canal Street to the bridge like some dumb circus trick, a slight of hand he couldn't quite figure out. Just as surprising was hearing as much English as Yiddish - except on Mott Street, and Grand Street where the language had become Italian - the Italians, moving in and taking away, so it seemed to Monk, valuable sources of profit that were, by birthright, his to exploit.

But what was really different - maddeningly disconcerting - nobody knew him. The look of awe, and fear his presence once inspired, was replaced by blank indifference. It made him feel invisible. And worse, he didn't recognize anybody.

It only been four years, he thought. *Not that I was expecting no fucking parade.*

He headed for The Pelham, Nigger Mike Salter's Saloon on Pell Street.

On that same morning the boys walked toward Zelig's flat on Broome Street where the body was to be brought from the morgue. From here the funeral cortege would proceed east on Delancey, over the Williamsburgh Bridge to its final destination, a cemetery in Brooklyn.

Abie was risking his life attending Zelig's funeral. Everyone who wanted him dead would be there. The boys thought he should stay on the lot. But Abie calculated the risk and figured it worth it. "Ain't nobody going to shoot me in front of Zelig's wife, and Mama, and the Rabbis," he said. "Even these bums got too much respect for that."

"It your life," said Klopper. Let's go."

Turning the corner into Broome Street the boys didn't believe their eyes. Thousands thronged the block. The street was cleared and the sidewalk cordoned by at least fifty coppers. Abie recognized Captain Kelly of the Clinton Street Station. There were also three Lieutenants and two sergeants.

All the luminaries from the underworld were there as were the politicians, and, the businessmen. In front of Zelig's tenement Captain Kelly was quietly conferring with a huge man in a top hat, black cape, and frock coat. He was leaning heavily on his cane. Abie recognized Big Tim Sullivan.

"Look like he waiting for his own hearse," said Klopper.

What surprised Abie were the thousands of ordinary East Siders who had come just to get a glimpse of the coffin. He was also impressed by the silence. "How so many Jews be so quiet?"

Suddenly there was a deep ominous rumbling - the sound of distant thunder. Thousands of eyes looked to the sky. Not a cloud. Then a sibilant murmur raced through the crowd. "The hearse. The hearse. The hearse."

Abie heard his own voice join the others. The empty hearse turned into Broom from Grand. Behind it came the carriages, also empty. One after another they came. The procession seemed endless. Abie counted thirty carriages as they lined up in front of the tenement.

"It costs somebody two hundred dollars - easy," said Sheeny Mike.

Nineteen: Unbound.

Monk wasn't surprised Nigger Mike's joint was closed - it was 8: AM. He began to knock. Nig lived upstairs and was sure to hear the racket. Suddenly monk's head was bashed violently against the door. His knees went out from under him. Powerful hands grabbed his right arm, twisting it behind his back and lifting it upward with such force his feet lurched off the ground. His arm, supporting all his weight, felt as if it was going to separate from the rest of his body. Only one man on the East Side had the strength to tear a man apart.

"It me, Nig," he screamed, "Monk."

Monk was sitting at the bar now. Nigger Mike Salter was pouring him a beer.

"What you do, Monk, bust out?" Nig asked.

Monk explained how he offered the DA an enormous campaign contribution. "Everything I stashed. Money talk Nig - here I is."

Nigger Mike Salter - swarthy and gigantic - a former strong man in a Coney Island freak show, could be trusted to listen sympathetically and keep his mouth shut; he knew everything worth knowing on the East Side.

He gave Monk the post mortem on his empire. How his old gang, the Eastman's, split into three factions, with Zelig, Dopey Benny Fine, and Kid Twist Zweiback fighting over the spoils. How The Kid was shot dead in a fight over some whore in Coney Island. How just yesterday Zelig's brains were shot out on a Delancey Street trolley.

"It over, Monk. These kids got no respect for nobody. Even you. You name come up, it a joke. Tammany still don't want no part of you. Where your power? Go back to Brooklyn, Monk. Open up a bird store. Fly your pigeons. Retire."

In the old days nobody spoke to Monk Eastman like this. Not Even Nigger Mike Salter who stood six feet six, and had the strength of ten men. *I just blows his brains out, and Tammany clean up the mess,* Monk thought.

GOD'S RAT

Nig showed Monk Zelig's front page obituary in *The Tageblatt*. Monk remembered Zelig as a baby faced punk who stole pocket books from old ladies. *OK*, he thought, *he pretty good with his fists and the ladies they loves him. But a hero? 'The Peoples Protector', yet?*

Monk left Nigger Mike's for the funeral on Mott Street. Nig told him half the East Side would be there. Good chance he'd find the kid Abie Isaacs. First thing he had to do, cook this kid - Lena's kid. Too bad about that, but he was proud he could take a life without a second thought. Without remorse. Killing was his gift, like being able to sit down and play the piano, or handle a cue stick. *When you enemies knows you's a killer,* he thought, *it break their will - take away their heart.*

He remembered Big Tim Sullivan coming to bail him out after he bashed some poor bastard's skull in at Silver Dollar Smith's just so he could put the fiftieth notch in his club. "You's dangerous, Monk," Big Tim said, "that why we wants you working for us."

Monk realized Nig was wrong: his power didn't come from Tammany; Tammany came to him because of his power. *They be back,* he thought.

He put his hand in his pocket and felt the cold steel of his gun. He bought it from Nig for twelve bucks. *Cheap bastard should've give it to me - a welcome home present,* he thought.

Heading toward the funeral, Monk began to walk with his old East Side strut.

As the thirtieth empty carriage sidled up to the curb, completing the cortege in front of Zelig's tenement, two ladies dressed in black came through the front door. One, about twenty, thin, plain, almost mousy, an eight month old child in her arms; the other, much older, heavy set with strong chiseled features that bore a striking resemblance to Big Jack Zelig. Behind them came other family members, all somberly attired. They stood on a concrete stoop about ten feet above the ground. From the sidewalk leading to the small landing were twelve steps. A choir, six men with beards, skull caps and flowing black robes, emerged from the crowd and climbed the steps - they claimed two steps, three to a step, and began chanting Hebrew lamentations for the dead. Many in the crowd prayed with them. As is the custom, the men edged their way to the front, the women to the rear. The men *davened*, rocking rapidly back and forth as they prayed, eyes scrunched closed. Some of the women prayed quietly, most just sobbed.

"All this for a gangster," Abie thought proudly, "one of us."

Abie scanned the crowd searching for Zelig's associates; the gangsters, gamblers, *gonifs*, and pimps - the "boys". He found them standing in a tight-knit group, on the sidewalk, next to the stoop, in a space reserved for the local dignitaries. They were *davening* passionately. He tried to imagine them as small boys, in Poland, Russia, Galacia, Lithuania - Big Alec, Joe the Greaser, the Boston brothers - going to *schul* on *Shabbis* with their papas, wearing skullcaps, and maybe even side curls--

His daydream was broken by a tap on the shoulder.

A gruff voice asked, "You's Abie Isaacs?"

In front of him stood one of the strangest men he had ever seen. In spite of the ninety-degree heat he was stuffed into a heavy plaid woolen suit at least two sizes too small; his face was a mass of scar tissue; his nose flat. He was wearing a battered black derby so small it seemed balanced on his head rather than worn.

"I knows you Mama," he said.

Then he turned and disappeared in the crowd.

"Jesus," said Klopper, "knows who that is?"

"Some friend of Mama's," he said. "Creepy looking."

"It Monk Eastman."

Abie was astonished. "You's shitting me," he said.

"You mama know Monk Eastman?" asked Freak Show. "Who else she know, the President? The King of England, maybe?"

Abie basked in the glow. Then the sadness came. He hated missing Mama; hated feeling like a kid.

"Funny," said Klopper, "Monk Eastman suppose to be in jail."

GOD'S RAT

By now the choir had stopped singing, and those who were going to accompany the body to its final resting place were arranging themselves in the carriages. The crowd was thinned, most to go about their business, some to join the cortege on foot and follow the carriages at least as far as the Williamsburg bridge.

The boys were bone tired, not having slept for eighteen hours. Abie and Klopper headed toward the lean-to. Sheeny, Sugar Davey, and Freak Show headed home.

Walking back to the lean-to Abie and Klopper inadvertently became part of the cortege as it wended its way north on Broome Street toward Delancey. Once on Delancey hundreds more joined the procession. Coppers were everywhere; the street was cleared of traffic; thousands stood silently on the sidewalk.

If a dago kill Zelig there be a riot, Abie thought.

Twenty: River of Fire

Abie noticed an interruption in the pedestrian procession. The crowd, like a stream confronting an obstacle at its center, thickened then eddied to the left and the right. Getting closer he saw the problem; one of the carriages had come to a halt, falling far behind the others. As he and Klopper passed the stalled carriage a familiar voice called to them.

"Boychicks, *ve geittus?*"

They stopped and faced the voice. Peering out the window, smiling broadly was Sammy Boston. Leaning over Sammy's shoulder was Meyer Boston's unsmiling face. In his hand, a gun. It rested on his brother's shoulder for leverage. From the corner of his eye Abie could see Klopper's right hand move toward his pocket.

"No, Klop," said Abie.

Sammy pretended he didn't notice.

"Don't be such strangers," said Sammy. "Come closer, we shouldn't have to shout." The boys moved closer to the carriage. "Abeleh, Klopper, my favorite *gunzils* come join us." Meyer gave the gun to Sammy and pushed open the door. "Come aboard. On such a hot day, Why should you walk?" The boys climbed in the carriage.

"Boychicks," said Sammy with surprising sincerity, "this is such a sad time."

Klopper shrugged. "Zelig was a gangster." He looked out the window as if more interested in Delancey Street than the man facing him with the gun.

"Ain't what sad," said Meyer.

"I ain't afraid of dying," said Klopper.

"What about you, Abeleh, you afraid?"

Abie said nothing. He felt his entire life was about this moment. He had chosen lawlessness. Death was part of that choice. Not that he wanted to die; not that he wasn't terrified. But from the first time he rolled a lush. Took the man's wallet. Kicked him in the face when he protested. From that moment he was owed nothing. He had lost his right to expect more than violent death. The only question; how would he face the inevitable?

Now there was silence. Only the hypnotic clop of hooves.

Everybody was listening to everybody's breathing.

Finally Sammy spoke, "It personal, boys. This ain't no contract. You should know that. Abie it was no fucking joke I makes you a *schtarker*. You come from nothing. A little *momser* what got a whore for a mama. A fucking mutt. I takes you in Abeleh; I makes you one of us. What you do? Snitch to Herman. I looks like a *schtumie*, a boob."

Sammy's pig face was without guile. Quizical. Hurt even. Abie remembered standing next to Klopper as he pointed the guns at Sammy and Meyer, the two of them lying there helpless, ridiculous; feeling pain like a belt of broken glass tightening around his intestines, fighting an impulse to grab the guns out of Klopper's hands. He could still smell the piss that ran down Sammy's leg; feel his shame.

They were on the bridge now a million feet in the air. It was Abie's first time on one of the huge structures spanning the East River. He was stunned. It was not like looking out of a tenement window, seeing only other tenement windows. Or rooftops. Now he saw what a bird saw. Or an angel: the river on fire as it ran into the sun and off the edge of the world. For a second his fear was as pure as if he were actually falling.

"Scared, Mr. Abie Cracks?" asked Meyer. "Sammy, look at Abie. Our little *schtarker* scared shit."

Sammy ignored his brother. He was staring at Klopper; eyes narrowing. "Nu Klopper," he said, "you didn't have the *kayich* to shoot us in the head. Worse for a Jew - not even the sense. Think we's going let you live? Die easy?"

Abie saw Sammy's face redden. Mottle, actually. Crimson splotches appearing on his forehead and cheeks like a fever soaring out of control. He reached over and grabbed Klopper by the collar;

pressing the gun to his head, screaming now. Wetting his face. "Behind my back I's 'Sammy Piss Pants.'"

Then Klopper did the unthinkable. He laughed out loud. Abie heard the sound of his own laughter. *We crazy?* he thought. Tears ran from his eyes. In his ears the words "Sammy piss pants," taunted any effort at restraint

Sammy's blotched face turned blood red.

Meyer was shouting, "Sammy, don't shoot. Give me the fucking gun. Not here. A million witnesses - blood." The brothers were struggling for the gun. Rage seemed to expand their bulk; their struggle consumed every inch of the cab.

Abie had no recollection of opening the carriage door and getting out. He remembered looking back, making sure Klopper was behind him. The two of them running back toward the city, squeezed between two lanes of traffic, dodging the trucks and cabs coming at them from opposite directions.

Above them they heard the familiar jingle of a junk man's bell. A squat, filthy, muscular Jew driving two battered drays hauling an open truck full of mangled metal was signaling them to climb aboard. On the truck Abie tried not to think of Sammy's words; but the words wouldn't go away. "Behind my back I's Sammy Piss Pants; Sammy Piss Pants; Sammy Piss Pants--" The laughter came again; he wanted to hold it back, but it exploded with a life of its own.

The junk man looked at him and shrugged his shoulders. "*Americaneh.*"

Klopper wasn't laughing. "Wanna hear something really funny Abie - what Meyer says to Sammy when I gets out of the taxi?"

Abie stopped laughing. For the first time he saw fear in his friend's eyes.

"'Sammy,' says Meyer, 'What for you worrying? If we don't kill them, Monk Eastman will.'"

* * * * *

GOD'S RAT

January 25, 1915, 6:06 am, and 24 seconds, Sing Sing.

Hands loosened the straps fastening Becker to the chair. It's over, he thought. They realize they can't kill me. Two doctors examined him. Their metal stethoscopes cold as ice. Gravely they shook their heads. Fear tore through him. "They think I'm dead. I ain't dead you dumb croakers." The guards began to refasten the straps. Mama came to him. She kissed his forehead. "They know you're alive, son. Let them take you. For God's sake - let go." Becker was on Second Avenue and Third Street, just as the Yiddish theatres let out. Abie Isaacs, his newsboy hat pulled over his eyes, was hawking the New York World. "Massacre In East Side Brothel," he screamed. Becker approached Abie and knocked his hat off. There was a bloody hole directly over the bridge of his nose. Becker cried. "Forgive me, Lena," he said.

Twenty One: *Lena's Room*

Early August, 1914. Albany.

From the moment Blanche switched on the electric light, Lena Isaacs felt she was losing her mind. Electricity brought light without soft shadows. Not a flicker. Unrelenting light piercing her eyes; forcing them shut. When she opened them, Blanche was gone; she gazed at her room. After twenty-four years everything was spotless, as if the tools used against dust, dirt, cobwebs, and grime used often enough could also fight time. But time; its passage; its depredations were made more stunning by the desperate effort to make it stand still. The room was a shrine. A museum. A tomb. She could almost picture the desiccated corpse of seventeen year old Lena Isaacs lying peacefully on her bed, scrubbed clean to the bone. Shutting her eyes she ran back to the light switch, couldn't find it and frantically moved her palms in a circular motion against the wall. "Fucking switch; where the fucking switch?" Finally her hands connected and moved it down. Darkness filled the room bringing some comfort But her mind could not hold the darkness. Compulsively she recalled everything she had seen in that frozen second. On the shelf, still in size places, her porcelain dolls, immaculate.

On her bed, their heads resting on the silk pillow case, her three favorites; Juanita from Spain, Hilda from Germany, and poor Natasha, the Russian - its left nostril still bearing the space where it chipped when she dropped it. Even now she felt the sadness, remembering crawling on her hands and knees, desperately looking for that tiny piece of porcelain.- "Did I think it would heal after twenty four years?" Otherwise the dolls were perfect - porcelain, unbroken, is eternal. But their brightly hued costumes were scrubbed colorless. On the wall, over her bed, the school flag hung, its deep royal blue cloth worn - the flowered wallpaper showing through; the once bold yellow threads spelling **The Albany Academy for Women** in gothic script, now the color of dust.

I must sit down, she thought, and squatted against the wall. Her body drenched in sweat; her eyes flooding. There was a knock on the door.

"Can I come in, Lena darling?" It was Mama.

"Of course Mama," she said. The door opened. The lights came back on. An old lady came in.

Where my Mama? Lena wanted to ask. The old lady spoke, "Why did you shut the lights, darling? I kept the room for you. Every day I made sure Blanche was in here cleaning. 'When Lena comes back I want it to look just the way it did when she left.' I always knew you would come back to us - even when everybody lost faith. And the lies. My darling Lena do you think for a moment I would believe the things--" As the old lady spoke, Lena closed her eyes. Mama's voice swept over her like a embrace; the familiar cadences, the clipped affected sentences, the voice itself harsh, nasal - forced through her nose, a deliberate process, extruding it of all its history - no trace of an impoverished girlhood in a tiny *schtetle* in the Ukraine; of her first language -Yiddish. Mama's voice cracked by time; but Mama's voice.

Lena opened her eyes. Now she could clearly see Mama's features hiding behind a mask of wizened flesh. *Take me into your arms mama; press my face to your breast; make me seventeen again; cleanse the filth Mama; bring back my clean white teeth Mama. Don't be this old lady.* I broke my mama; dropped and broke her just like Natasha.

And from this old lady pours mamas voice, "--living in poverty, in that terrible ghetto, in that filth. My daughter a student at the most prestigious school in Albany, living like the child of someone who slaughters chickens; peddles buttons; who presses pants--"

We sit here in this tomb with the stinking corpse of her memories. How many conversations did she have in this room with poor Lena? *Did we talk about my handsome wealthy husband; my beautiful children; did we laugh over my D in math; did we marvel how I almost ran away with that horrible New York White Slaver, Mr. Schiff; did we plan the wedding; argue over the guest list?*

Mama, Mama your beautiful brown eyes are unfocused - permanently confused - the left one lost behind a cloud; Who do you see in front of you? Lena grabbed Mama. The old lady felt so small and fragile and cold in her arms; an oversized porcelain doll--

"and your tante Hilda from the ghetto, she recognized you from the picture we sent; but she wouldn't see you; wouldn't give you my letters - said she did, but I knew she was lying - then I sent money. I knew she would give it to you; or else send it back. (Hilda would never keep money that wasn't hers.) It gave me so much comfort, the money--"

mention of the money broke Lena's self control - for twenty four years; thirty dollars a month; sometimes it arrived in an envelope under the door; other times a street urchin would come up to her, ask her name, give her the money, and run. Always the first of the month, always the same amount. In the beginning she thought the money was from some uptown admirer - then it became part of the fabric of her life. With all the hardship and the pain and the degradation, Why not this too? None of it made any sense. *Mama, you did all this behind Papa's back - how did you manage this my darling mama?*

The tears came. "Mama," she said, "You kept me and Abie alive. Why mama? After everything I did to you, the shame, what I'd become--?"

The old lady pulled herself from Lena's arms. Now she held Lena's face in her hands. "Lenaleh," she said through tears, even the bad eye produced perfectly good tears, "You were a victim. There is nothing to be ashamed of; there was no shame. When you say things like that I don't understand."

"I love you, mama," said Lena

After Mama left Lena tried to sleep. But sleep held the promise of peace. And Lena Isaacs would know no peace in the home of her birth. Emotionally and physically she was exhausted. But mere exhaustion was a whore, a seductress, a taunting mirage; not sleep. "Come, Lena," it said. "I will deliver you from the pain of consciousness." But there was no deliverance; just fatigue drenched visions; psychic regurgitation's of everything that had gone wrong over the last twenty four years.

She needed a beer.

Eleven year old Abie came to her with a bucket of beer. He was crying. "Morris shoots me mama; but it OK; now you can come home." She drank the beer and tasted blood. It was the last thing she remembered before losing consciousness.

Twenty Two: Yussie's

the East Side, NYC. August, 1914

    Pursued by a raging wind, rain, like a million frightened feet, raced across deserted streets. Abie Isaacs was on his way to Yussie's Pool Hall. It was three in the afternoon, and as dark as night. Yussie's, like most pool halls, was once a horse parlor where a pool of phones was in place to get the results from race tracks up and down the east coast. Clerks took the calls, posting the odds and the winners on large blackboards. Gaming at billiard tables, supplied by the house, was a way to pass the time between races. Of course, ten percent went to the house. In 1910 horse parlors were declared illegal. The owners realized they could make good money on just billiards, without the hassle. The clientele remained the same.
    When it rained Klopper Benny slept at Yussie's. Yussie liked Klopper. "Tough kid, smart too," was the verdict. Not that Klopper didn't earn his keep. "Just knowing the Klop could walk in any time, keep the *gunzils* in line," said Yussie.
    The *gunzils* were thirteen to eighteen year old coke sniffers, laudanum guzzlers, pick pockets, lush workers, professional beggars, street fighters, pool hustlers, brothel towel washers, and pimps. Their mama and papa, the gang; their dreams, plunder; their *shul*, Yussies; their Rabbi, the adult gorillas and thieves that were its clientele.
    Walking in the rain, thoroughly drenched, Abie felt safe for the first time since Rosenthal's murder. *Nobody want me dead bad enough to walk in this,* he thought. When he reached Yussie's he hesitated, reluctant to seek shelter; to leave the security of the deluge.
    He entered, closed the door quietly, and waited for his eyes to adjust to the darkness. Abstractly, he gazed at the room's ten pool tables. Hanging lamps illuminated each table creating shimmering tents of smoke and light, transforming the players into spectral shadows of grace and intensity. He was comforted by the sound of

wooden cues against marble balls, the way they hissed when rolling on velvet, the clack of their collision. With pleasure he inhaled the familiar miasma of cigar smoke, beer, sweat, and resin.

Finally he walked toward a door at the rear of the room; it was barely visible to the naked eye. Over it was a hand printed sign; **NO WOMEN**. He pushed and entered. The brightly lit room was almost as large as the pool hall. There were five tables where men loudly played stuss. A little snake-eyed hood, dapper in white linen with gold accessories - including three front teeth - stalked the tables, a roll of money in one hand, a wooden club in the other. He looked up when Abie entered and quickly vanished.

In the back, past the stuss players, a crap game was going on. As Abie entered, Sugar Davey was about to roll. Abie watched him crouch, shut his eyes and massage the dice with both hands. Everyone knew what was coming.

He began to chant a prayer in Hebrew. His voice, with a resonance surprising for his youth, filled the backroom and drifted to the pool hall. To pray over dice was an act of such profound blasphemy that even here, among the low lifes, it caused palpable, if momentary, discomfort. The dealers stopped dealing; cue sticks were lowered as the pimp, Sugar Davey Saperstein, disgraced son of a Torah scribe, sent a message to his papa.

He rolled the dice.

"Seven," a voice screamed.

"You make Papa proud, Davey," shouted one of the stuss players in Yiddish.

Everyone laughed.

Klopper Benny caught Abie's eye.

"They arrest the copper Becker," he said.

Monk Eastman felt his woolen suit shrink as he walked through the downpour. Even in the rain Monk walked his East side strut; he never ran. "Gangsters don't run," he said. "Ain't nothing that important. Besides, maybe someone think you's scared."

MICHAEL BOOKMAN

He was on his way to Yussie's Pool Hall to kill Abie Isaacs. Killing Abie was more than fulfilling a contract. It was a statement. Nigger Mike Salter was right, his name no longer meant anything except maybe to kids - a fucking legend, past tense. Wherever he went he was greeted with indifference. Even worse. Pity.

I kills this kid in Yussie's, in front of everybody, they remember Monk Eastman. Knows I's back, he thought.

He knew Abie was at Yussie's; got the call in his new flat on Pell Street from Little Farfel Cohen one of the few old Eastman's who stayed loyal.

Walking the deserted rain swept street toward Yussie's Monk was exhilarated. He was stalking prey, anticipating deadly violence, taking a life simply to get what he wanted. It was something only he, Monk Eastman, could do. And God. A deep peace enveloped him, a feeling he shared with no one. Monk heard someone coming up behind him. He stopped, turned, scanned the street and saw nothing. He turned again, facing the direction he had been walking.

No wonder I don't sees nothing, he thought.

Freak Show Barovick was already ten feet in front of him and moving fast. Without knees to flex, Freak Show didn't exactly walk; he jumped from stump to stump.

Freaky kid, Monk thought, amused. *Like a baby duck waddling after its mama.*

Abie was about to roll the dice when the door burst open. It was Freak Show, as wet as if he had just climbed out of the East River fully clothed.

"Monk Eastman coming," he shouted.

"Shit," muttered Little Farfel.

All eyes turned from the dwarf to the diminutive hoodlum in white linen. Klopper drew his gun and began walking toward the hapless Farfel. Knives drawn, Sugar Davey and Sheeny Mike Levine backed him up.

GOD'S RAT

Monk thrust his right hand in his pocket and gently clasped it around his gun. With his left hand he opened the door to Yussie's. Upon entering he stopped a moment to get his bearings. Last time he was in Yussie's it was a horse parlor.

Finally, gun drawn, he moved quickly to the rear door, opened it and stormed into the room, "I wants the snitch," he screamed.

The stuss players paid him no mind. Cards and money were moving across the table as fast as the eye could see. The *gunzils* were gone. Little Farfel was sprawled on the floor hands tied behind his back. Monk rushed to his side, and rolled him over. His face was covered with blood still pulsating from a deep cut running from the corner of his right eye to the top of his lip. His white linen suit was ruined.

"Sorry, Monk," he whispered. "The little freak warn them."

The card players continued their game as if nothing happened.

Confused and humiliated Monk glared at the gamblers.

They ignored him. Finally Duddy Tarnoff put his cards down. "Nu Monk," he asked, "Now kids' you killing?"

Another player at the same table, Louie "Boo Boo" Goldman, put his cards down. Doing a fair imitation of a parrot he squawked, "Monk, you's the best, Monk, you's the best, Monk, you's the best."

The men giggled, then chuckled, then, finally, laughed hysterically.

Monk lifted his gun, took aim, and fired; Boo Boo's last guffaw turned into a blood gelled gurgle.

The laughter stopped.

Monk left, without saying a word.

Twenty Three: Fugitive

Within hours every low life on the East Side knew Monk Eastman was stalking Abie Isaacs. And everyone knew why. Nig Mike Salter explained: "Monk want to show he ain't washed up. Kills this little snitch and we's all shitting in our pants. One thing sure, Boo Boo ain't gonna to laugh at him no more."

Abie and Klopper were sitting in front of what was left of Klopper's lean-to after the deluge. The army blanket roof had buckled from the rain, forming a miniature lake suspended three feet off the ground. Fractured sunlight danced on the surface like hundreds of ten dollar gold pieces. *Why ain't it leaking?* Abie wondered.

Squatting with his back against the remnant of wall supporting his lean-to Klopper had fallen asleep. Abie looked around the vacant Delancy Street lot; the weeds and wild flowers - now seared by eight weeks of summer heat - had lost their frail promise. He thought of Rosie Saperstein coming to him on his first night under the lean-to. *She risk her life for me.* But she was a fish seller for the pimp Nigger Bialick. Thinking of her fucking men for money - old men for chrissake - was like piercing an exposed nerve somewhere deep within his stomach, or his brain, or his soul. The pain became rage. Rosie on Allen Street, arm and arm with some fat sleazy geezer; he pulls her away and slaps the protesting john hard across the face. Rosie is crying; her eyes pleading for his forgiveness. "I loves you Rosie," he says.

"I loves you, Abie." She closes her eyes like she did in Seward Park. They kiss. She smells of cheap perfume, and sweat. He feels her tears, warm, against his face.

Suddenly powerful arms pushed him violently into the ground. He felt something hard pressed to the back of his head. A voice with a slight Irish lilt, screamed, "Abraham Isaacs, you's under arrest."

Two huge coppers hauled him to a waiting taxi and wedged him between them; he realized they never put handcuffs on. *This ain't no regular arrest,* he thought.

GOD'S RAT

The taxi turned north into Baxter, a narrow, torturous street. It wended slowly Downtown toward City Hall, the Tombs, and The Criminal Court Building. Finally they stopped in front of a huge, hulking, Romanesque structure adjacent to the Tombs. Abie recognized The Criminal Court Building. The coppers, one in front one behind, ushered him through crowds of agitated Jewish, Italian, and Irish mamas, papas, brothers, sisters, aunts uncles, Priests, and Rabbis waiting to see their young man have his day in court.

Why they care what happen to us? Abie wondered.

Quickly moving up a broad marble sweep of stairs Abie and the coppers arrived in front a mahogany door; its upper half a rippled, frosted window inscribed in somber Franklin Gothic, **The Attorney for the Eastern District of the State of New York, The Honorable Charles Whitman.**

Hours earlier, the Honorable Charles Whitman looked at his watch. He was waiting for the cops to bring in the two men who would help persuade the kid Abie Isaacs to cooperate with the Prosecution. If they were the right men; if his hunch was right. Where the hell were they?

Sitting behind his huge intricately carved black mahogany desk, an unexceptional Victorian imitation of a Ming Dynasty treasure, Charles Whitman was worried. On one hand things were going better than he ever imagined. By selectively releasing Grand Jury testimony directly to the New York World's star reporter, Herbert Bayard Swope, he had generated a fine hysteria against Becker. The entire City was fixated on the **"Killer Cop."** The only missing piece was Abie Isaacs, and that, he thought, was being taken care of. But just this morning he learned the kid, Abie, was still alive. Not only had Monk Eastman botched the execution, he turned it into a bloody spectacle.

The damn rogue is using this as an opportunity to regain his reputation, he thought. *And what if he succeeds?* The murder of a fifteen year old by an infamous hoodlum recently released from prison on a technicality would generate as much publicity as the

Becker case itself. Not to mention the questions it would raise. Monk Eastman was a mistake.

There was a knock on the door.

"Bring them in," he yelled.

The door opened; a suffocating stench of piss and booze filled the room. Two men, accompanied by a cop entered. Whitman had to fight an almost irresistible impulse to puke.

One was over six feet tall, his hair so matted by filth it seemed like a horse hair wig; his face was pocked by open sores; the busted veins in his eyes made them look like wounds about to bleed. The other, short and pudgy, was even more filthy. At first Whitman thought he was shirtless until noticing only part of the caked filth covering his upper torso was flesh; the rest, remnants of what was once an undershirt.

"Gentlemen," he said brightly, extending his hand, and then quickly reconsidering. The men were too terrified to notice the slight. They reminded Whitman of roaches suddenly exposed to light. Looking at the two moldering creatures in front of him, he wondered if their presence was such a good idea after all.

They came to his attention when he bumped into a police reporter for the Tribune who told him a strange story about two bums who ran screaming into the Essex Street Police Station swearing a kid had shot at them in a Delancy Street lot. Every time the cops threw them out they came back demanding protection.

"Probably the DT's," said Whitman.

"Nah, Charley," said the reporter, "just drunk."

"They know who did it?" Whitman asked.

"For what its worth, Charley," the reporter said, "they said it was a friend of Klopper Benny. This Klopper's a bad kid, runs a rough gang, The Stanton Street Boys; carries a gat. According to the bums Klopper jumps the shooter; he keeps screaming his name; 'Abie' ".

"Any follow up?" Whitman asked.

"They're bums, Charley." The reporter shrugged, "Who cares about bums?"

GOD'S RAT

Standing in front of Whitman's office, tightening their grip on Abie's arms the cops hesitated; Whitman was their boss and one of the most powerful men in the City. Finally one of them knocked.

"Come in," came a voice.

The copper opened the door.

Abie couldn't believe his eyes, "The rat eater's!"

The bums, seeing their young tormentor unarmed and in custody, convulsed with rage. They roared and they howled. "It him. Arrest the little Jew bastard." Spit flew from their mouths. They stamped their feet causing the accumulation of caked filth on their body and clothes to crack, crumble and fall to the floor.

A fucking avalanche, thought Abie.

A man he recognized as DA Whitman, motioned toward the third copper in the office.

"Get them the hell out of here."

The bums, still screaming and sputtering were pushed out.

Whitman looked at Abie and pointed to a seat in front of his huge desk. Abie felt very small.

Whitman turned toward Abie's two police escorts and pointed at the door; they left. He and Abie were alone. Across the desk Whitman glared at him. His faded blue eyes reminding Abie of the rat he killed in front of Sugar Davey's tenement. Intelligent, deadly. The DA cleared his throat making a sound so raw Abie winced, visualizing the phlegm. "I have nothing but respect for your race," he growled wetly. "You Jews have taken the myth of chosenness to heart and developed a healthy contempt for us benighted gentiles. But no matter how hard we smite you, you come back stronger. We are outraged at your damn resilience. Even more; we are driven to bloody madness by the suspicion that our minds, our hearts, our God are second rate." Abie was stunned. Where this going? "This East Side of yours is but a temporary setback. One day the poverty, the filth, the criminality will be forgotten. You and your ilk, Mr. Abraham 'Abie Cracks' Isaacs, will be less than a footnote. Not even a memory. Already there are almost as many Hebrews in City

College as are in the Tombs." Abie's eyes wandered to the huge flag hanging behind Whitman; he began counting the stars.

"Am I boring you?" asked Whitman. "Perhaps this will wake you up. You, Abraham Isaacs, are under arrest for the attempted murder of two Delancy Street vagrants; not to mention violation of the Sullivan law." Abie looked at Whitman. Whitman laughed. The laugh instigated a fit of phlegm clotted coughing. He pulled out a soiled handkerchief, spit, examined the result, and looked up at Abie; his eyes warmed. "You think I'm a hard man young Mr. Isaacs? Devoid of compassion, mercy? Perhaps even an enemy of your race? On the contrary, I am well aware of the tribulations that put a young Abie Isaacs on the wrong side of the law. A Mama who indulges the balm of alcohol to dull the pain of a degraded past - a past of which you are painfully aware. No Papa to guide you, give you the succor of a firm manly hand. From birth the absence of adequate nourishment; a gnawing in your belly, the debasement of dire poverty--"

Abie felt his eyes fill with tears. He was being seduced, surrendering to brilliant deception. It felt strange, feminine. His will to resist overwhelmed by a desire to be understood; protected; loved. "--yet," Whitman continued, "in spite of these unholy privations you had the moral stamina to risk everything just to save the life of the gangster Herman Rosenthal. I am impressed young Mr. Isaacs--"

Enough, thought Abie. "Excuse me sir," he interrupted, "I mean no disrespect. But what you wants from me?" Whitman stopped, frowned. Silence. A piercing stare. *The rat's eyes again,* thought Abie.

"Young Mr. Isaacs, Why, were you so far from the well trod path of your East Side on the fateful evening of the demise of Mr. Rosenfeld?"--Abie felt a glimmer of comprehension.

"--Perhaps," said Whitman, "you heard something to send you to 43rd Street; something to make you doubt the guilt of the rogue cop Charles Becker?" Abie saw himself hiding behind the wall at the Occidental, listening to Sullivan, Morris and Becker. He remembered Becker saying 'Herman gets killed Mr. Sullivan I take the rap. Who has more reason to kill him then me? I'm out of this.'

"--Lieutenant Becker," Whitman continued, "is a sewer of corruption and brutality. In its blighted history, the constabulary of this City has seen no worse. The People and I, fully intend to convict Lieutenant Becker of masterminding the murder of Herman Rosenthal--" Abie realized Morris could have easily put two and two together - figured out he overheard that conversation. Whitman leaned forward; he lowered his voice to a whisper forcing Abie to lean across the desk in order to hear what he was saying. They were inches apart; Abie smelled bourbon.

"--I will brook no interference from a young Hebrew scamp with an impulse to snitch." Now Abie understood "Whitman put Monk Eastman back on the street to kill me. The DA and Morris is working together." Whitman smiled. "I mean you no harm, young Mr. Isaacs. Allow yourself to forget what you think you heard and I will forgo the very serious charges against you."

Fuck Becker, he thought. *I don't wants to go to jail.* Then he remembered what Mama said to Zayde, "Morris ain't his Papa." *What if Becker is?* he thought. His head throbbed. Abie looked the DA in the eye. "Frankly sir," he said, "I don't know what you's talking about. I went Uptown to work the Tenderloin. Everybody know it where the money is." Whitman glowered.

Abie saw beads of sweat form on his forehead. "So that's how it's going to be young Mr. Isaacs?"

Now or never, Abie thought. He made a dash to the door, flung it open and ran into the hall toward the stairway. Abie was fast. Since ten he could easily outrun the average fat copper. Behind him were screams, then footsteps. "Stop him, damnit." It was Whitman's voice. Then another voice, even more frenzied, "Stop, or you's dead." It was the copper who arrested him. People seemed to evaporate before Abie's eyes. He wondered what a bullet felt like and thought about death and lowered his head to make himself smaller, but felt ten feet tall, clumsy, fat and pathetically slow. He didn't see the marble staircase and pitched forward. *I'm flying,* he thought.

Now he was tumbling down the marble steps, desperately trying to shield his head. The fall was interminable; it felt less like falling than being hammered endlessly by violent blows from a black jack. He muttered the ancient *Hebrew, Shema,* the only prayer he knew, "*Sh'ma Yisroal, adonoi alehanu, adonoi echad."* It was Zayde's voice, not his. Finally the blows stopped. As he got to his feet, someone hit him hard in the left shoulder. He turned; no one was there. Moving toward the revolving door and the street, his feet became numb; a euphoric peace swept over him, like drinking laudanum and beer. *I's falling asleep,* he realized. "Sweet dreams, Abeleh," Mama said.

GOD'S RAT

Twenty Four: Bottom

August 19, 1914. Albany.

These were the strangest days in Lena Isaac's life. The house in Albany was a sealed chamber of childhood phantoms. Everything she did and saw reminded her of her former life. Twenty three years on the East Side ceased to exist. Her reflection in the mirror was a constant source of shock and pain; too brutal a reminder of the lost years.

Gertie Halpern's calls were not returned.

What would I say? She wondered. *Well Gert, I fucked strangers for money; gave birth to a bastard whose father's a killer; lived in a filthy rat and roach infested flat without hot water or a toilet; associated with thieves, pimps and, whores; and, of course, drank myself into oblivion. What have you been up to?*

Hours were spent in her old room looking out the window while she spoke to ghosts: mama, papa, her sisters, Gert, the *schiksas* at the Academy. Sometimes she imagined Abie visited her; a respectable young man born here in Albany; going to school and getting A's; a star on the baseball team; excelling in math. His father, her husband, always at work making a comfortable living. She and Abie having long relaxed chats about school, girls, triumphs on the baseball diamond. As she spoke to herself, Lena noticed her speech lost its East Side edge; the "aint's"; the "youse,"; the double negatives; the profanity; the gangster Yiddish.

Everyone but Mama and Blanche treated her as if she were invisible. Her sisters never introduced her to their husbands, or children. She took her meals in the kitchen, alone. She craved her only salvation, alcohol. The problem was how to get it? Fearing she would run into someone she knew, Lena never went outside. But she did manage to convince a reluctant Blanche to buy it for her. The price; a lecture.

"You gots to get out of here, Miz Isaacs," Blanche said. *Same smell,* Lena remembered. *Soap; vegetables; chicken fat.* "This ain't you home no more," Blanche continued. "I hears you talking with yourself, conjuring spirits; making yourself crazy. You Abie a nice boy - he look like his grampa and he love his Mama. He be you home."

"I can't go to Abie, Blanche," she said, "I'm a danger to him."

"Y'ssm," said Blanche. She turned abruptly, and walked away.

Lena began reading her old romantic novels. She couldn't imagine she was ever moved by these characters; beautiful goyishe *putzim* in outlandish costumes; saying things no human would say - even think of saying. *Who was that little girl who read this garbage; believed in it?* she wondered. Even her past was slipping away.

I'm losing my mind, she thought. Lena needed more liquor than Blanche could reasonably supply, and began drinking whatever she found in Papa's liquor closet. Mama gladly provided the laudanum for her "migraine headaches." Glassy eyed, and stinking of schnapps Lena was fulfilling the family's worst expectations.

One night while lying in bed, staring at the ceiling, wondering if all the liquor and laudanum in the word could stifle her pain, a car backfired loudly; it sounded like a gun. She saw Abie collapse on the street. The neighborhood dogs barked and snarled in fear; to Lena, in her semi-stupor, their barking became human: "Kill him; kill him; kill him." Klopper Benny came to her. "They killed Abie, Mrs. Isaacs," he said.

Badly shaken Lena got out of bed, stumbled downstairs to the liquor cabinet, reached for a bottle, and without looking, lifted it to her lips; it was empty. Frantically she felt for another. There were no more. The cabinet was empty. Papa had removed everything, except the bottle she finished.

Time to go, she thought.

Lena packed her few things, mostly stuff her sister Birdy had left behind when she married. She called the Albany station; the next train to Grand Central Station was 12:01 AM; plenty of time. Her preparations to leave were deliberate and efficient. The month long alcoholic haze quickly evaporated under a blaze of purpose.

There was no reason to say goodby. Blanche would understand. Mama wouldn't. And Papa would happily resume mourning the memory of his beautiful seventeen year old daughter.

She felt nothing. Neither sadness, nor joy. "Abie a nice boy - he look like his grampa and he love his Mama. He be your home," Blanche said. Lena was going home.

She climbed down the steps as quietly as she could, using the banister to brace her weight. As she walked through the parlor toward the front door the light went on.

"Lenaleh." It was Papa.

She froze; then turned to face her father. The harsh electric light accented his age. He was sitting in his favorite chair; it seemed bigger than she remembered. *Papa's shrinking,* she thought.

"You're going to Abie?" Papa asked. It wasn't really a question. Lena saw his tears. "I'm not Job," he whispered. "I'm not without blame. Protect your son."

She didn't want to answer; just to turn her back and walk out. "I will Papa," she said.

He stretched out his right arm in the gesture of a hand shake. Lena saw he was holding money. She hesitated.

"Please," he said. His voice trembled. Tears streamed from his eyes.

She took the money.

"Go in health, my daughter," he said in Yiddish.

Lena left.

GOD'S RAT

Part 3

GOD'S RAT

One

Sunday August 20th, 1914, 8:AM

Lena woke up in her Rivington Street flat somewhat confused, but stone cold sober - not even a hangover. Albany was a dream. *I'm home,* she thought. Along with the stifling waves of August heat, the muffled sounds of Rivington Street drifted through the front parlor into her windowless bedroom. "I buy old clothes," sang Bennie the rag man in Yiddish; a horn blared; a trucker cursed; a chant from the girls jumping rope, "Old Mr. Kelly had a pimple on his belly/his wife bit it off and it tasted like jelly."

It comforted her to know that somewhere Abie was hearing the same noise.

Lena was aware her return to the East Side posed a danger to her son. From the time she left Albany Abie's words to Papa rang in her ears; "Morris want me dead; he'll go through Mama to get to me." On the long lonely ride from Albany to Grand Central Station Lena saw one possible answer to her problem. Sitting on her bed, dressing in Birdie's high school clothes, she thought of her old friend Manya Bluma. *Manya owes me a favor,* she thought.

Manya Bluma was her only friend on Allen Street. A chunky sweet face girl, as swarthy as an Arab, who came from an Orthodox family, and could never reconcile her life on the street with her upbringing. When she wasn't working, she was crying. Sometimes she even cried *when* she worked. This endeared her to some of the older greenies who enjoyed treating her like a daughter, even forsaking sex. Others were not so kind and complained bitterly to her pimp who beat her viciously. Even worse, she was tormented by the young boys in the street; "Manya, Manya, watch her cry/watch her unbutton an old man's fly," they chanted, not stopping until rewarded with a flood of tears, curses, screams of rage, and, if they were lucky, the flash of the rather large knife she kept in her purse. Lena who was only two years older, comforted her like a mother. Manya would call Lena "Mama" and, over tea and schnapps, tell her how one day soon she would *schtup* the Angel of Death and find Everlasting Peace. One of Lena's regular customers was a young Rabbi from Romania. Lena spoke to him about her Orthodox friend, "She an angel Rabbi, drowning in unholy slime, *traif*, maybe you can bring her back to God." She arraigned a meeting.

The Rabbi gave Manya lessons in Torah; they prayed together. Soon Manya and the Rabbi disappeared. Then, after ten years, while shopping on Pitt Street, Lena heard a familiar voice, "Hello Leanaleh," it said. She starred at a swarthy middle aged woman wearing a babushka over her wig. It was Manya Bluma. She told Lena how she and the Rabbi married and moved far away to Boro Park in Brooklyn. But her husband was just offered a position as head Rabbi of the large new synagogue looming behind her. "Such an honor, he couldn't refuse," she said. Abutting the synagogue was a brand new brownstone.

"Yours?" asked Lena.

Manya smiled and nodded. "Who would've believed?" she asked. And added, "Maybe I should cry?" The two old friends laughed; exchanged a few more pleasantries; felt equally uncomfortable, and went about their separate ways. Afterward, when meeting on the street, they nodded cordially, nothing more.

* * * * *

9:30 AM

As she stood in front of the great oak door of the huge new brownstone on Pitt Street - attached to the newest and perhaps grandest synagogue on the East Side - Lena wondered how her old friend, the fancy *rebbitzen* would react to her strange request.

Manya Bluma answered the door. Not surprisingly, upon seeing Lena she wept. "Lenaleh," she choked through her tears, "What you want from me? What if the Rabbi see you here?"

Lena said simply, "Manya, my life is in danger; much worse my son Abie's life. I need your help."

Manya Bluma was silent; she bowed her head as if in prayer; then took her old friend's hand.

"Please come in."

When Lena entered she was startled to see furnishings similar to those in her home in Albany: the same heavy oriental carpets; the same dark mahogany furniture; the same velvet curtains, and the same chandelier that sheds a thousand cut glass tears.

Lena took her hands, "You've done well, Manya. I'm very proud."

"With Ashem's help - and yours," Manya said. Then she added, "You speak differently, Lena."

"I've been home, Manya. It's a long story."

Manya smiled, "Time, I got plenty -- sit, please," she said, leading Lena to a large brocaded yellow wing back chair facing two huge rolling mahogany doors separating the parlor from the rest of the house. The doors were shut fast.

"But the Rabbi, you were worried--" Lena weakly protested as she took her seat.

"Nu," Manya said with a shrug and a mischievous smile. "The Rabbi, ain't he your friend too?"

As they spoke, Lena became aware of another presence in the house. She heard running water, the sound of someone washing clothes. Lena smiled to herself, *Why shouldn't a fancy Rebbitzen have help?*

Suddenly the two mahogany doors in front of her began to roll on their tiny hidden wheels back into their respective walls. Behind the doors pushing them apart, her face made even more gruesome by the effort, was Mushy Bum.

"Oh my God," Lena whispered. She didn't know which was worse, the sight of Mushy Bum - the rags, the toothless grin, the hideous scar that Morris gave her, the scummy film covering her eyeballs; or the stench - beer, piss, and the sweet sickening odor from years of undisturbed, decomposing filth.

Lena looked at Manya.

Almost apologetically Manya explained, "Poor Mushy Bum; some of the girls take her in as a towel washer; so I bring her here to wash for us - the least I can do. The Rabbi think it's a *mitzva*."

It was 1899 when Lena found seventeen year old Mushy - just Mushy, - "Bum" was added as her situation declined - dazed and bleeding on the street; she - Lena - was with Monk then, his number one trotter; young, beautiful, and the bearer of a fine East Side pedigree - having whored for both Morris the Pimp, *and* Rosie Hurtz. Monk was pleased with Lena - almost as proud strutting down Broadway with her on his arm as he was with Louie on his shoulder. So when Lena found Mushy, and dragged her home to Monk, he grunted, shrugged his shoulders, and allowed Lena to care for her. The two whores grew close. When Lena was knocked up by Monk she confided in her young friend. Soon afterwards, Mushy's wound healed and Monk threw her back on the street. Over the years Lena heard of Mushy Bum's plight, but had not seen her since that day.

Mushy Bum was all over Lena; holding her hands, her filthy face against Lena's breasts, crying - not like a woman - like an infant, staining Lena's blouse with her tears; her spit; her snot. Gently Manya pulled Mushy Bum away from Lena and escorted her, still crying hysterically, back to her wash.

"So Lenaleh," asked Manya Bluma returning to the parlor, shutting the two huge mahogany doors behind her - muffling, not silencing Mushy Bum's screams - "How can I help?"

The friends lost their heart for conversation. Mushy Bum's weird infantile outburst had brought the past back to them like puss from an infected wound long thought healed; had destroyed the illusion of time's restorative powers. Manya Bluma wore the pained expression Lena hadn't seen for fifteen years; she feared her friend would begin to cry and never stop.

Lena explained what she wanted.

Now looking at herself in Manya Bluma's full length mirror Lena was shocked. The combination of the severe brown dress covering her ankles and wrists, and the dyed black horse hair wig under a white babushka reminded her of her mother's mother, bubba Milka. *Maybe I'll start lighting candles,* she thought.

She hugged Manya and left. Stepping out of the brownstone Lena felt comfortably invisible.

* * * * *

9:45 AM

Walking north on Pitt toward Broadway Lena knew exactly where she was going; what she was going to do. Had to do. She knew it from the moment she saw the headline in Papa's paper in Albany: "**NYC Lieutenant Indicted for Murder.**"

Why did she feel she had to see Charley Becker? Did she still love him? He was innocent after all. She knew that. Abie knew that. And, of course Morris, knew that. None of this would have happened, she realized, had Becker not followed fifteen years of pain back to her door on Rivington Street. Abie wouldn't have been sent to find Morris; wouldn't have overheard the conversation at the Occidental; wouldn't have squealed to Rosenthal. *What would have happened,* she wondered, *if I accepted Charley's marriage proposal; moved upstate New York; had his children; became a Catholic?* Her head began to throb. What if? What if? What if? And most of all she wanted to ask Becker if he knew anything about Abie. "Charley, Charley, we've always been together. Abie should have been yours. Help me Charley. Help me save my kid."

* * * * *

January 25, 1915, 6:06 am, and 59 seconds, Sing Sing

Becker was under water now, deep in a fathomless sea. He thought he was rising but the darkness was unrelenting. There was no surface. No end. No way to know for sure which direction he was moving. He held his breath until his lungs revolted, forcing open his mouth. But instead of water, a burst of oxygen. *My punishment is life*, he thought. His wife Helen came to him pregnant. She took his hand and gently placed it over her womb. "Feel your daughter, Charley." He felt life. Tears ran down his face. "She died before she was born Helen. Father and daughter sentenced to death." "I'm sorry, Charley," Helen said. "You needed me alive. We sacrificed our child to save your life." She showed him a copy of The World. "Remember what they said about me Charley?" **"MRS. CHARLES BECKER MURDERS UNBORN CHILD"** *"It wasn't you,"* he said. "It was me, Helen, I couldn't let you die - couldn't let the doctors let you die. Couldn't be alone. I made the choice, our child had to die." "It was both of us, Charley," Helen said. "I would have made a good father, Helen," Becker said. Helen was gone.

Two

Sunday, August 20th, 1914 7:00 AM

First, Abie heard noise. Sound without meaning; human voices as a fly would hear them. Then a scalding pain, as if someone was pouring boiling water on his shoulder. Reaching for the source of the pain he felt rags drenched in blood. Opening his eyes, he saw light and shadow and a billion black spots; he quickly closed them. Then he remembered someone hit him in the back. Now he realized it was a bullet.

I gonna die? he wondered.

"He coming around," said a voice. It was Klopper.

Then a female voice, "Thank God." A hand holding something cool and wet was soothing his forehead. It was Rosie Saperstein.

Where's I? he wondered. *Why ain't I in jail?*

When Abie could finally keep his eyes open Klopper assured him he was going to live, then explained what happened.

"After the coppers throws you in the cab and it takes off I runs after it; sees them bring you into the Criminal Court Building. It don't make no sense. Still don't. I finds a telephone in the lobby and calls Yussie's. Sugar Davey there. I tells him to get here fast. So now the two of us is on the street, pacing; not knowing why the hell you's here; we sees all these boobs getting out of the paddy wagon; got cuffs on; been booked at the precinct like a normal criminal; not like no fourteen carat gold *macher*, getting out of a cab with no cuffs - **escorted**, for chrissake--" The cool damp towel in Rosie's hand caressing his forehead gave Abie great comfort. Hope even. His life was being squeezed from him. Death wore too many faces. Jewish killers; Irish killers; and now the law.

"--What you thinking Klop," said Abie, "I's doing a job on you, a double cross?" He was trying to speak in a normal voice, but it came out a whisper. Klopper's eyes narrowed.

"Bug off Abie, OK," he said. "Me standing there like a geelick, a gat in my pocket what could get me a deuce upstate, and I's looking at more coppers than flies on dead meat, but I ain't going nowhere till I knows what happen to my friend who a lot of mugs thinks is getting soft and who was escorted like a fucking blue blood into the Criminal Court Building. So I don't want to hear nothing about what I's thinking."

He would kill for me; die for me, thought Abie.

Klopper continued, "I sees them two lushes you shoot at in the lot come out of a wagon. They ain't got no cuffs neither. I figures they's there to ID you. Now we's waiting - me and Davey - seem like forever. Coppers looking at us real queer - like we belong in the building, not on the street. Then there's a shot from inside. Everybody look; we sees some kid staggering out the door. It you. You falling forward like someone push you hard from behind. I runs to you; you got this smile on your face; make me think you's gone; seen God or something.

Like I'm drunk on beer and laudanum, Abie remembered. And Mama's voice; "Sweet dreams Abeleh." Abie winced. *Did I ever have a Mama whose breasts were a pillow; whose arms were strong enough to die in?*

Now Klopper stood and began to pace around the bed as if trying to keep up with the blur of events racing through his mind. "I grabs you just before you fall - you dead weight. Funny, you hanging on with your chin what's hooked on my shoulder like a claw. I looks for Sugar Davey he ain't there. Now the coppers is closing in with their guns; I takes out mine; figures we dead. I's still moving backward, but what for? Ain't no place to go--"

It was hard for Abie to believe this happened to him; that he was there, but with no recollection; as if Klopper were talking about someone else; someone who died.

"--then this fat Italian Mama come running out, from the crowd," said Klopper, "she screaming at the coppers- right in front of them - jumping up and down, 'donna' shoots them kids youse bastid cops.' Now the whole crowd - the Jews the micks, the dagos, the priests, the rabbis, for chrissake - they's all jumping in front of the cops screaming like we's their kids. Then someone poke me on the arm and points. I sees Sugar Davey sitting in the front seat of a cab. He yelling out the window at me. But I can't hold you no more with one arm; you falls on the sidewalk - on your face. Blood coming out your back. Some big guy run out from the crowd scoop you up, carry you to the cab. I get in after you. Davey screaming at the driver, 'Move you dumb mocky. Move.' Got his knife at the guys throat; tells him to drive here."

Here? thought Abie.

"I got my own place now," said Rosie.

Your own whorehouse, he thought. "That nice Rosie," he whispered.

Klopper, still furiously pacing continued, "The ride here, it maybe twenty minutes, seem like forever, with you bleeding, and maybe the coppers' chasing us. The cabby a Yid, a political greenie, talking to us in Yiddish; figure we's in Russia and the coppers is Cosacks - we's the good guys - tell me take off my shirt and press down hard on where the blood coming out - you owe me a shirt Abie - it stop the bleeding. We gets here and the cabby help us carry you up the stairs. Won't take no money; wants to help; so we sends him to get Doc Greenbaum. Should be here any minute."

Greenbaum's old, thought Abie, *a hop head lush; his hands shake.* " Shit," he whispered.

"Sorry," said Klopper, "we didn't get no fucking surgeon from Mt. Sinai."

Rosie bent her head in front of Abie's face. Her kimono was loosely tied; her breasts fully exposed; he saw the rose tattoo. She smiled. Abie closed his eyes. "Don't worry Abeleh," she said, "Doc Greenbaum could take out a bullet after three bowls of hop and a bottle of *mash'ke* - been doing it forty years." Her voice is as soft as petals. She kissed his forehead. Her breath smells of beer and tobacco.

"Like I says, Abie," said Klopper, "You gonna live - the question's for how long."

Klopper reached deep in his pocket and pulled out the gun he had taken away. "You needs this *schtunk*," he said affectionately.

"Don't shoot at no drunks this time." He placed the gun under Abie's pillow and left.

"Don't let Nig sees it," said Rosie. "It his gun."

Abie fell asleep.

He dreamt of a hatless Monk Eastman standing over him holding his derby like a bucket - it was full of steaming hot water. Mama shouted, "No Monk." Monk tilted the hat in Abie's direction. Boiling water poured on his wound.

* * * * *

8:00 AM

Abie woke up screaming.

"Through pain comes healing," said an old man's voice. "Through suffering, redemption."

Doc Greenbaum was leaning over Abie doing something to his wound that caused waves of unspeakable pain. Abie tried to push the old man away, but his arms were tied to the sides of the bed. The old man was breathing hard. Grunting. Pulling. Leaning backward. All his weight leveraged against the huge forceps inserted in the wound. Abie had the feeling a piece of himself was being torn from his body: a bone; a sinew; a vein.

"You's tearing me apart," he screamed at the Doctor.

Suddenly the old man fell backward clutching the forceps. Blood was flying everywhere. Abie felt some relief.

"What a mess," said Rosie from somewhere behind him. "Nig'll kill me."

Doc Greenbaum was standing over Abie now. Smiling. *He look a little like Zayde,* Abie thought. *If Zayde was a lush and a hop head.*

The old man held out his open hand to Abie. Swimming in blood was a tiny, battered metal ball.

"Mazel Tov," the Doctor said. "Like delivering a baby."

He stinks of schnapps, but his hand steady, Abie thought. *Must've just banged the gong.*

The Doctor held the spent bullet in front of Abie's eyes. "Maybe a souvenir you want?" he asked.

Abie didn't respond.

"I knew your Mama," he said. "Such a beautiful girl. A little like you she looks." His thick glasses exaggerating the opium induced pin point contraction of his irises. "She OK?"

Everybody knows Mama, Abie thought.

"What she almost did to herself, a *shandeh*," said the Doctor. "Tell her I says Hello."

The mystery of Mama's life was deepening. Every revelation more disturbing. "They call your mama 'Lena the Lake'. Ask her why," said Lieutenant Becker.

After dressing the wound the Doctor left, promising to be back in a week, "To clean up."

Abie's shoulder was throbbing dully. Attempting to soothe it he moved his arm and felt the pull of the rope. He looked for Rosie to untie him. She was on her hands and knees with a rag, trying to scrub away the blood stains.

Abie smiled. The blood was virtually invisible against the deep red of the carpet. Like all whore houses everything was red. Even the ceiling.

"What you worrying, Rosie?" he asked. "The blood matches. Maybe that why whore houses is red."

"Maybe you should shut up Abeleh, and appreciate you got a roof over your head," Rosie said.

"Nig ain't exactly happy you's here."

"You pimp know I's here?"

"He pay the rent, Abie," Rosie said.

GOD'S RAT

Three

Sunday, August 20th, 1914 1:40 PM

Nigger Bialik, Rosie Saperstein's fifteen year old pimp, was walking at a brisk pace, going west on Houston; he was not happy. Rosie was his best whore. She understood seduction was power, and power was money. More than just a pretty face, great tits and a sweet ass, Rosie was a sexual predator who thought like a man; used her pussy like a dick. Even her capacity for pleasure was a measure of profit against loss. "It what bring them back," she once told him. And smart; could run a whore house - keep everybody in line: the whores, the johns, and the coppers. Best of all, like him, she was burdened with no soft spots destructive to the smooth operation of business.

Except for maybe one; Abie Isaacs.

"Her fucking childhood sweety," he sneered. "Thought he out of the picture once the money start rolling in. Now she got him holed up in my place of business for chrissake"

Worse, having Abie around meant the Stanton Street Boys, especially the *schtarker* Klopper Benny and Rosie's goddamn brother Sugar Davey, the only other kid pimp on the East Side worth worrying about.

Like the locusts in the Bible, Abie and the boys descended from nowhere to turn his world into shit. Nigger, so preoccupied with his anger, failed to realize he had reached his destination, and was in the middle of Gopher territory. He was here to find Terry Jackson, leader of the Gopher's. They owed Abie one - the way he busted Big Jim Toohey's arm with his bare hands - and had been searching for him for weeks. Nigger was here to inform them their search was over.

To make sure the job was done right he'd pay a hundred beans. On the East Side it was considered bad form to hire goys to kill a

GOD'S RAT

Jew. But Jewish killers would do it just for the money - the Gopher's needed to kill Abie Isaacs, a matter of honor.

Even a pimp realized there was more to life than money. Still, he was a Hebe pimp in the middle of Gopher turf. He tensed. The Gophers weren't known for asking questions before smashing heads.

Or gouging out an eye. One of Terry Jackson's lieutenants, Dandy Johnny Dolan, refined the technique of eye gauging into an art by inventing a cutting apparatus made of copper. Worn on the thumb, it enabled the wearer to perform, unbidden, radical ocular surgery with amazing neatness and dispatch. Dandy Johnny Dolan was considered a genius.

Venturing into their turf Nigger was taking the biggest gamble of his life.

He felt a sharp pain on the left side of his head.

Just a blackjack, not no bullet, he thought before losing consciousness.

Four

Sunday August 20th, 1914 10:00 AM

This was not Lena's first visit to the Tombs. She had been here years ago to visit Monk Eastman when he was her pimp and lover. Then she was an Allen Street whore visiting her pimp.

No big deal.

Now she looked like someone's orthodox Jewish wife here to see Lieutenant Charles Becker the most despised man in New York City.

Her visit did not go unnoticed by the horde of reporters assigned to cover the Rosenthal murder. Gallons of ink were spilled speculating about the "Mystery Woman" who visited the "Killer Cop." The name she signed on the visitors form was Mrs. Sarah Levine. **"Sarah Levine, Who Are You?"** screamed the *New York World* in exasperation. *The World's* star reporter Herbert Bayard Swope wrote: "Today, a well dressed Jewish housewife visited Lieutenant Charles Becker in the Tombs. One can hardly begin to speculate on its meaning. All efforts to locate the woman, Mrs. Sarah Levine, have been to no avail." The mystery was never solved

As Lena walked down the narrow corridor to Becker's cell she tried to ignore the taunts and catcalls of the inmates. Desperately she focused all her attention on the large key that dangled from the belt of the copper who escorted her. But she could not ignore a voice from one cell. It spoke to her in Yiddish.

"Mama," said the voice softly, "Don't be afraid, I mean you no harm."

She turned. A young man, his paints around his ankles was pressed against the bars of his cell holding his erect circumcised penis.

"It kosher, Mama," he said.

Even dressed like a rebbitzen, she thought, *they can see the heart of a whore.*

Facing the exposed young man, she feigned lust and whispered in East Side English, "Money talk, tough guy, for three beans we has a party."

She never forgot his expression. Like he had seen the ghost of his dead *bubba*.

"Got a visitor Lieutenant," announced the copper as he placed his key into the lock of a cell. Lieutenant Charles Becker was not surprised he had a visitor. Lawyers dropped in all the time. And, of course, reporters. He did not, however, expect to see an orthodox Jewish woman. "Who are you?" he asked.

"Take a close look, Charley," Lena said.

He recognized her. "You find God, Lena?" he asked.

"I have a good reason not to be recognized," she said.

He motioned her into his tiny cell.

She entered and sat on the three-legged stool brought in by the copper who escorted her. The stench of raw excretion mixed with extreme moisture, fear, and a lack of air was repulsive yet strangely familiar. *It smells like a zoo,* she realized.

From the windows high on the opposite walls soft dusty beams of light seeped into the windowless cell transforming Becker into an ominous shadow. Caged, he projected naked power. As always, it frightened and excited her.

"I'm sorry Lena," his disembodied voice said, "I had no right to hurt you." She could almost taste the blood as it dripped into her mouth where he hit her with the gun just a few short weeks ago.

"I made you bleed too, Charley," she said.

"I know why you're here, Lena," he said.

She said nothing.

"I'm a copper. Still got some loyal snitches. I know who's going to kill Abie."

Lena's eyes burned him.

Becker looked away. "Monk Eastman," he said. "Whitman sprung Eastman early. Abie saw Morris shoot Rosenthal. The deal is, Monk kills him."

Lightning bolts of pain tore through Lena's head. She swayed, then fell off the stool; she didn't remember falling, just lying on the cool, dank filthy floor. She felt Becker lifting her up. *Only Monk has more strength,* she thought, returning to the stool.

"I was pretty sure Monk was Abie's father," Becker said. "When I heard he broke some punk's arm with his bare hands, I knew."

Lena was sitting again.

"You've got to talk to Monk, Lena. Tell him Abie's his kid."

Lena was staring at the floor. Becker followed her gaze. Something was moving.

"A mouse, Charley," she said indifferently.

"A rat, Lena," Becker said. "A baby rat. Look at the tail."

"I can't go on, Charley," Lena said. "I'm so tired. I want to lay down on the floor with the rat."

Lena stood up. Becker went to her.

"You'll beat this thing Charley," Lena whispered.

They hugged fiercely. Becker felt his cock harden. "Why? She laughed at me; she's fat and broken."

Lena smiled. "I love you too, Charley," she said.

"See Willy the Shiv," Becker said. "He'll tell you where to find Monk. Hangs out at Yussie's."

* * * * *

January 25, 1915, 6:07 am & 48 seconds, Sing Sing.

Charles Becker felt nothing - he was numb; this sudden lack of pain had the impact of a terrible and profound silence. Death was near. My mind is breathing, *he thought.* My body is dead. *Before him stood an orthodox Jewish woman. She was well dressed, not like the usual East Side scum. Blood was oozing from a wound in the side of her head.* "Are you Death?" *he asked.* "I'm Lena, Charlie," she said. "Remember?" He remembered smashing her on the head with his gun, and he remembered her visit; the horrible message he had to deliver. "I'm sorry about Abie," he said. She said nothing. "Join me, Lena," he said. "We'll never be lonely again." He reached for her wig. "Let me take it off, Lena; let me touch your hair; your beautiful hair," he said. He removed the wig. Her hair was matted with sweat, half the blond strands were gray. "I'm sorry, Charley," she said, "nothing stays the same." "I love you, Lena," he said. "Why, Charley?" she asked. "I spit in your face. I trotted for a killer, Monk Eastman; flaunted him in front of you; had his child," she said. "Come to me, Lena," he said. "We mustn't die alone." Lena came to him; she sat on his lap; he felt nothing. He buried his face in her hair and breathed deeply; he smelled nothing. Lena disappeared. His second wife Helen came to him. "You're not alone, Charley," she said. "I've always loved you. I did all I could to save you." "I know you did," he said. "Be Lena for me, Helen." "I can't do that, Charley," she said. He reached out for her hand. Helen was gone. "Mama, Mama," Becker said. "Please don't leave me too."

Five

Sunday, August 20th, 1914 11:00 AM.

Woman were not welcome at Yussie's. The second Lena crossed the threshold separating the poolhall from the world, she was greeted by a wall of silent rage.

Please, God, she thought. *Nobody should recognize me.*

"Yusseleh," one of the players screamed.

A fat little man came tearing out of the back room.

Lena tensed; she knew Yussie Tunafish from the old days. He was one of Monk's *schtarker's*.

When Yussie heard one of the boys shouting his name he expected trouble and grabbed his favorite weapon; a foot long solid steel pipe with a knotted leather thong threaded through a small hole an inch from its base. Now, twirling the steel pipe by its leather thong, he confronted Lena, his hard eyes demanding an explanation.

"Please, sir," Lena said - assuming the more formal Yiddish of the Orthodox - "as He, whose name is not to be uttered, is my witness I mean neither you nor your establishment any harm. I am merely here to request a bit of information and I will be on my way."

Yussie said nothing.

She continued, "I would like to speak to a gentleman by the name of Willie the Shiv."

Yussies lips began to quiver. "Who," Yussie asked, the quiver resolving into a smile.

"A Mr. Willie the Shiv," Lena repeated, realizing how ridiculous her request must seem, but seeing no way out.

Yussie turned from Lena and shouted, "Boys, the rebbitzen want to talk to Velvel."

One of the pool players shouted back, "Willie ain't here, but if she want someone killed she come to the right place." The speaker still holding his cue stick walked up to Lena. He was well over six feet tall with close cropped graying red hair and a fighter's ruined nose. Lena recognized Rochle "The Mocky" Steinwolf.

"Missus," he said - playing to the room. "Why you want some poor bastard he should die? Smoke on Shabbis?"

Lena felt tears rush to her eyes. *This was supposed to be the easy part,* she thought, and walked out, oblivious to the peals of laughter in her wake. Back on the street Lena felt lost. There was a gentle tap on her shoulder, she turned and faced a sharply dressed young man of about twenty.

Probably a pimp, she thought.

"Excuse them bums," he said. "Ain't go no respect for God or women." He smiled, "Georgie Pittell at your service."

She asked if perhaps he knew where a Mr. Monk Eastman lived. The young pimp knew exactly where Monk lived. As Lena began to walk toward Monk's flat on Mott Street, she wondered if her luck had begun to turn.

Six

Sunday, August 20th, 1914 11:30 AM

Monk Eastman was about to bang the gong for the third time this morning. Turning into a goddamn hop head, he thought, trying to generate real concern, half not giving a shit. Monk's reputation, after the debacle at Yussie's, had sunk even lower, in spite of cooking the strong arm guy Boo Boo Goldman. And now opium was turning the sinews of his implacable will into mush. Before Sing Sing, hop was just one small part of his life. Pure pleasure. No sweat. Something to look forward to at the end of the day. Jail changed that.

In jail Monk finally found something he couldn't control: Time. Sentenced to eight fucking years behind bars! Time, a tactile presence; a malevolent insect spawning 76,400 seconds a day - an eternal storm of larval dust jamming his nose and filling his lungs. Breathing death; suffocating on Time. He thought of suicide. But Monk wasn't suicidal. He lived for pleasure; felt no remorse. Why die? Yet he thought of nothing else. Then he found there were more drugs in jail than on the street: laudanum, morphine, cocaine, marijuana. Time became a rather swiftly flowing river of dope. But there was no opium in jail - pure unadulterated opium. Too complicated to prepare - had to be cooked. He missed opium. First a little; then desperately. No matter what he smoked, popped, or drank it was all a poor excuse for hop. While the other cons thought of pussy, Monk thought of opium. Not just any opium; *li yuen*, the good stuff that costs a dollar a "pill". He imagined himself in the back of the pet store holding his pipe over the lamp, watching the "pill" melt in the bowl, becoming the brown sludge of pure hop. Filling his lungs, making his thoughts lighter than air. Soaring. Free of logic. Time. And Rage.

Monk carefully set his opium paraphernalia out on the kitchen table. He thoroughly enjoyed the ritual of cooking hop. Some Americans dispensed with the complex Chinese ritual. Not Monk.

GOD'S RAT

It reminded him of his older brother Zalman chanting his morning *bruchas* while putting on the *t'fillin* - two long thin leather straps each with a small leather box containing strips of parchment with hand scripted prayers; the reverential way Zalman placed one box on the inner side of his left arm and coiled the strap around his forearm exactly seven times; tied the other box around his forehead, securing it by knotting the strap at the back and then winding the arm strap around his middle finger three times. All the while rocking back and forth, losing himself in the dark music of Hebrew prayer.

Gingerly, Monk opened the elaborately carved yen hop, the opium box, and extracted some of the dank brown hop; cut off a small piece with a tiny intricately carved ivory scissors, the *kiao tsien*; rolled it between his thumb and forefinger into a "pill", or *yen pok*; punctured it with the *yen hock,* a long thin needle; then lifted the *yen pok* and carefully placed it into the bowl which had already been meticulously cleaned with a special sponge, and a *dao*, a sharp narrow saw-toothed knife. Finally he was ready to strike a match, ignite the lamp, cook the *yen pok* - inhale its rapturous fumes. *Zalman, you schmuck,* he thought as the opium distilled into his brain, *hop is so much fucking easier then t'fillin.*

* * * * *

11:45 AM

When Lena arrived at Monk's tenement, 941 Mott Street, she froze; it was sixteen years since she first stood at his front door.

She was still a kid, twenty four years old and had just left Morris after he brutally beat her for fucking Becker; she felt lost. A whore with no pimp was raw meat. Becker was gone; she couldn't go home; and she wouldn't return to Morris. Who could she turn to? Monk Eastman was the most powerful thug in the city. His gang, the Eastmans, took up where the Irish Whyos left off. One thousand strong, they plundered every corner of the East Side. The epic gun battles waged against their only important rivals, the Italian Five

Pointers Gang, were banner headlines in every paper in the city. Lena remembered her first meeting with Monk at Silver Dollar Smith's. He seemed to find her attractive. She felt safe in his presence. One day she simply showed up at his front door.

Now - sixteen years later - Lena was frightened.

The young pimp, Georgie Pittell, told her Monk was on the second floor. She proceeded up the old wrought iron steps. On the landing between the first and second floor she was met by an overpowering sweet, musky fragrance. Opium. The scent of burning flowers.

Normally, to provide some protection against the distinct aroma, wet towels were placed where the door meets the floor. *Not Monk*, thought Lena. She could hear his gruff voice, "Let the world know I's cooking hop, fuck 'em.." The thought he hadn't changed wasn't comforting. On the other hand there would be no violence. Hopped up, nobody was violent - not even Monk Eastman.

Monk was now comfortably prone on his couch. He lifted the pipe to his lips and took another deep draw. To Monk, smoking hop was a little like sweating it out in the murky hundred and twenty degree water in the pool of an East Side *shvitz* - feeling his tension and anger liquefying as he became one with the sweat that poured from his body. He imagined himself sinking beneath the scorched water of the pool. All laws of nature suspended; causality, dissolved. His mind, infused by euphoria, binding thought to wish. Suddenly, like a breath, pure light shimmered before him; gradually it composed into the form of an angel; it hovered above him, its wings -in repose - were wrapped around its body like a gossamer web as fragile as a dream, its expression peaceful, beatific; its eyes closed. In the center of its forehead was a small bloody hole. Monk recognized Abie Isaacs. He smiled.

Lena stood trembling before the door to Monk's flat. She knew the door was unlocked. Monk never locked his door. "Don't need no lock. Someone come in what shouldn't be here, I blows his fucking head off. Lock can't do that."

GOD'S RAT

Lena didn't bother to knock. Hopped up, Monk wouldn't answer. She opened the door slowly, walked through the kitchen and stood at the entrance to the windowless parlor. The main source of light was the small gas lamp used to fire the opium. Monk looked at her as she stood at the entrance. Pulling deeply on the pipe, his eyes glowed.

"Hello Mama," he said his voice occluded, flat; barely audible. Lena remembered her disguise; she looked Old Country. *Like everybody's Mama,* she thought.

"Hi Monk," she said carefully.

Monk ignored her. "First an angel; then the ghost of Mama," he thought. "Maybe I gets the Zeigfield girls next."

"Sit down Mama," he said.

Lena sat on a old rocking chair facing him. Monk was speaking to her in the language of his mother; Yiddish. His Yiddish was high caste, Germanized, reflecting proper middle class origins. Monk put down his pipe. "Surprised I'm still alive, Mama? Didn't think I'd live past twenty. Should have been dead, though. Shot fifteen times. You were right about jail. Did five years. Bet you read about me. Sorry I didn't make your funeral. Nobody told me you were dead. Zalman could have found me, told me. I didn't find out 'till a year later."

Lena removed her wig.

"I'm not your mama, Monk. I'm Lena Isaacs."

Monk smiled benignly. He was on another plane of reality. Everything was possible. Nothing really mattered.

"You was my best whore. Damn good fuck too," he said. "Want to come back to work?"

This was the Monk Eastman Lena remembered. "Hear you're trying to kill my son Abie, Monk," Lena said.

"It what I do," Monk said. "Ain't nothing personal." He lifted the lamp and held the pipe over the flame, inhaled deeply and looked directly at her. The glow of burning hop in the bowl transformed his eyes into two brilliant embers. Monk was on edge. Normally he smoked hop alone. It was a theater of his mind. There was no place for pain.

Lena took a deep breath. Now or never. Her stomach felt like she was about to leap off the roof of a seventh story tenement. "Abie Isaacs is your son too. I'm sorry, Monk."

Monk froze. A minute passed. The remaining hop in the bowl turned to ash extinguishing the fire in his eyes. The only source of light was flame from the lamp; Monk's face was insubstantial - fire and shadow. It seemed to float. Lena saw his hand at the base of the lamp, he turned the knob that controlled the flow of gas. Darkness. She heard his breathing, and imagined his rage; a gale whipped sea crashing through opium's torpor.

"I should have told you Abie was yours, Monk," Lena said - she could think of nothing else.

Silence.

Then she heard a sound that frightened her even more than the outraged scream she expected; the sound of irregular breathing.

Oh my God, she thought. *He's crying.*

When Monk felt the tears coming he switched off the lamp. To cry in front of someone is like shitting in public. "You tells me it was Morris' kid," Monk said. "That you was knocked up before you come to me." His voice was normal; he had willed the opium from his brain; the tears from his voice.

Now Lena was crying. "I'm sorry," she whispered uselessly. *What can I tell him?* she thought, *that he terrified me. I didn't want my son to bear the name of a monster?*

"Tell me something, Lena," Monk said. "Morris know?"

"Yes, Monk," she said. "Morris knows."

* * * * *

12:10 PM

After Lena left, Monk was overcome by a fatigue so heavy it felt like death. He slept.

His dreams were always violent. Faceless adversaries armed to the teeth seeking vengeance for offenses whose nature and origin were never clear. Often he awoke feeling more exhausted than when he went to sleep. This time the usual bloody tableau was interrupted by the opium induced vision he experienced before Lena's visit. The same pure light shimmering before him, gradually composing into the form of an angel; it rose and hovered above him, its wings - in repose -wrapped around its body like a gossamer web as fragile as a dream; its face peaceful, beatific; eyes closed. It was Abie Isaacs. In the center of its forehead, a small bloody hole.

Monk was jolted awake; the vision that had given him so much satisfaction just a short time ago now seared his brain like a hot coal. Furiously he shook his head as if that would somehow dislodge the martyred angel, "My son - with a goddamn bloody hole in his head."

He left his house and began to walk to Nigger Mike Salter's saloon. *Nig know everybody goddamn business,* Monk thought. *He know where my kid is. My kid, my son for chrissake.*

* * * * *

12:41 PM

Monk left Nigger Mike Salter's saloon with the information he needed. As expected, he ran into some resistance. "It my business to keeps my ears open and my mouth shut," the big man said. "You knows that Monk. Half the drunks here is here for one reason; to yap to Nig. I talks to you I's out of business."

"You's`out of business you don't," said Monk laying his gun on the counter.

Nig told Monk what he knew, which was a lot more than where Abie was holed up. "More guys out there wants him dead than you, Monk," he said. "You's got your work cut out."

When Monk stepped out of the saloon he saw the poster:

****

**Hear
<u>DA Whitman</u>
Expose the Criminal Anarchy
Destroying our City!
Rally at Cooper Union,
1:00 PM Admission $1.00**

****

Monk stopped and reversed direction; now he had two stops to make before going to the kid-whore Rosie Saperstein's place.

GOD'S RAT

Seven

Sunday, August 20th, 1914 1:00 PM

DA Charles Whitman had spoken at political fund raisers before; but this was different. The crowd rapidly filling the huge auditorium in the Cooper Union Building in Greenwich Village was there for one reason only. To see him; to cheer him; to pour even more money into the coiffures of the Fund for the Prosecution of Lieutenant Charles Becker.

Whitman read somewhere more words had been written about the shooting of Herman Rosenthal in ten weeks than had been written about the Spanish American War over its duration. He knew Herman's murder was a rallying point for the Good Government Anti-Tammany burghers; real Americans who felt overwhelmed by the European trash - the micks, the wops and the kikes - flooding their city; and how the ensuing criminal explosion, magnified by a hysterical press, became the focal point of their rage. Now this; a brutal cold blooded murder committed by scary little Hebe killers who hid behind corrupt Irish Tammany hacks. And worst of all the whole thing masterminded by a copper, Lieutenant Becker.

Whitman realized Becker's crime - he never thought of it any other way - had, in the eyes of the public, created a bloody and dangerous fissure in the blue wall protecting them against the toxic horde pressing at the gates. For this Becker had to pay - pay dearly.

Sitting on the stage in the chair of honor - it was bigger, its seat and back cushions a rich, brocaded blue velvet compared to the faded red cloth of the chairs inhabited by the other, lesser dignitaries - Whitman felt himself merging with the crowd as it rapidly filled the auditorium; feeling their anger; their frustration; their bloodlust.

A huge banner was unfurled over the first balcony. Whitman had to squint through the dense veil of cigar smoke to make it out. In red white and blue it read, **WHITMAN FOR GOVERNOR**. To its left another was unfurled; its legend: **BECKER MUST DIE**.

GOD'S RAT

Perfect, he thought.

Whitman moved his eyes from the balcony to the first three rows of the center section. Here sat some of the most powerful men in the city. Perhaps the world. JP Morgan was here. Andrew Carnegie. Jacob Schiff. Jay Gould. And John D. Rockefeller, for chrissake. They were the vanguard of the The Society for Prevention of Crime and had already contributed, and raised, enough money for Whitman to hire his own investigative army of Pinkertons. Today's fund raiser would allow the DA to turn a suite at the Waldorf Hotel into the prosecution's Center of Operations. He smiled down at them. *I can never have your wealth; yet you, the richest men in the world, are here paying respect to me, bequeathing me coin from your sacred vaults. Why? Because only I have the power of life and death. Only I can kill the animal who stains the soul of your city - the corrupt cop Charles Becker; the killer cop Charles Becker. Only I can purify this besieged metropolis and drive the barbarians back.*

Suddenly Whitman felt compelled to look beyond the first three rows. He noticed a gruesome little man with a scarred and battered face- an undersized derby balanced precariously on his head. But mostly he noticed the eyes, unblinking, burning with hatred. He was badly shaken.

Sitting amidst the screaming throng of scrubbed, powdered, and pampered Episcopalians Monk Eastman felt like a gob of green phlegm on a white linen tablecloth. He wasn't sure what he was doing here. Just that he needed to see Whitman. To glare at the son of a bitch; to let him know that even The Beast Monk Eastman wouldn't kill his own kid. And maybe to let himself know. Monk never before backed out of a contract. Coming here was a formal cancellation. And something else; he was sending a message to Morris. *The DA gonna tell the little mocky prick I's out of it. Morris'll know why; he know I find out the truth; he know I tear his fucking head off.*

Eight

Sunday, August 20th, 1914 3:00 PM

After the Cooper Union rally DA Charles Whitman had his driver take him to the 53rd Street Prison. He went directly to the Warden's office and summoned Morris.

It was now three weeks since Morris, Vallinsky, and Bridgey Webber were locked in jail as material witnesses. The papers were full of stories about the good life they were living. Which was basically true except for the first brutal week in the Tombs when Morris told DA Charles Whitman, "--me and the boys'd rather die quick in the chair than wait months for Becker's trial in this fucking dungeon which is worse than dying because it worse than hell." Whitman moved them to the new 53rd Street prison between Ninth and Tenth Avenue where they devoured five course meals delivered from their favorite joints, and welcomed their many visitors: tailors, barbers, manicurists, bookies, lackeys, wives, and girl fiends. In their spare time they read the transcripts of depositions from "eyewitnesses" for the Prosecution sent to them, through their attorneys, by the DA to make sure everybody's' story jibed . The People needed witnesses who were *not* participants in the murder of Herman Rosenthal. (The testimony of Morris, Bridgey, and Vallinsky was not enough to make the DA's circumstantial case against Lieutenant Becker stick.)

So"eyewitnesses" kept crawling out of the woodwork with stories that just happened to add weight and substance to the People's case against Lieutenant Charles Becker. Invariably these public spirited witnesses had their own cases pending under the jurisdiction of the the Attorney for the Eastern District of the State of New York, The Honorable Charles Whitman. There was no shortage of criminals willing to trade jail time for truth. "Goddamn genius this Whitman," Morris said to Bridgey. Listen to this." In his hand was a sheaf of mimeographed papers his lawyer just delivered from the

DA's office. "It a deposition," Morris explained, "from a small time skeemio, Samuel Lubin, facing 3 to 5 for forgery; swear he overhears Becker in The Lafayette Baths, bragging how, 'I forced those, kike pimps to shut Herman Rosenthal's big mouth forever.' "

"What Lubin cop to?" Bridgey asked.

"Whitman knock down his time to three months with a year probation," Morris said. Bridgey was impressed: "This Whitman think like a criminal." He could conceive of no higher compliment for an officer of the law.

Morris had not seen Whitman for weeks, *So what the hell that farbissener wants from me now?* he wondered as he walked, unescorted, down the broad, brightly lit corridors of the modern 53rd Street facility. Suddenly, Morris knew exactly why Whitman wanted to see him: *It got to do with the kid, Abie. He ain't dead yet - Monk ain't honoring his contract; Monk always honor his contracts.* He stopped walking; his head felt light; his body oozed sweat. *Monk know the truth about Abie,* he realized. *Maybe he know I know?* Death froze Morris' heart. He imagined Monk Eastman's face when he discovered Abie Isaacs was his kid. Vomit splattered at his feet.

Darkness came. Morris awoke to the smell of vomit. And the sound of DA Whitman's voice. He was sitting in the Warden's office facing Whitman across a battered desk. "The Dietary Laws of the Hebrews are quite clear, Morris," he said. "You are strictly forbidden the indulgence of shell fish, yet crustaceans of every ilk are your favorite repast. As they say, God punished you." The phlegmy laugh; the ice cold eyes.

The DA's expression articulated neither amusement or disgust. Just anger. Morris' head was throbbing; his stomach ached; his throat burned from acid. Whitman cleared his throat. "This evening Mr. Eastman let me know, in his own inimitable way - he's not without style, hoodlum panache - that he will not be fulfilling his end of our bargain. Your choice of Monk Eastman, was to say the least, unfortunate." Morris' head began to clear. "Our problem - young Abie Isaacs," Whitman continued, "is still is very much with us." Sodden with vomit, Morris was finding it difficult to regain his composure, or even a shred of dignity. "I had the pleasure of meeting the young scamp," Whitman said. "Deceptively intelligent. And, as you suggested, demonstrates a curious adherence to the Truth. In a word dangerous. Consider this Morris, Young Mr. Isaacs' well developed conscience directs him to the offices of the Times, or the World where he divulges what he heard at the Occidental--" Whitman leaned across the desk, his face two feet from Morris' face -- "Intolerable!" he hissed. Morris flinched. For a second the smell of bourbon overwhelmed the reek of puke.

"--If Abraham Isaacs is not dead within 12 hours, I will drop the case against Lieutenant Becker and pursue the one that is incontrovertible. You, Bridgey Webber, and Hyman Vallinsky will stand trial for causing the murder of Herman Rosenthal. Young Isaacs, as the State's star witness, will be encouraged to indulge his penchant for truth telling. He will testify as to what he heard at the Occidental and *saw* on 43rd Street. Whitman smiled. "Gotcha," he wheezed. Morris stomach roiled. "One way or another I gonna croak," he thought. "Either Monk, or the chair."

Whitman opened a desk draw and retrieved a 32 revolver which he laid on the desk. "The young fugitive, Abraham Isaacs," he said, "is presently recovering from a bullet wound to the shoulder at a tenement bordello - 122 Hester Street - rented to the procurer, Mr. Jacob "Nigger" Bialick, and presided over by a Miss Rosie Saperstein. You will be released for twelve hours. The gun Mr. Schiff is yours; use it."

* *** * *

January 25, 1915, 6:08 and 10 seconds, Sing Sing.

Becker was five years old, on his father's farm. One Eye was alone on the path that led from the chicken coop to the house. One Eye had been around ever since he remembered - her left eye gone, covered completely by scar tissue as if it was never there - as if she popped out the egg with just one eye. Like the magic Mama read to him in books - pigs that talked and cows that flew over the moon. He didn't know why he wanted to wrestle with the chicken - just that he did. Not to hurt her; to feel what it was like. He followed her for about ten feet until he got the nerve. He jumped on top of her and it was all feathers and claws and chicken smell and a strength much greater than his - a strength that comes from terror. One Eye's claws were tearing at his face and her beak trying to eat his eyes as if they were kernels of corn. And Becker realized he was not wrestling a chicken at all; it was Samual Luban - forger and con man who had spent half his adult life in jail and was facing five more years for forgery and embezzlement, and whose sentence was reduced to one year parole for his sworn testimony for the People against Charles Becker. Luban was on the stand now and his scrawny Jew face was One Eye's face and his voice was Luban's. When Luban answered a question fed to him by DA Charles Whitman Becker felt the same pain he felt when he was five and the chicken was tearing up his face and trying to eat his eyes.

DA: Mr. Luban would you recognize Lieutenant Charles Becker?

Luban: Yes.

DA: Please point him out.

Luban: That's him

DA: Thank you. Where have you seen Lieutenant Becker before?

Luban: At the Lafayette Baths, in the steam room.

DA: Was he aware of your presence.

Luban: He never noticed me.

DA: Was the Lieutenant alone?

Luban: He was with another man; they were speaking.

DA: Did you hear what they were saying?

Luban: Yes I did.

And Becker was rolling in the dirt with One Eye again - the same feathers and claws and the chicken smell and strength and One Eye's claws tearing at his face and - because Becker did not *resist this time - his eyes were torn from his head and consumed; and One Eye's voice was Luban's voice.*

One Eye: He said, 'I finally got those Jew pimps to kill that rat Rosenthal.'

DA: Speak up Mr. Luban.

One Eye: 'I finally got those Jew pimps to kill that rat Rosenthal.'

DA: Thank you. No more questions Your Honor.

And Becker screamed at the DA, "Your lies killed me sir. You destroyed the life of an innocent man." And Whitman faced him and was One Eye, and the jurors were One Eye, and Luban was still One Eye, and Judge Goff was One Eye. And Becker laughed. Not because it was funny. Because it was true.

GOD'S RAT

Nine

August 20th, 1914 12:45 PM

Abie woke up with the smell and taste of Rosie Saperstein. He reached for her. She was already up. He didn't want to leave the bed - not even to take a piss; to rinse his mouth; to do anything to disconnect himself from her sweat, her come, her perfume. The wound in his shoulder still throbbed; he looked at the bandages and saw the impression of Rosie's lipstick. He smiled.

It happened after he asked her to cut the ropes tying his arms to the bedposts. She came to him, dropped her kimono, bent over him and pressed her lips to the bandages, causing a sensation of such exquisite pleasure it was as if the wound were a sexual organ.

Now he sat up and placed his fingers on the bandages. Pressed hard. There was just pain. He closed his eyes.

She climbed on top of him, pressing her lips to his mouth. He pushed her away. "Rosie, cut the fucking rope," he shouted. Desperately he wanted to hold her, turn her over.

"Abeleh, relax," she whispered. "Accepts the pleasure." Her voice was heavy, occluded. She was all heat and breath; she kissed him again; he felt the beat of her heart against his chest. She lifted her lips from his mouth; her body squirmed downwards, her lips at his throat; her thighs hugged his leg, leaving a trail of moisture as she moved lower. Her mouth was now on the level of his bandages; again he felt the pressure of her lips against his wound; he came; she wrapped her mouth around his cock. Pure fire; he dissolved. She left the bed, returned with a knife and cut the rope. They fucked. He held her and said he would always protect her. "Be my pimp Abie," she said. "We be bigger than Rosie Hurtz."

"You don't has to be no whore Rosie," he said.

"Abeleh, I **is** a whore," she said. "I don't **has** to be nothing."

A knock on the front door broke his trance. "Heshey, I be right there," Rosie shouted from the kitchen; the shuffle of her slippered feet; the door opening. "Hesheleh, my *zeesein schtup*," Rosie chirped. "Sorry I's dressed. Didn't know you be here this early."

A male voice: "With you clothes on is better Rosaleh. I likes to watch you take them off."

Rosie laughed. A hard dry cackle; a whore's laugh.

Abie never cried - not since he was five. But if he did, he would have.

Suddenly the door to the bedroom began to open. *Shit, they's coming in here,* he thought. Reaching for the gun under the pillow he pointed it at the opening door - cocked it. *This fucking Heshey dead.* The door opened. A woman in rags stood there. Under one arm she held four or five clean towels.

Rosie's towel washer for chrissake, he thought. Her free hand was pressed to the side of her face. She reeked of piss and booze. *It the old whore from Seward Park, Mushy Bum.* He remembered how her insane babbling stopped and suddenly she spoke coherently: "He home Abeleh. Papa's home."

Mushy Bum froze, as shocked to see Abie as he was to see her.

"Mushy," he whispered, "Who my Papa?"

She shuffled toward him, stopped, and peered into his eyes. He was gripped by the eyeballs; how they pierced their cataracts like angry suns. Then she squawked the same words that killed Boo Boo Goldman. "Monk you's the best -- Monk you's the best -- Monk you's the best---" Mushy was in a sort of trance - eyes scrunched so tightly her entire face seemed to converge at the bridge of her nose. *Jesus, she look like a fucking parrot,* Abie thought in amazement. Suddenly she stopped; her face calmed, her eyes faded to dark clouds. She turned and left the room

What that about? Abie wondered. Then he knew. The nightmare memory - being held out a window six stories up; a powerful hand clutching a fist full of his hair. Wishing the hand would release him so the pain would stop. Knowing he wouldn't fall, but fly away like a pigeon. Nearby Mama was sobbing. In the background a male voice rolled like thunder. It was the voice he remembered - not its sound, but its ferocity. Hearing it again, only last week, at Zelig's funeral; the gruff voice asking, "You's Abie Isaacs?"

My Papa's voice. Monk Eastman.

He wasn't shocked; or terrified; or consumed by anger. It was just knowing that mattered. As if he spent his entire life without a hand; or an arm; or a nose and suddenly it was there. *My papa's Monk Eastman.*

His next thought: *My name's Abraham Osterman.* Like everybody on the East Side, Abie knew the story of a kid named Edward Osterman from a religious family in Williamsburg, Brooklyn, who, at sixteen, moved himself to the East Side and invented Monk Eastman, its most famous and feared gangster.

Painfully, Abie raised himself to a sitting position and got out of bed. He stood before Rosie's huge rococo mirror - it reminded him of Zayde's house - and looked for a resemblance to the great Monk Eastman. There was none. He realized why. *Monk face look like it hit by a truck.* So with his right hand he pushed in his nose; he scowled darkly, and imagined himself in a tight plaid woolen suit, wearing a derby too small for his head. Now Abraham Isaacs was Abraham Osterman. He felt invincible; larger than life. "My papa was shot fifteen times; my papa kill fifty men." He saw himself, Abie Cracks Osterman, strutting down Delancy Street enjoying the pall of fear his presence cast. "That Monk Eastman's kid; got the heart of a killer just like his pa." He had an impulse to run into the adjoining room and pull the old man, Heshey, off Rosie, watch his cock shrivel in fear; scream in his face, "I's Monk Eastman's kid and I fucking kills you."

Moving quickly, on impulse, he ran back to the bed, grabbed the gun under the pillow, returned to the mirror and pointed it at his reflection.

He was Abie Isaacs again - a scared kid holding an adult's gun, stalked by his father, a man who kills humans as easily as most people swat a fly. He lowered the gun and for the second time in a day felt an impulse to cry.

Monk Eastman my papa, he thought. *And my papa wanna' kill me.*

This time the tears came. The sight of his tears terrified him. Even more than the thought of his deadly father.

* * * * *

2:40 PM

By the time Abie arrived at the Delancy Street lot he realized he should never have gotten out of bed. His wound was throbbing badly, feeling like a dam about to explode; every step was excruciating. He became light headed.

A flurry of black flakes clouded his vision. Becoming a blizzard, they blinded him. He heard Klopper's voice; it seemed far away. "Schmuck, you's trying to kill yourself? Doc don't want you out of bed for a couple of days. Chrissake, Abie yesterday you's bleeding like a chicken with it head cut off."

Looking up, over Klopper's shoulder, Abie could see Sheeny Mike and Sugar Davey. They appeared to be far above him, as if he were in a hole looking up. *Like from a grave,* he thought. Now, feeling a little better, sitting in front of Klopper's new lean-to, Abie told them what Mushy Bum said; how Monk Eastman was his father.

"You's sure Abie?" asked Davey. "This old whore Mushy Bum, she meshugeh."

"Monk Eastman my Papa," Abie said.

The boys were convinced. Not because Abie said it; but the way he said it. With fear.

Klopper took charge. "First we gets Abie back to bed. Then I finds Eastman, tells him he trying to kill his own kid."

"Maybe he know, don't give a shit." said Sheeny Mike.

Klopper shrugged. "I looks him in the eye and tells him anyway," he said.

Ten

August 20th, 1914 2:35 PM

There was always a crowd in front of Auster's Candy Store, on the corner of Stanton and Clinton Streets. It was "Home of the Original Egg Cream" - one of the most popular hangouts on the East Side.

Auster's Candy Store. A triumph of the Jewish predilection for confection over booze.

Which is why Monk Eastman hated candy stores. Candy stores were too soft for the gangsters who were among their best customers - a Jewish aberration. Tough goyem hung out only at saloons, not candy stores; bragged of their capacity for chugging shots, and buckets of beer, not egg creams - "Our Yid boilermakers," sneered Monk.

So it was with surprise that the boys - the *paskudnyaks*, the bookies, the *gunzils* and pimps - welcomed the arrival of Monk Eastman, here, at the core of the East Side's sweet tooth - a nondescript joint on the corner of Stanton and Clinton with the faded and peeling hand painted sign, **"Home of the Original Egg Cream."**

Suprise. And, of course, fear.

Greetings were mumbled through clenched lips. Eye contact was averted. Except for Rochle "The Mock" Steinwolf, Lena's tormentor from Yussies - who extended his hand. The Mock like all the aging *schtarkers*, once ran with the Eastmans. "Never had no fear," remembered Monk as he reached out to accept his old lieutenant's hand.

"*Ve gettus*, Monkeleh," said The Mock. "What you's doing here? *Mash'keh* they still don't put in egg creams - pure dairy. Maybe in jail you get a taste for sweets? Like in jail you learns to be a hop head."

Why's they still testing me? Monk wondered. *Look what happen to Boo Boo.* At that moment he knew his time had passed; he could kill a hundred Boo Boo's, it wouldn't matter.

"Mock," Monk said - his nose practically touching The Mock's; his voice more a hiss than a whisper, "wanna know what I learns in jail? I learns to eat the shit they feeds me for breakfast, lunch, and dinner, and the shit the screws feeds me a hundred times a day. In jail I develops a strong stomach for shit, which is why maybe you's gonna live another day."

The Mock looked away, grateful for Monk Eastman's gracious gift - unsure why he provoked his anger in the first place.

"You seen the Bostons?" Monk asked. The Mock moved his head in the direction of the candy store. He looked sick.

Monk smiled. *I still turns a man's face green,* he thought. "You don't look so good Mock. Come on, I buys you an egg cream," he said. Then turned and entered Austers.

Monk had never been inside Auster's. It was quite dark and not particularly clean; it reeked of chocolate syrup and slightly soured milk, making Monk nauseous. The floor hadn't been mopped for days, the little white and black triangular tiles a *schmutzick* gray. But the fifteen foot long mahogany counter - the kind usually found in the finest saloons - shone with a gleaming oiled veneer. And, fronting the counter, the eight intricately trellised high backed wrought iron chairs glistened with fresh coats of black paint. The chairs - sporting brand new red leather seats - were empty.

Behind the counter was a little man with a full, well trimmed, black beard - formally attired in a black on black stripped suit and white on white shirt - idly wiping the counter with a clean white towel. Monk recognized Joseph Auster, inventor of the Original Egg Cream.

Auster greeted Monk with a big smile that looked only slightly forced - and announced, with the ingenuous eloquence of the true huckster, "I am Joseph Auster sir, proprietor. It is truly an honor to meet the East Side's most legendary rogue and benefactor. What is your pleasure?"

Monk immediately liked Auster. "I too Mr. Auster is pleased to meet a legend," he said. They shook hands.

"Monk, I know our egg cream is not your favorite drink," Joseph Auster said. "Maybe you accept a glazle shnapps?"

Monk was impressed. The inventor of the Original Egg Cream was offering him whiskey. Not it, seemed to Monk, out of fear - but respect. He smiled, and nodded.

Auster retrieved a bottle of slivovitz from under the counter and placed it in front of Monk for all to see. Next to it he put a glass.

Monk reached for his wallet. Auster shook his head. "Please," he said.

"I understands the Bostons is here," Monk said.

GOD'S RAT

Eleven

August 20th, 1914 2:25 PM

    Nig Bialik was blind. The horror, the finality of his sightlessness, competed with - and almost neutralized - the pain induced by the surgical removal of his eyes. Someone was yanking him up by the scruff of the neck, pushing him forward; a handkerchief was tied around his head covering the gaping wounds that had been his eyes.
    After Nig regained consciousness - the last thing he remembered was a blackjack smashing into the side of his head - he found himself staring up at least thirty Gopher's - a weird terraced dome of black derbies. In the evil intensity of their eyes - in the snarling curl of their lips - he realized that no matter what he had to offer - one hundred dollars, Abie Isaacs' living pulsating Yid heart on a platter - it would not ransom his life, or sate their lust for **his** blood.
    "Look who we's got here," growled Terry Jackson, Gopher boss - his shocking blue iris' bobbing in a bloody soup of ruptured veins. "You's far from Jew Town, Nig. Looking for another Irish moll to turn into a trot you sheeny pimp bastard?"
    "Shit," thought Nig, "I forget about Maggy Duffy." He recalled a beautiful freckled faced Irisheh, about fourteen, who tripped into Auster's one day, pressed up against him and whispered into his ear, "I hear you's the best mack on the East Side; I's looking for work."
    "Mr. Pimp," said Terry Jackson, "I likes you to meet Mr. Joe Duffy, perhaps you knows his sis."
    A freckled faced kid about sixteen was standing over him - on the thumb of his right hand was hooked a finely tooled cutting apparatus that looked like a copper claw. Nig didn't remember much after that. First, talking - talking fast - telling them where they could find Abie Isaacs; how he'd pay a hundred beans they cook the kid, two hundred chrissake, three -- every penny he had; finally pleading, flat out begging, for his sight. Closing his eyes on the last thing he'd

GOD'S RAT

ever see - that fucking copper claw; then the pain - feeling tears running down the side of his face, realizing it was blood. Seeing, picturing, dreaming of him and Ikey Gotteinker, the time they were running on a roof, the coppers behind them; the roof ending at an air shaft - a six foot jump to the next roof, 70 feet to the ground; the boys stop, frozen; Nig jumps first; he makes it; Ikey jumps, still holding the fucking pocketbook, doesn't make it, not even close; but it's he - Nig - who's falling; the perverse thrill of pure terror; he screams and puts his arms out - as if that would brace gravity's tyranny - screaming and screaming and screaming until all is black. For now and forever.

Twelve

August 20th, 1914 2:30 PM

"The Monk Eastman," said Mr Joseph Auster with raised eyebrows, "is looking for those two *tsedrayter* kops, the Bostons'?"

Monk nodded.

Auster glanced toward a heavy blue velvet curtain that separated the public Auster's from the private. Behind the curtain, in almost ritual secrecy, the Original Egg Cream was concocted. Also, it was where Mr. Joseph Auster - in partnership with the pimp Nigger Bialik - jerrybuilt two plywood rooms in order to profitably quench another even more pressing thirst.

As Monk turned toward the curtain two pretty, very painted, fourteen year olds sauntered out.

"See you tomorrow, Mr. Auster," they chirped.

The Bostons followed after them; both buttoning their flies.

"All class," muttered Auster.

Sammy was the first to see Monk.

His mouth broke into a broad grin; his eyes looked toward the door. "Monk, What you's doing here? Thought you hates egg creams?"

"I does," Monk said. He took a sip of slivovitz.

Whiskey was *traif* in The Home of the Original Egg Cream. So the Boston's were shocked, to see Monk proudly imbibing his schnapps, obviously a gift - more than that, a formal tribute presented by Mr. Joseph Auster himself to the aging gangster king. This, even more than the killing of Boo Boo Goldman, was proof Monk Eastman still had teeth.

For Monk it was pure pleasure to watch these pig faced bulvans squirm.

"We's been meaning to see you since you got out," piped up Meyer.

Monk took another sip.

"We was gonna visit you upstate Monk," said Sammy weakly.

"Yeah," chimed in his brother with even less conviction. "But things kept coming up."

"You mugs want something to drink?" Monk asked.

"Sure," Sammy said. Relieved at monks generosity. "Bet schnapps tastes even better in Auster's."

He was feeling more comfortable; could almost taste the whiskey.

Monk smiled at Sammy who was pushing the limits of his wit. Then he called to Auster: "Mr. Auster, egg creams, for the boys." The brothers cringed - predators dissolving into prey.

"Boychicks," Monk said, still smiling, "I hears we got something in common, Abie Isaacs."

"Yeah," Sammy said. "We hears you wants him dead too."

Then Meyer - just to make conversation - asked, "So Monk, What the kid to you?"

Monk whispered, drawing the Bostons in, his smile expanding. "Youse won't believe it, turn out he's my kid." Laughing now.

The Bostons, not understanding - but desperately wanting to accommodate Monk, joined the laughter.

Now, not laughing, Monk asked, "Think it funny, youse's trying to kill my kid?"

The not too bright Bostons didn't get it. It was the last thing they wouldn't get.

A short time later, Joseph Auster explained to the coppers why there happened to be the brains of two dead *schtarkers* splattered all over his shiny mahogany counter which was accustomed to much less exotic *schmutz*.

"So officers, these two Italian hoods come in," said Auster standing behind the counter - his dignity intact in spite of the gore covering his ruined black on black suit and white on white shirt. "Now this in itself ain't too common - don't get me wrong officers, everybody welcome here - just let's say I was surprised. One thing sure; these dagos ain't looking to buy no egg cream. Right up to the poor Bostons they walks - don't say nothing - just pulls out their guns and bam -- bam shoots them in the head. Two shots each one fires.

Then they turns, still holding their guns just in case some of the boys objects which of course ain't the case except maybe nobody too happy dagos coming here spilling Jewish blood. Even this Jewish blood."

Auster glanced at the mess on his counter. Then back at the coppers. "Hope this don't stain," he said.

The cops knew this was the first truthful thing Mr. Joseph Auster had said. But so what?

Whoever killed the Bostons deserved a medal.

GOD'S RAT

Thirteen

August 20th, 1914 2:45 PM

As the boys - Abie, Klopper, Sugar Davey, Sheeny Mike, and Freak Show walked west on Delancy nearing their destination, 122 Hester Street - Rosie's place - they saw the pimp Nigger Bialick lurching toward them.

Blood - oozing through the hanky that covered his raw, gouged ocular holes - poured down his face like tears. Frantically he waved his arms to protect himself against the million deadly obstacles only the sightless can imagine. His mouth was open, but emitted no sound.

Horrified, the boys ran to Nig. When they reached the corner, Sheeny Mike grabbed hold of him.

Suddenly twenty Irishers wearing black derbies rounded the corner, trapping them in a locked circle. A very tall - surprisingly effeminate - twenty year old blond kid smiling brightly - gun drawn - walked up to them. Abie recognized the Gopher boss, Terry Jackson - the resemblance to his younger brother, Kenny, was striking. Jackson pressed the gun to Klopper's head and spoke so amiably the boys almost forgot the gun, "Greetings me kiddies, Where the boyo what busted Big Jim Toohey's arm like twas a toothpick?"

Silence.

Jackson turned and looked at his kid brother. "Kenny, who the kid?"

Kenny smiled at Abie like an old lost friend - he was holding a six inch dagger which he waved in Abie's direction. "How you's doing Abie Cracks?" he asked.

Jackson turned to Abie and greeted him like a Tammany hack out for votes: "Glad to finally meets you Abie Cracks, Let me introduce myself. I's Terry Jackson, boss of these motley thugs."

"What you's wants from us?" Klopper growled.

Jackson ignored him and placed his gun against Abie's head. "You don't look so good Abie Cracks," he said. "I hears the coppers shoot you. Look like you should of stays in bed. But don't worry Abie--" He turned and looked at his boys, then back at Abie, "--we's gonna makes you feel a lot worse."

He cocked his gun.

But before Abie could register the terror he felt. Even before Terry Jackson had the opportunity to glower, there was a blinding flash, then another - two fierce explosions followed. Then the acrid stink - a white gust of burning gun powder. First Terry Jackson crumbled. Behind him, his kid brother spun - gracefully at first, a slow pirouette, arms raised high - in shock; surrender - his right hand still clutched the dagger. Then, without grace, he stumbled forward until he fell hard on his face.

The surviving Gophers ran like hell; some dropped their weapons. They all held their hats.

Only the two dead boyos were left behind.

Expressionless, Monk Eastman watched them run; his gun at his side, still smoking. Abie and the boys were all motion, without purpose - running in circles, screaming at the top of their lungs, reminding Monk of a gang of mangy mutts scared shitless by the backfire of a combustion engine.

"Youse's a bunch of girlies," he shouted. "They just loses their best - ain't gonna be back for a long time."

The boys relaxed. For the moment Monk was the *Masiach* who haunted their Mama and Papa's dreams. "You," he screamed at Klopper. "Pick up the weapons they drops." Klopper scurried to collect the slung shots, knives, and knucks abandoned by the retreating Gophers. Had the order been to jump in front of an oncoming trolley the Klop would have happily complied.

Sheeny Mike put a protective arm around the blind pimp. "You," Monk screamed at him. "Take the poor bastard to the hospital."

Abie was sitting on the sidewalk. The dam of Doc Greenbaum's bandages had burst. Monk scooped him up as if he were an infant. "We goes to the kid whore - Rosie's," he said to Klopper.

And to Sweet Davey: "Get the Doc."

In his father's arms Abie looked up and saw the fear; saw his ridiculous woolen suit become stained with his blood; felt his left hand pressing on the wound to stanch the flow.

"Papa," he whispered. "You didn't drop me." And he smiled, and was unafraid of the darkness.

The four of them, Klopper, leading the way; Monk - Abie in his arms; Freak Show bringing up the rear were heading south on Hester Street.

* * * * *

January 25, 1915, 6:08 and 55 seconds, Sing Sing.

Becker was drenched with sweat. *I hope they don't think I'm crying.* The newsmen in the witness box were getting bored. Some yawned. Herbert Bayard Swope looked at his watch. Another looked toward the exit, as if preparing to leave. *They came to see my death,* Becker realized. *But my agony offends them.* "Sorry boys," he said. "I'm dying the best I can."

Abie Isaacs entered the witness box. He carried a stack of newspapers under his right arm; his newsboy cap pulled low over his eyes. "Becker dead!" he shouted. "Death Letter to Whitman say he innocent!"

They published my letter, Becker thought. "Thanks boys," he said.

DA Whitman entered the witness box wearing a blue silk dressing gown. He was drunk. "I'll take a paper son," he said. Abie handed him a paper. Whitman faced Becker. "I'm impressed Lieutenant Becker," he said, "that on the day of your death you could compose an epistle so brilliantly answering the vile and very public defamation's I heartlessly made against you on the day before your death."

Whitman, newspaper in hand, stumbled toward him. "I should take your place on the chair Lieutenant," he said, "but my sense of justice does not run quite so deep." Standing next to Becker now, he turned and faced the newsmen in the witness box. "Listen gentlemen," he declaimed drunkenly, "Listen to the truth. For you, as surely as I, have murdered an innocent man." Whitman dissolved into light, his voice a supernal mist enveloping and caressing Becker like a breeze - Whitman's voice began: "Ossening NY, January 23 - Charles Becker sent this challenging letter tonight to District Attorney Charles Whitman; he wrote it today on the day of his execution in his cell in the death house in Sing Sing." And now the voice was no longer Whitman's; it was his own voice, and it was clear and true and righteous. "Sir: You are credited in the public press his morning with these statements concerning me, each of them wholly untrue and unwarranted: First you said I agreed to plead guilty to murder in the second degree. Standing on the brink of the grave, I ask you solemnly to name the person I agreed to plead guilty to murder in the second degree, or any crime whatever. It would be too shocking to suspect that the District Attorney of this State could stoop to assail with unfounded charges a helpless man in the very shadow of death--"

And now the voice was no longer his, or even a voice but a source of pure sound that wafted toward him like a shadow and the shadow took the form of the reporter Herbert Bayard Swope and Swope was crying, paper raised, reading the last words Lieutenant Charles Becker wrote "--I am as innocent as you" - tears stopped flowing from Swope's eyes and entered his voice - "of having murdered Herman Rosenthal or of having counseled or procured or aided in his murder, or having any knowledge of that dreadful crime.

"Mark well sir these words of mine. The skein of lies you have created through the encouragement of false testimony, and with the connivance of a judge who viewed me as a symbol of corruption, and with the eager assistance of ambitious reporters who flung me as raw meat to the masses starving for vengeance - you have proved yourself able to destroy my life. And believe me I will surrender it without rancor. But not all the judges in this State, nor the country, nor the District Attorney; nor disingenuous reporters, nor all of them combined can destroy permanently the character of an innocent man. Posthumously Yours, Lieutenant Charles Becker." And Herbert Bayard Swope having finished, disappeared.

GOD'S RAT

Fourteen

August 20th, 1914 11:15 PM

A brand new horseless truck coughed and sputtered out of the parking area of the Fifty Third Street Prison - on its sides, in bold black letters, was printed the word, **Morgue.** At 53rd and Ninth it turned west toward the river, passing three blocks of anonymous warehouses, until finally coming to a halt at a roughly cleared cargo area adjacent to the Hudson River. Facing the river, its headlights flickered a pitiful protest against the rolling, leaden, vastness.

The driver, a copper, emerged, walked to the rear of the truck, released the latch, grabbed the handles of the two steel doors and swung them open. A lone figure climbed down. The copper ignored him, closed the doors, and climbed back into the truck.

Morris "the Pimp" Schiff watched the red tail lights disappear. He was blinded by the night and mistakenly walked toward the river, tripping on the wooden abutment that marked land's end.

Terror tore his body; he screamed, flailed his arms as if they were wings, and somehow regained his balance.

Maybe I's better off in the river, he thought. *Better off dead.* Morris was depressed at the thought of shooting the kid, Abie Isaacs. He had killed once already. But shooting Herman Rosenthal was an act of passion - impulse. His only regret, getting caught. Shooting Abie Isaacs was an act of cold blooded murder. It was easy giving Monk Eastman the contract - killing the kid, himself, was something entirely different. "I knows this kid since he was a baby. Coulda' been mine for chrissake."

"Even you pimp," said Monk, "wouldn't kill your own kid." What if Abie was his kid? Would he still pull the trigger? The answer came easily. "Ain't nothing worse than dying. You do what you gotta do." One thing he knew for sure. "I shoot his kid, Monk gonna get me. Tonight. Tomorrow. Next year." The thought no longer terrified him. In a strange way it was comforting.

He put his hand in his pocket and felt the pass key Whitman gave him - "What if it don't work," he asked the DA. "These things ain't fool proof."

Whitman looked at him and smiled. "Then my little friend," he said, " you'll kick down the fucking door." Morris turned, squinted, made out the street lights on Eleventh Avenue and began his long trek to Hester Street. He was walking very, very slowly but soon picked up the pace.

* * * * *

11:57 PM

Abie couldn't sleep and it wasn't just the pain from his new, clumsily tied, stitches - Doc Greenbaum was so nervous stitching him up in front of Monk Eastman he needed a bottle of laudanum on the spot. Rather it was the thoughts and images that teemed in his brain: Terry Jackson's gun against his head; Monk's violent intervention - ferocious but precise, as if Monk himself was fired from some dark hidden place to pierce the hearts of the Jacksons; the look of panic on Monk's face as he tried to stanch the blood pouring from his son's wound; Rosie's hysteria when she saw him, bloody, in Monk's arms; and, incessantly, the inner voice reminding him he was Monk Eastman's son - his name, Abraham Osterman.

Exhausted, he found sleep and dreamed. He was with Mama in Zeyde's house. Mama and her Mama, the ancient aristocrat - lighting candles, incanting the Friday evening prayer welcoming - as their mothers, and their mothers before them - the Bride Of The Sabbath--

* * * * *

11:58 PM

Mushy Bum - in a drunken stupor - was curled in a fetal ball on a pile of blankets in Rosie's kitchen. She heard the sound of Morris' pass key in the lock to the front door - a momentary fumbling until the bolt flipped. She pulled a blanket over her head. Who was at the door? Only Rosie and Nig had keys. Rosie was in the bedroom asleep with Abie; poor blind Nig was at the hospital.

Very slowly the door opened. Footsteps. Tentative at first, then more sure.

Mushy Bum, like an animal who never forgets the scent or sound of a long gone, but brutal master, began to tremble. "It Morris." She heard him cock his gun; heard Rosie shriek.

Mushy Bum scrambled under the sink.

* * * * *

11:59 PM

--suddenly Mama turned from the candles, faced Abie in fear and horror, and emitted a piercing wail that continued after he opened his eyes; continued as he watched a screaming, Rosie - naked, and clinging to Morris like a cat - tearing at his eyes. He heard Morris' labored breathing; saw the gun as he fended off the onslaught of nails and teeth. "I don't wants to hurt you, girlie," Morris said, flinging Rosie off. He pointed the gun at Abie. Rosie was back on him - silent, now.

Abie, fully awake, was frozen.

Morris and Rosie in a silent death struggle - breathing like lovers.

There was a shot. Rosie's naked body shuddered - pressed against Morris. He flung her aside and pointed the gun at Abie.

Abie looked into Morris' eyes and felt no fear. Only surprise at the sadness he saw.

* * * * *

12:00 AM

Mushy Bum heard the second shot; the sound of Morris' feet running toward the door; the door slamming. Like a wounded beast, she crawled toward the bedroom

part 4

Yis bor - ach V' yish tabbach V' yis po - ar V' yis ro - mam V' yis nas seh --
      Kaddish, the prayer for the dead.

GOD'S RAT

One
Kaddish

The tiny cemetery was the first thing you saw entering Brooklyn from the Williamsburg Bridge. No larger than one square city block it was crammed with unbroken rows of soot stained tombstones; an eternal slum for the East Side's Jewish dead.

A small group of mourners surrounded a freshly dug grave. Under the sky's unblemished dome, the late August sun poured upon them benedictions of light and warmth.

Monk Eastman removed his hat and with the back of his hand wiped the sweat from his brow. Lena was leaning on his shoulder sobbing. Facing her, holding her white gloved hand, Manya Bluma spoke softly. Next to the open grave Rabbi Leonescu - Manya's husband - was supervising the workers about to lower the coffin into the ground. At the Rabbi's side, Zayde, a white silk prayer shawl draped over his head prayed fervently, tears streaming down his cheeks. Behind him - hovering protectively - was Blanche who insisted on accompanying the old man to the funeral. Klopper and the boys were there. Except Sugar Davey, who was attending another funeral. The boys looked uncomfortable in their suits and yarmulkas. Sheeny Mike Levine lit a cigarette - Klopper knocked it out of his hand.

The Rabbi walked among the mourners. He approached Lena and Monk. "I'm so sorry, Lenaleh," he said. "At least it's a beautiful day." He squeezed Lena's hands tightly - then walked away. Monk told her it was a lousy day for a funeral.

"It suppose to rain at funerals," he grunted.

"Then nobody could see your tears," Lena said.

Again, Monk wiped the sweat from his brow. He couldn't believe it was only yesterday when Lena came bursting through the door interrupting his dinner. She was still dressed as a *rebbitzen*, but her wig had fallen off - leaving her natural hair clumped and matted. She bore the expression of a woman about to reveal a grief so profound she can neither take comfort, nor give any. Grabbing hold of him - her body dank and stinking from sweat and fear - she screamed, "Abie's dead Monk. Our son is dead. Morris killed my baby."

"Chrissake Lena," Monk said, "Morris' in jail." Then, behind her, he saw Mushy Bum covered with blood, whimpering like a puppy, mumbling what sounded like gibberish until he made out the words: "Abie - - Rosie - - Morris - - " Monk remembered arriving at Rosie's front door, kicking it open, knowing before he put on the light that his son was dead - fumbling for a match, lighting the lamp and seeing the hole between Abie's open eyes, his lips slightly pursed as if to ask a question. Monk reached down and closed his eyes. Near the bed, Rosie's naked body was sprawled on its back, Mushy Bum squatting next to it, Rosie's head in her lap - playing with her hair while rocking back and forth, her lips moving rapidly as if in prayer - making no sound. Monk saw the rose tattoo; he covered Rosie's body with a sheet. Lena kneeled next to the bed, her arms wrapped around her son's waist; her head on his silent chest. She sobbed quietly. Monk knew he should console her; he didn't know how. He felt helpless and sought his only consolation. Rage. Morris killed his son. And one day he would kill Morris; but it gave no comfort.

The squeaking from the wheels and pulleys lowering the coffin into the grave tore Monk from his reverie. Rabbi Leonescu began to chant Kaddish.

* * * * *

January 25, 1915, 6:09 am & 00 seconds, Sing Sing.

The desire to fight Death was extinguished. "You've let go son," said Mama. There was only darkness now and the voices of the jurors - voices that cleaved the earth. And the end was upon him. And the promise of silence was sweet, but still a promise. And each voice was a sea filling the ragged valleys of the newly riven earth. "Guilty", "guilty", "guilty", --twelve times. And the waters swallowed the earth. And there was silence. And Becker heard the silence. And it was sweet. And hope left his body as if it was his departing soul.

Printed in the United States
729500001B